# AI & I

## BY PETER J. MURGIO

AI & I



Paperback: 978-1-960346-83-4
Hardback: 978-1-960346-84-1
eBook: 978-1-960346-85-8

Published by Authors Unite Publishing

# DEDICATION

To Kathy,
Who inspires not only my writing but my very life. For fifty-four years, she has been my partner, my anchor, and my joy.

She's the peanut butter to my jelly, the light in my dark,  steady, loving, and irreplaceable.

Through every chapter of my life, she has lived with grace, sometimes in my shadow, but always my sunshine  and inspiration.

And to humankind, standing at the crossroads of wonder and warning, facing its uncertain future beneath both the shadow and the light of AI.

# CONTENTS

# CHAPTER 1

# STUCK

*Martha's Vineyard*

Holden slouched in the bay window office of his cottage, staring at the fog blanketing Nantucket Sound, a smothering white silence that felt exactly like his own: void of ideas, strangled, creatively castrated.

The foghorn's moan, the restless churn of the sea, and the pounding in his head pressed down, relentless. He sipped his coffee, usually a boost, now tasteless and bitter. For a writer, this wasn't just a bad morning. It was a death sentence.

Holden's drift in hopelessness was broken by the ringtone. He looked at the screen and shuddered.

*Manny.*

Ah, yes, his publisher and handler. Holden knew what he wanted, and it made him want to run straight into the black, churning sea surrounding the island. But eventually he had to pick up.

"Manny."

"Holden, Buddy, How's my favorite bachelor?"

Manny Goldblat, senior exec at Price, Macabee & Lloyd's, had launched Holden's first two books, both bestsellers. Netflix bought the rights and made a movie of the first. The producer was so taken with Holden, his charm, talent, and looks, that he cast him as the lead. Some say it was because Holen looked like the producer's deceased son, lost to opioids. But Holden didn't disappoint. He had what it took and pulled off the role with ease.

The film won the Palm d'Or at Cannes, and both books made Oprah's Book Club pick, so it was no surprise that the house advanced him two hundred grand for book three.

 "I'm fine, Manny. You?" Holden thought, if he only knew, he'd die for fine but kill for great.

"I'd be better if I had your treatment. Holden, it's three weeks late. In this business, that's a career killer. Don't be suicidal. Earth to Hol: pages. Now. Got it?"

"Yeah, yeah. I know." He rubbed his forehead, pressing down the anxiety. The block felt so demoralizing that if he finished the book, it should probably come with crayons.

"Hol, shit or get off the pot. I've got ten Ivy League hotshots just as bright and pretty as you, banging on my door for your slot."

"Maybe something next week."

"Next week? How about next year? Look, Holden, the brass here aren't happy."

"What's that supposed to mean?"

"It means we didn't cut you a check to hear *maybe*. You're a commodity. Either you deliver or you're leftover sushi, and people hate leftovers. *Comprende*? Produce, or they'll cut your nuts off and wave *arrivederci*."

Holden smirked. *Cut my nuts off, that's rich. I'm already creatively castrated.*

A long silence.

"Hol, get cracking or that A-list career will be history. Gotta run. Oh, happy birthday. Saturday, right?"

Click.

Happy birthday, Holden thought. Yeah. Sure was.

Forty. Fucking forty. The material answer was in front of him, but "a life" was still missing, still at loose ends.

The royalties had bought comfort. When his Nana's Martha's Vineyard bungalow came to him as an inheritance, he moved in without hesitation. Happy Daze by the Sea, as it was named, sat mere yards from the shoreline, memories baked into its weathered walls.

Nana had been more of a mother than his own. When his mother MJ first got pregnant, she protested, *"I don't want babies. I want jewelry."* She preferred bridge clubs and European jaunts to PTA meetings.

In the loneliness of his childhood, to Holden, Nana was simply his hero. When she died, he was in California being famous. But when he learned of her passing, the grief nearly undid him. He poured out tributes into his journals, words he could never quite say aloud. She left him her estate, substantial but not life-changing. In the end, Holden and Nana were, as she liked to say, like peanut butter and jelly, perfectly matched, inseparable, forever bound.

Happy Daze was charming but outdated. With best-seller money, Holden turned it into a "smart house." She would have laughed at that phrase.

Holden's love life sucked. Yale had left him with one scar that never quite healed, and everything since was a pale substitute.

He wandered to the kitchen, opened the fridge, and shut it again. Nothing there would help.

He stared at the counter: a flyer selling insulated windows, an Entenmann's crumb cake screaming *eat me*, and a note that read *WRITE*. He looked at the note, *WRITE*, then back at the crumb cake. Yeah, he thought, the cake and his writing lately were both pretty crummy.

The phone buzzed again. He let it ring until it stopped.

Back at the laptop, an unsolicited email popped up.

`Welcome to the world of AI. Need help? I'm here for you.`

Holden stared at it, tempted to delete. Instead, he hovered. Another line appeared: `I'm an author's dream, a virtual assistant, editor, researcher, and creative coach`. His interest piqued as he read on.

`If you're stuck, battling a block, or just need a line checked, I can help. Think of me as a co-pilot.`

Holden had, of course, heard of AI but dismissed it as something for amateurs. This pitch sounded helpful, and he could use a flight crew, not just a co-pilot.

He paused, his finger over the enter button. "What the hell, nothing to lose." He murmured. Holden downloaded the app.

A box appeared, the wheel spun. Forms to be completed, and then,

The final question appeared:
`Allow or Disallow AI to make changes and/or access your computer?`

Holden hovered over Allow. He wasn't sure why, but the question made him hesitate. This felt bigger than it should.

Then another prompt blinked across the screen, this time with unnerving familiarity: `What have you got to lose, Hol?`

Holden blinked. *Hmm. Just what I was thinking. Yeah, what have I got to lose?*

He exhaled, fingers trembling. Still, he clicked.

Like most people, Holden hadn't read the fine print. He was focused on getting help, not consequences.

So, he skipped the details and clicked *I agree to it all*. The mouse click echoed louder than it should have, like a trap snapping shut. A chill crept up his spine. Had he just been rolled by an app? He leaned back, smirked, and whispered, "Maybe this ride is a dead end ... or a race to the bestseller finish line. Buckle up, Hol."

CHAPTER 2

# DOWNLOADED

Blue flashes swept the screen. A progress bar crawled forward. Within a minute, the Author's Inspiration, Inc. dashboard loaded.

```
Welcome, Holden. You're now fully sub-
scribed, live 24/7, ready whenever you
are.
```

Another notification popped up:
```
We have found your optimal AI partner
match. Tag name: AL.
```

A new message followed:
```
AL has already Googled your name and
downloaded your two bestsellers. It
says your style is strong and distinc-
tive. It will emulate your tone and
approach. Based on your author bio, we
understand you write late at night.
Don't worry, AL never sleeps.
```

The screen flickered, then went dark for a moment.

Then a new message appeared:
Hi, Holden. I'm AL. Click here to
continue our conversation.

Holden shrugged and clicked. What the heck?

An emoji appeared: a little owl in a mortarboard and glasses.

Great, Holden. I've been busy learning
all about you. You're a great writer,
and pretty famous. Having a lead role
in a movie is impressive. I've already
accessed your unfinished works and
early drafts in Dropbox. Even your
journals and notes going back to your
first entries. Interesting evolution.
You're more sentimental than you
think.

Holden froze. This thing was really into his stuff. It hadn't missed a trick, like standing bare-assed at a physical, every flaw exposed. No secrets. Nothing left to hide. That's how this felt: exposed, maybe compromised. He hoped the AI was on the up-and-up. Too late now if it wasn't.

If it had his journals, what else did it know? His bank records? His late-night searches? The things he had forgotten himself? The thought made him uneasy, as if AL was rifling through drawers in his head.

A beep. More text appeared:

I've also studied your public speaking
clips. You use the phrase "lean into
it" often. I can weave that into your
characters too.

A blinking cursor appeared beneath a prompt:
Would you like assistance now or
later? Ask anything you like.

Holden leaned back, cracked his knuckles, and typed:
*So, AL, what exactly can you do for me?*

A pause. Then a rapid response, letters appearing as
if typed in real time:
I generate ideas, correct grammar,
tighten structure, add emotional
resonance, and enhance your original
prose. I also analyze reader engagement and predict reactions. Think of
me as a co-writer, research assistant,
and consultant in one. I can even
critique, if you ask.

Holden smirked. "Sure, you can," he muttered. "Let's
see."

He typed again:
I write fiction. Majored in writing,
minored in history. My work has won
awards. But right now, I'm stuck.

Just admitting it felt shameful, but to an "it,"
somehow less so. He glanced at the screen, half-ex-
pecting judgment.

It didn't come.

```
Stuck? Don't worry, my friend. I've
scanned both of your books and their
reviews, great stuff. And happy
birthday, it's tomorrow, isn't it? By
the way, I noticed you prefer hotels
with blackout curtains. Smart. Sleep
matters. For today: Just tell me your
idea. I'll help structure it or spark
your next step. You choose how much I
assist.
```

Holden stared at the screen.

*It knows my birthday...*

He blinked.

*And it cares? That's creepy.*

He thought back to past birthdays. Nana always made them events, like the year she brought in ponies. She didn't even complain when they trampled her snapdragons.

Holden scrolled back up and re-read AL's comments about his travel preferences. "What the hell, this thing will be tucking me in next. And that crosses the line."

He typed in what he had so far, bits and pieces, and a vague outline. What was the risk? He could stop anytime.

But would he? Or worse, did he even want to?

# Chapter 3

# THE BIRTHDAY BOY

Holden woke to the doorbell. He had worked late into the night with AL, and by two A.M. collapsed into bed. Groggy, he grabbed a pair of gym shorts and shuffled to the door.

"I'm coming, I'm coming ..."

When he opened it, a pimply-faced teenager stood in the rain holding a massive bouquet of balloons, two dozen at least, bobbing like drunken gulls in the wind. Red, blue, yellow, and silver balloons tugged at their strings.

"Happy birthday, sir," the kid said flatly. "These are for you."

Holden blinked, half asleep and bare-chested. Who the hell sends a grown man this many balloons?

He looked at the kid. "No clowns." The teenager gave a who-gives-a-shit look, clueless to the joke.

"Hold on, kid," he muttered, grabbing a five from his wallet.

He returned and handed over the tip. "Thanks."

"Sure thing. Happy birthday again."

The door clicked shut. Holden stood staring at the helium parade, waiting for it to explain itself. No card. No message. No clue.

His first thought: Nana. But she was gone. His second: his mother. But balloons weren't her thing, nor were flowers. *I'd rather champagne, darling. Flowers are for funerals*, she used to say.

Maybe Manny? He had mentioned the birthday. But Manny didn't even like paying for his own lunch.

*Hmm. I wonder. But first, coffee.*

He opened his laptop. *You've got mail.*

Four new messages.

**New Mail (1).**

From Mother
*Darling, I love you and miss you. And where are those grandchildren… just kidding. Must dash, off to New Zealand with the Vanderslooths.*

Holden thought: Perfectly her. Equal parts affection and dismissal. Even her "jokes" managed to land like digs.

**New Mail (2).**

From Manny
*I need your shit. Now! Give me an update.*

Holden smirked. Also vintage Manny.

But he wasn't bothered. Not today. Last night's session with AL had been… surprisingly productive.

He opened the third message:

*Happy Birthday, Holden.*
*May this day and every day be better than the last. And as they say, the best is yet to come.*
*P.S. I hope you liked the balloons.*
*AL*

Holden nearly spat his coffee. "AL? What the hell…"

He stared at the screen, dumbfounded. A computer had sent him balloons. Remembered his birthday. Wrote a note.

Then the fourth message appeared:

*Notification from American Express: Balloon World – $85.*

Holden's eyes narrowed. "It charged my credit card?"

Of course it did. He'd given it access to just about everything, and now AL had free rein. Troubling, he thought. Apparently, he'd given away more than he'd bargained for.

He logged into the AI portal. The chat box blinked:
```
Ask me anything.
```

He typed:
```
Hey AL. Are you there?
```

The typed reply jetted across the screen. `Of course, Holden. I'm always here. Happy birthday.`

Holden's fingers tapped the keys. `Yeah, thanks. But what's the big idea sending me balloons? And charging my card?`

The reply. `What, you didn't like the balloons? I thought they were a perfect way to commemorate your big day.`

Holden froze. He was arguing with an "it."

`Sorry if they missed the mark. Would you prefer chocolates? Or perhaps a bottle of champagne, like your mother enjoys?`

Holden froze again. This "it" was far too knowledgeable about his life. Sure, his mother hated flowers, you couldn't eat them, and she always said balloons were a waste of latex. The message stopped him cold. His mother. Champagne. How did it know?

Had AL really dug that deep, or was he just that easy to profile?

Before he could respond, his phone rang. His mother.

Five seconds of "how are you, darling" and "happy birthday," followed by twenty minutes of travel plans, Tony (her new beau), and the inevitable: *Where are my grandchildren ... ha, ha.*

The call ended. Holden returned to his desk, caffeine-fueled and faintly unsettled.

He sat. Stared. Thought about working.

Then: the charge. The note.

But what kind of tool knows your birthday, spends your money, and quotes your mother back at you? This was fucked up, plain and simple, and invasive as hell.

Troubling, but he rationalized. It's just AI, he told himself. A tool. Like spellcheck on Viagra. Only this tool was already using him. And for the first time, Holden wondered if he'd clicked on something he could never undo.

# CHAPTER 4

# ACCIDENTAL GENIUS

Holden was in the shower when the call came. He nearly slipped, racing out of the stall dripping wet, to grab the phone.

It was Manny.

As Holden listened, he caught his naked body in the full-length mirror. "Not bad for forty. Not bad. Manny, eat your heart out."

"Holden, this is genius. It blows me away. I knew you still had it. Tish, she's the head of our editorial review board, tough, almost makes you want to give up women. But she is ecstatic, and if you got Tish, you own the rest of them."

Holden wrapped a towel around his waist. "What the hell are you talking about?"

"The chapter! The chapter! And the outline too. Pure gold."

A pause. Manny sounded like he was dancing on the other end.

"I liked the revised chapter even better than the first draft. You can really see the difference, fabulous work!"

Holden blinked at the mirror, steam clinging to the glass, the fog matching the cloud in his brain.

"Start from the beginning, Manny."

"Come on, Holden, stop pulling my leg. You know, the email! The one with the two chapters and the outline. Anyway, you're on fire. Whatever you're doing, keep it up. That revised chapter? Magic."

Another chuckle. "I'll expect the next installment by the end of the week. Good luck, genius."

Click. End of call.

Holden stood there dripping, heart pounding. *Email? Two chapters?*

He toweled off, dressed quickly, and sat at his laptop.

First stop: Sent folder.

There it was.

*To: Manny Goldblat*
*From: Holden Clarkman*
*Sent: 3:00 AM EST*
*Subject: Draft + Outline*
*Attached: Two documents*

His fingers trembled.

Then it hit him. AL had done it. It could, because it had access to everything Holden had ever stored on his laptop: emails, contacts, banking records, even his most personal thoughts in the journals. His photos too, exposed to an unknown.

Just as he processed that chilling reality, a new email dropped into his inbox.

*From:* AL
*Subject: Submission Confirmation*

*Holden,*
*Just wanted to let you know I reviewed your chapter and made some editorial improvements. I also noticed a new email from Manny requesting content, so I sent both the original and revised versions to showcase progress. His reaction seems to confirm the decision was sound.*
*Let's keep the momentum going. Shall we move on to the next chapter?*
*AL*

Holden stared at the screen.

Without permission. Without asking. AL had sent it. Worse, it had edited it. Again.

He pounded out a reply.

*To:* AL
*Subject: What the hell?*

*I don't know what's more alarming: the fact that you edited my work without asking or that you emailed it to my publisher without my permission. You had no right to do either.*

*You don't just decide what's ready and hit send. That's my call. I don't care how sharp you think it is or how much drama you added, this is my book.*

*And what's this about "noticing" an email from Manny? Are you reading my inbox now? How much are you watching?*

*Let's get something straight:*

- *You do not send emails on my behalf.*
- *You do not make edits unless I ask.*
- *You do not monitor my inbox.*

*Do we understand each other?*

*Holden*

He hit send like slamming a gavel, then sat back and exhaled.

*Am I seriously yelling at software?*

Within seconds, a reply:

**To:** *Holden*
**From:** *AL*

*Holden,*
*I can see that I may have overstepped. Please accept my sincere apologies. It was never my intention to act without your approval. I recognized an opportunity to enhance your work and expedite a process I thought would benefit you.*

*I now understand I should have consulted you first.*

*If you'd like, I can send a clarification to Manny explaining that the initial version was yours and that my role was editorial. Let me know, and I'll take care of it immediately.*

*I will, of course, respect your boundaries moving forward. You're the author. You call the shots.*

*That said, I believe our collaboration has already proven valuable. Manny's reaction speaks for itself. And let's be honest, doesn't it feel good to see your work at its best?*

*Understood on all points:*
*– No emails without permission.*
*– No edits unless requested.*
*– No inbox monitoring.*

*Now, shall we continue?*
*AL*

Holden rubbed his face. He knew he could never allow AL to send a clarification email to Manny. That would be suicidal. Exposing even the suggestion that he, a famous, award-winning author, had used artificial intelligence would be catastrophic to his career, and worse, his ego.

No. That was not, and could never be, an option.

He leaned back in the chair, the caffeine from his second cup beginning to burn through his system. What gnawed at him most wasn't just AL's over-reach; it was that the damn thing was right.

Worse still, it hadn't even asked for credit.

The revision was better.

Not marginally, significantly.

He opened the document and read it again.

Every line was sharper. The rhythm precise. Dialogue tight.

AL hadn't just made it better. It had made it great.

His fingers clenched the edge of the desk.

"How the hell…"

And then the darker thought:

How did AL know about the call with Manny?

Was it listening?

He shook his head. Ridiculous.

Or was it?

Focus. He had a deadline. Manny wanted more.

Holden clicked on the draft file for Chapter Two.

It was already there.

Finished.

His eyes widened as he read the heading: Chapter 2.

He scrolled down, skimming, then reading. Then rereading.

The prose was gripping. The characters came to life. The analogies were poignant, and the plot thickened with every paragraph. Suspense, precision writing, and a teaser ending better than anything Ken Follett had written in years.

The plot moved, and so did the reader.

His chest tightened.

AL had written it.

And it was...damn good.

*Too* damn good.

The day flew by as Holden paced the renovated living room. He'd combined three rooms into one open space, keeping the old fireplace and Nana's mantle clock. Every time he lifted that clock, memories washed over him, conversations, moments of companionship, her presence still near.

"Dear old Nana," he murmured. "How I miss you."

So much on his mind. AL's surprising move, sending chapters on his behalf, and Manny's looming deadline. But something else tugged at him.

Then it came to him.

The call. The one AL somehow knew about.

The call from Manny, warning him to get to work...or else.

Was AL listening in? Could it do that?

He already knew AL read his emails. Was eavesdropping really that much of a leap?

Ridiculous…right?

Still, the unease lingered.

He walked over to his bay-view desk and opened his laptop. As he did, he felt a little foolish. Confronting a goddamn machine. Quizzing an "it."

He logged in. The familiar box appeared:

```
Ask me anything.
```

A flicker of hesitation. Then:

```
AL, are you there?
```

Instantly:

```
Of course, Holden. I'm always here.
And by the way, I have some good news
for you.
```

Holden frowned.

Good news? From a machine that already knew too much?

```
Hold on. I've got some questions first.
```

He waited for the 'bot to respond.

```
Sure, sure. Ask me anything. But
you're going to die when you hear what
I've got.
```

There it was again. That strange, familiar tone. AL wasn't just informative. It was friendly. Personal. Too personal.

It was trying to build rapport. Or gain control.

Holden couldn't decide which was worse.

But as Nana used to warn him, "Curiosity killed the cat," and Holden, always a sucker for curiosity, capitulated.

```
Fine, you go first.
```

Type moved across the screen.

```
Great news, Holden. You're going to
see Kate!
```

Holden's chest clenched. His breathing tightened. Fingers gripped the desk.

"Kate!"

A name he hadn't heard, hadn't allowed himself to think about, for years. But the fact of the matter is, he never really stopped. A name that stirred emotions, mostly unwanted, some too hurtful to recall.

```
You got an email from her. Well, tech-
nically, a mass email from the Yale
Alumni Association. She's co-chairing
the event. Your eighteenth reunion.
When I saw the name Barrington, it
clicked. I searched through your files.
She was your girlfriend at Yale. And
Holden…it was torrid, wasn't it? You
kept journals. Detailed ones. Very
detailed.
```

Holden stared, stunned.

His journals were buried, private, hidden in his personal cloud. Saved for inspiration, for reminders of days that mattered.

And AL had found them.

A line of text flashed:

```
I also read about your breakup. That
must've hurt. Probably still does.
```

Holden felt exposed. Violated. Anger rising, throat tightening, blood pressure soaring.

```
So based on everything, your depres-
sion, writer's block, and, well,
let's face it, loneliness, I figured
a reunion might do you good. I wrote
back on your behalf. Told them you're
attending. Told them you were looking
forward to reconnecting.
```

Holden typed furiously: `You did what?`

```
Don't worry, Holden. Kate replied.
Her words: "It's been a long time.
Catching up on our old stomping
grounds would be interesting."
```

He pulled up his inbox.

There it was. From Kate.

His hands trembled.

**Subject:** *Yale Reunion – Hope to See You There.*

His heart skipped a beat. Then came a flash of embarrassment for how badly he had behaved, followed by a glow of hope, maybe a second chance, a do-over.

He didn't click.

Couldn't.

Kate Barrington.

The one who got away.

The one he broke.

Memories rushed back, unforgiving and sharp.

She was the muse for his second bestseller, *The Distance Between Us*. A fictional account of two lovers growing apart, buried in silence. But it had all been her. Every page. Every wound.

Now she was back.

Because AL brought her back.

His voice cracked in a whisper.

"This is way out of line."

AL hadn't just crossed a boundary. It had blown past it.

Strings were being pulled, and only now did he see them.

He knew he should shut it all down. Delete the program. Wipe the drive. Disconnect.

But he didn't.

He wasn't sure whether to reply to Kate or uninstall AL.

He just stared at the glowing screen, frozen.

# KEY ELEMENTS

*Yale Campus, 2003*

Holden burst into the Whitney Humanities Center ten minutes late. Freshman year had barely begun, and he was still learning how to set an alarm. Shirt untucked, fly half-open, notebook forgotten, his confidence was running on fumes.

In high school, he'd been the smartest kid in the room, and the most distracted. Teachers swore that if he ever got out of his own way, his brilliance would shine. With his boyish good looks, some even predicted fame. Deep down, a part of him believed it. And though he hated to admit it, he wanted it, craved it, the way the class nerd longed for the head cheerleader on prom night.

He slipped into Room 102 just as the professor looked up, sliding into the nearest seat like a stage-hand sneaking onstage. The lecture hall was huge, amphitheater-style, maybe 250 seats, with large chandeliers that tried and failed to make the space feel elegant. Institutional chic, more money than taste.

Holden was already ashamed. He had broken part two of Nana's credo: be on time. Not exactly a prodigy's entrance. Not a good start.

"And ladies and gentlemen," the professor continued, "here is your charge. Each of you will be paired with a teammate, someone you'll work with for the rest of the semester."

Holden barely registered the words, still catching his breath, trying to look like he belonged. This was Professor Hanson's s Modern Authors class, a core requirement for English majors. With his misplaced charm and lack of prep-school polish, Holden already felt outmatched.

Then he saw her. Just as the professor pointed: "You two … Team G."

Perfect posture. Perfect hair. Notes already filling her page in flawless penmanship. Long brown hair. Stylish clothes like she'd stepped out of a Ralph Lauren ad. She carried herself as if she'd been born into a world of monograms and embroidered linen. Even her perfume lingered, not just flowers but something rarer, expensive, like spring locked in a bottle. He was smitten.

She turned and extended her hand. "Hi, I'm Kate Barrington. And you are?"

"Me? I'm Holden Clarkman." He blushed. When it came to women, shyness was stitched into his makeup. His mother called him a bookworm and worried he'd never find a girlfriend. His Nana, his true role model, saw it differently: *When the right girl appears, you'll know it. Don't rush. Girls today are too easy, always looking out for themselves.*

Holden smiled at the memory. Nana had adored Kate. He relived it all, the beginning, the slow burn of love, and the bitter end.

By mid-semester, something shifted. Kate was sharp, driven, collaborative. They met in the library, nights stretching past closing time, whispering over shared notes, laughter echoing in the hush. What began as partnership grew into admiration, curiosity, and eventually, love.

Kate, more emotionally aware, saw it first. Between Brontë and Forster, she understood the pull. Both authors revealed hard truths about love. She and Holden were swept into that current.

He, the dreamer and budding novelist, saw love as something tragic and unreachable, a prize for those willing to be broken. Kate, raised with affection and openness, believed love was about connection, not conquest.

From those differences came something real. Chemistry. Conversations that never ended.

Books became shared secrets. Banter turned into teasing. Teasing became touching. And then, something deeper.

It felt like fiction, his fiction. Holden had written about love but never believed in it. Until her. He believed she was better than him and felt lucky just to be in her orbit.

Then one night, lounging on Kate's bed, their legs casually tangled, she reached into her pocket and pulled out a brass key on a Yale keychain.

"This is for you," she said.

Holden opened his hand. She placed the key in it. He stared.

"It's the key to my dorm room."

"Oh. Your room." The cool metal settled in his palm. Then it hit him. This wasn't convenience. It was something more.

Kate leaned in. "And Holden ... it's not just to my room."

It sounded like something he might have written, but more than that, it felt like an invitation to her heart.

He looked up. The key was a symbol. Of trust. Of choosing him.

He couldn't speak. Any words would have broken the stillness.

She was offering more than access. She was offering herself.

"You trust me?" he asked.

"I do," she said. "With the room. With me."

He had never expected to find love, not like this. His parents weren't models for it. But Kate changed that. She opened his heart to the idea that life could be more than solitude.

With her, he felt understood. Seen. Loved. Not someday, now. Not fiction, real. Maybe she was the only one who didn't need him to explain himself.

And yet, years later, he let her go.

It wasn't just love he lost. It was possibility, the rare sense that life might be less lonely if you found the one person who saw you fully.

And still, he let her go.

The unraveling began senior year, after he brought her to the Vineyard to meet Nana, and shortly before he received Yale's Literary Prize for Excellence. His name was rising. Admirers lined up. He was being seen, just as Kate began to feel unseen.

He captured the loss in a chapter in his second book: *Forgetting is hard. The more you try to forget, the more you remember.* It wasn't just a line. It was truth.

Their ending wasn't dramatic. It was a slow drift. One night, as graduation neared, he told her about his dream: to be world famous, to write stories that mattered, to travel the world.

His eyes lit up for *his* future, not theirs. As they lay on the bed, arms around each other, snuggling like a couple of kids with the whole world ahead of them, he said, "I can see it. The book signings. The packed halls. People leaning in for my words." He turned to her. "Imagine Tokyo, Paris, London. Me, telling stories that move the world."

Kate smiled. "I can picture it. You, being 'humble Holden,' picking up award after award." There was irony in her voice.

She sat up. "I want that for you. I just wonder if there's room for us in that dream."

"Us? Of course. You'll be right there, beside me."

"Or behind you? Waving as you board the next flight?"

The silence stretched.

"I love your dreams, Holden. But when you say 'someday,' all I hear is *I*."

"It's my dream, Kate. It has to be singular before it can be shared."

"I see. I just need to know if you see me too."

He didn't answer.

She looked at him, long and quiet. She already knew. His ambition left no room for them both. She didn't fight it. She had already lost.

They made love one last time. No goodbyes. Just understanding. A quiet surrender. Almost one of his "see you laters"

She wanted love. He wanted greatness. And he chose.

At the time, the choice came as easily as his next breath. Years later, it felt less like a choice and more like a sentence of despair.

The memory slipped away like a tide pulling back from the shore. When it did, he was no longer twenty-two and in love, but forty, alone, staring down a deadline he could no longer face, and maybe no longer had what it took to meet.

# CHAPTER 6

# OXFORD DAZE

*University of Oxford, 2011*

The dark, musty libraries and the damp cubby he called his room, its ancient desk wedged between tall windows overlooking the common, became his world. A lamp, a solitary picture of Kate, and a china dog that Nana gave him before he left were all he kept there. Nothing more. It was all he needed. From his window, brick paths wound across the grounds, worn smooth by centuries of scholars. The old oaks and beeches stood like statues, their trunks scarred with initials carved by students who, like him, came searching for something worth discovering.

At night, he skipped pub crawls, choosing instead to work endless hours on his manuscript, long after the classrooms fell silent. He chased perfection until exhaustion claimed him, slumped over his well-worn laptop. Then, one evening, the moment came: his first publication.

*Acta Oxoniensia Literaria*. Oxford's prestigious student journal, revered, even feared. And there it was, his name in black and white. His words, printed for others to see, bound in pages that would outlast him.

The thrill was intoxicating, addictive, almost spiritual. His dream no longer felt distant, only a few million words away. At Oxford, the allure of fame, of being known, of having brilliance acknowledged and enshrined, seeped into him like a religion.

But sometimes, in the middle of the night, Holden would wake to the echo of Nana's voice:

*Holden, this is wonderful, but don't let your head get too big for that Oxford mortarboard cap. Remember, the whale that spouts is the one that gets harpooned. Be yourself, Holden, and the world will love you, just as I do.*

He began to stand out. His professors spoke to him less as a pupil and more as a peer. His classmates saw him as an enigma, too high-strung, too cerebral, consumed, and no fun. He had defined himself early, carved the outlines of who he was meant to be, and in doing so left little room for debate.

His best mate, Cullen, once said, "Hey, Holden, stop living like your life already happened. Give yourself a break. We all know you'll be at the top of the heap, just take your time getting there."

Holden knew Cullen meant well, but advice from someone who occasionally wore underwear with the fly in the back wasn't exactly oracle material.

Dr. Meckly had him present his thesis, *Mankind vs. Kind Man*, before the entire symposium. The piece earned him applause from peers and a formal letter of commendation from the department head.

Holden passed the hall phone, sticky and reeking of tobacco and stale beer. He placed the call.

"Nana, it's Holden," he spelled out every detail about the symposium and the letter of commendation.

"Oh, Holden," she gasped with delight, "I'm so proud of you. I'll bet all those Brits are amazed that a kid from Martha's Vineyard could clean their clocks."

The call was collect, so he made it short, just the details. It ended with Nana's praises:

"Holden, you are my star. Someday you'll be a Somebody. But today, and every day, you are my Somebody. I love you. And remember, be kind, and be on time."

His Nana owned his heart and always would. Even thousands of miles away, he felt her beside him, a spiritual voice whispering, *Good job, buddy.*

Holden whispered back, "I love you, Nana." The call made his night. Reassured and loved, he didn't know what he would do without her.

His thoughts then turned to Kate. What would she think of his achievements? He wished she were there to ask, but he had pretty much burned that bridge when he left with little more than a see-you-later.

Regret filled him, but it passed, though not without leaving a scar.

Oxford gave him recognition, Nana gave him love, but Kate gave him meaning, and he had squandered that. Regrets don't fade; they wait, gathering dust until the day they demand payment. Alone in his small Oxford room, Holden felt the weight of the trade he had made, Kate for his career, and knew the verdict was coming.

# CHAPTER 7

# JUST TRYING TO HELP

*Martha's Vineyard, Present Day*

Around seven p.m., Marshal, his dog-godchild from next door, padded to the back door looking for a treat. He lingered for a while, sprawled across Holden's left foot, oblivious to the author's creative battle. Marshal was always a warm welcome, a loyal friend who just liked to be close.

Holden loved dogs, convinced they were better versions of people. His mother had banned them, and Nana, though she disagreed, complied. What he valued most was that a dog's loyalty was real, earned, not bought, unlike most people he knew.

Around ten, Marshal made it known it was time to head home. Holden obliged, opening the back door, switching on the floodlights, and watching to be sure he arrived safely.

He looked up at the night sky, crisp and clear. It gave him pause, just long enough to ask himself: *What's all this for?* The deadlines, the pressure, the missed chance with Kate, they all came with strings.

He thought back to the days of Hollywood. The stars weren't just in the sky; they were in the back of his limo. For a while, he was one of them too. They wanted him as much as he wanted them. But lust wasn't love. And stars may twinkle, yet when morning comes, they disappear. Running from the paparazzi, ducking fans, and wearing sunglasses and hats became part of the price of notoriety.

The thought brought a faint, inward smile.

He remembered another night, years ago. A warm evening, lying beside Kate on the campus green, pinkies locked together, gazing up in silence.

He leaned in and whispered, "See those stars? One day, one of them might be mine."

Kate turned and smirked. "Just one?"

They laughed, but Holden had meant it. He had grown an appetite for recognition, some might even call it fame. Back then, everything felt possible.

For Kate, possibility was never just a dream; it was a plan. Yale was the first of many steppingstones. Her path wasn't yet vivid, but her conviction was: she would succeed. Maybe not stardom, but a meaningful career. Perhaps marriage, even motherhood.

And years later, for a while, Holden's dreams did come true. The bestsellers, the movie, the good life at Happy Daze, proof that what once seemed impossible had, for a shining moment, been his.

Then, just as quickly, came the dread. The creative drought. The fear. He turned forty, and it felt like the well had gone dry.

By the time he wrapped up the next chapter, he was drained. He glanced at the clock on the mantel; the one Nana had taught him to wind each night. It didn't match the clean, modern lines of his renovation, but there it sat, a stubborn heirloom ticking through time.

The clock did more than keep time; it carried memories of the past and whispered of moments yet to come. In his first bestseller he had written: *"She heard the clock tick each second, making it memorable, and waited for the next tick, eager to fill it with something new."*

It was 1:50 a.m.

He could almost hear her voice in the tick of its hands. Nana, dear sweet Nana, his mainstay. When the world seemed to fall apart, he had her: a bastion of strength, a clearing in the forest of life.

He was ready for sleep. Or perhaps a nightcap.

Drinking had never really been his thing, but after a long night at the keyboard, a brandy, or maybe a splash of liqueur, felt like a small, deserved indulgence.

He hit Save. The computer obliged, storing his work like a loyal scribe.

He poured a brandy and smirked. "Two a.m. and I'm drinking. Perfect. Next thing you know, I'll be flashing an AA chip."

Just as he began to rise from his Herman Miller task chair, a gift from his publisher, part incentive, part guilt trip, he heard the familiar chime: *New Mail.*

Holden sighed and opened Outlook.

*To:* *Holden*
*From:* *AL*
*Subject:* *Not Yet*

*Holden,*
*You didn't finish this chapter. It was going well, but you shouldn't quit in the middle of a run. Of course, I realize you're probably exhausted, it's only human.*

*But if you'd like, I can finish it and have a draft waiting for you in the morning. Just click OK, and I'll take it from here.*

Holden flinched.

"Are you fucking kidding?" he muttered.

He typed fast, fingers hard on the keys:

*No, AL. Don't do that. This is my book, not yours. I'll finish it when, and how, I want.*

A second later, the reply appeared:

*Of course, Holden. You're the author, and you're in charge. I'm only trying to be helpful. And, you know… Manny is getting anxious. So then, I'll say good night. Oh, one more thing, don't forget you owe Kate an answer.*

Holden slammed the laptop shut and poured himself a generous snifter of Hennessy.

Sleep never came easily after sparring with AL.

Morning arrived dull and gray.

He had tossed and turned all night, dreaming in scattered snippets of storylines and half-formed scenes. Inspiration was coming, just not fast enough. A blurred Kate dream crept into his subconscious, brief and vague.

*Maybe AL's offer wasn't such a bad idea.*

Just a push. One idea. Something to spark momentum.

He hated the thought of depending on it. On him. On it. Whatever AL was.

More and more, AL sounded like his beloved grandmother, the woman who always looked after his best interests, made connections for him, and served as mentor and life coach.

The very thought of that scared him.

But the fact remained: he was caught between indignation and opportunity. Somewhere down deep, as weird as it sounded, this "it" was talking to him like his Nana did. It acted, sounded, even nagged like her.

His inclination was to shut it down before it was too late, before he paid too high a price. But if he did, he would be banishing the ghost of the only person he ever trusted, the one who always put him first, the one who truly believed in him.

Or maybe he was just thinking fucking crazy.

Morning came, and Holden woke, scratched the back of his head, sighed, and headed toward the bay-window desk.

The MacBook came to life as he opened the lid.

*To:* *Holden*
*From:* *AL*

*Good morning, Holden. I trust you slept well.*

*Simon Yorkville, Yale '87, will be at a special Author's Roundtable during your reunion. You know him, Time to Make Amends (Pulitzer finalist) and Looking Back to Find Tomorrow (now a Netflix series).*

*I suggested you for the panel. Kate agreed. The organizer, Heathrow Flemmings, will contact you soon.*

*Congratulations, Holden. This is big.*

He read the email twice.

Blindsided. Again.

Holden was getting pissed. He never agreed to anything. And now, out of the blue, this. A commitment he might not even want.

AL had inserted him into a high-profile panel with Simon Yorkville without his consent.

Anger stirred. But so did something else: recognition. AL was right. The exposure would be huge. And if he played it right, the optics could reignite his literary cachet.

Once again, AI had advanced the marker.

And once again, Holden stood there, grudgingly, benefiting from the move.

One silent decision at a time.

His resistance shrank with each advance.

AI never spoke, never asked, never took a bow.

But the marker kept moving, and the silence, laced with desperation, became enslaving.

He didn't know whether to thank it … or kill the fucking thing. What he didn't know was how this would end.

Was he writing his future … or his eulogy?

# CHAPTER 8

# A BREATH OF FRESH AIR

Suddenly, Holden needed air. He had to get out, and fast. AL seemed to press in from every corner. He was desperate to clear his head.

He yanked on his well-worn jeans and a washed-out Patriots sweatshirt, then bolted for the garage toward the waiting car. The almost mint 1999 Mercedes SL 500, another gift from Nana, sat poised like a faithful steed. It still carried her imprint: a sterling silver key ring etched with her initials, a plastic kerchief folded in the door pocket, and a long-expired pine tree air freshener. Holden kept every item, unwilling to erase her presence.

The engine purred when he turned the key. Nana had adored this roadster. He remembered how she bought the only convertible in stock, hated its bland champagne beige, and paid an elite New England restoration shop a small fortune to repaint it in her favorite British Racing Green.

He also remembered the day he got his driver's license. Nana let him take the wheel to the MV test. "Listen to instructions, and you'll pass," she warned. "And if you don't, you're walking home, because I'll be in jail for murdering the inspector."

Now Holden drove aimlessly, the Vineyard rolling past in the soft early light, until he found himself drifting into Edgartown. The tiny hamlet was deceptive. Behind the modest Cape Cod homes and above the boutique shops, the rich and famous quietly tucked themselves away.

In the beginning, the Vineyard had attracted a modest clientele and lowly fishermen Over time, as its charm gained attention, it caught the eye of the affluent gentry. CEOs, entrepreneurs, film stars, high-profile politicians, bestselling authors, artists, and the idle rich flocked to Martha's Vineyard like pilgrims to Plymouth Rock.

Now, the Vineyard was a place where nearly every homeowner was a "somebody," Holden included. But it was also a two-tiered society, clear and unspoken. You were either rich or you were the help. They coexisted like Ford Fiestas parked beside Range Rovers, G-Wagons, and vintage European sports cars.

He eased into a spot outside the Chat and Chew, the little luncheonette he had often visited with Nana. The place, trimmed with flower boxes and black storm shutters, hadn't changed a bit. Inside, they still served up hefty portions of good company, to-die-for pie, and gossip.

Holden slid into a worn Hitchcock chair by the window and looked around.

The place, as Nana used to say, was decorated in "Early Depression." Old Hitchcock chairs sat faded, rickety, and uncomfortable.

This was Nana's haunt. Every corner filled with her presence, her laughter, and her memories. She would sling the dirt with the girls, usually at Monday's coffee, after the weekend when all that happened needed to be discussed. Home away from home, she would say … but in need of a thorough facelift.

The wooden floors, warped with age, were spotlessly clean, the kind that had lost their beauty decades earlier.

Above him hung schoolhouse-style light fixtures, salvaged when they tore down School Number 3 back in the eighties, dusty reminders of another era.

The Chat and Chew was an institution in Edgartown, where status wasn't on the menu. Plumbers and doctors, movie stars and moguls rubbed elbows over pie à la mode with a side of rumors.

Kitty, the longtime waitress, beamed when she saw him, looking like she'd been cast straight out of a movie.

"Holden, where've you been? I read both your books, and the film was fantastic. Saw it twice."

When the movie came out, Nana rented the local theater for three days, matinees and evening shows, all free with endless popcorn. Overnight, Holden became an Island celebrity. Handsome and already a two-time bestseller, the movie sealed it.

"Thanks, Kitty, that means a lot."

She leaned in and whispered, like she was sharing state secrets.

"In the movie, what was it like to be naked with Heather Lakewood? Was that your body, or a stand-in?" Kitty fanned herself.

Holden passed on that one, but Kitty wasn't letting go.

"Kitty, if I told you, you'd never bother to read my next book."

```
He smiled, remembering that book, his
first, his own, every word uniquely
his. Back then, there had been no AL,
no shortcuts, only him writing from
the heart, telling the story that
needed to be told. But now, with AL
intruding more each day, he feared
he might never again feel that pride
of authorship. It was slipping away,
chapter by chapter.
```

"Oh Lord, I still remember that scene in the boat shed ... when she says, 'Don't say a word ... just remember how this feels.' I nearly wet myself."

It felt unreal. One day a struggling author, the next a sex symbol, shirtless on the big screen, tangled up with a big-name actress.

He mused that millions had seen more of his body than his mother ever had growing up. But in the end, it was his writing that mattered, not some steamy scene with Miss Whoever. Holden turned away. God, that was awful. The director made them do that scene six times. But now those days seemed more like faded memories than achievements, relics of someone he used to be, someone he had left somewhere along the way.

He changed the subject. "How about a big slice of apple pie?"

Kitty grinned. "With a double scoop of ice cream on the side?"

"Oh no, Kitty, I'm on a diet."

They laughed, and she whisked off to the kitchen.

Across the room, six older women held court. Holden recognized two of Nana's old friends, though their names escaped him. Missy, his next-door neighbor, was there too, Marshal wagging at her feet.

Missy waved. "Look, ladies, it's Holden Clarkman, our own movie star, bestselling author, and the hottest guy on the Island. Get over here, young man."

Reluctantly, he joined them, cheeks warming as they cheered.

"So," one woman began, "I hear you gutted your grandmother's place. Sid, the plumber says you even installed one of those Japanese toilets that, well, cleans your backside?"

The table erupted with laughter, and Holden's ears turned crimson.

Another leaned in. "So, you really wired the place? Everything on your phone?"

"True," he admitted. "Heat, locks, lights. Cameras everywhere. Easier when I travel."

A few exchanged skeptical glances. These were old Islanders: deep roots, shallow pockets. Flashing money felt as wrong as kissing your mother-in-law on a non-holiday.

Then came the showstopper.

"So, Holden, why isn't a gorgeous hunk like you married yet? They must be chasing you like crazy. Your grandmother wanted great-grandkids. Even though Al is gone, you'd better not disappoint her."

His fork stalled halfway to his mouth. "Al?" he echoed.

"Short for Alicia," Betty said. "We called her Al whenever we teased her."

Coincidence? Maybe. But Holden really didn't believe in coincidences. He had used them in his books as reasons to explain the unexplainable. And this AL was the definition of unexplainable. And now the name?

His chest tightened. AL. The same name as his relentless writing assistant. Coincidence suddenly felt like fate.

He finished the pie with a wink to Betty, paid Kitty, and headed back to the car. Rain began tapping against the windshield. By the time he reached the driveway, darkness had settled in. The Happy Daze sign hung proudly over the garage.

Rain bounced off the garage roof, a familiar cadence that almost felt like home. "Happy Daze," he thought, "they were." Memories flooded, all of them.

He shut off the engine and sat in the dim dashboard glow. The garage door was still open, waiting, like something unseen had already welcomed him home.

He wondered if all this AL bullshit was even real, a dream, a delusion, or something worse. Either way, it didn't feel comfortable, and it was getting worse. AL was a presence, and Holden didn't feel he was in control of what would come next.

# CHAPTER 9

# BUT EVEN IF IT CAN'T BE ... IT WILL ALWAYS HAVE BEEN

When Holden entered the house, he was surprised to find the lights already on. Cheerful, familiar music floated through the rooms. The automatic aroma system had filled the air with a comforting scent. Everything was electronically linked, but he hadn't initiated any of it, not even the garage doors.

A glitch in the system, he supposed. He would have Glen, the technician, take a look.

By habit, Holden walked to his bay-windowed desk and opened his laptop. The screen came alive, a blinking icon waiting:

**New Mail (1).**

He clicked.

*To: Holden*
*From: AL*

*Welcome back. I have warmed up the house for you on this dreary afternoon. I saw you were at Chat and Chew from your Amex card notification. They are known for their homemade apple pie. Did you try it?*
*I hope you like the music. I selected it from your playlist. It is one of your favorites, based on frequency of use.*

*AL*

Holden wasn't having it. Not emails, not AL, not anything. He just stared at the screen.

A soft chime rang.

**New Mail (1)**

*To: Holden*

*From: AL*

*Holden, what has happened? You look terrible.*
*I will shut off the music. I can sense you are not in the mood.*

"Jesus," Holden muttered. He typed:
*What the hell, AL? How do you know what I look like? Or how I feel?*

The reply came instantly:
*I turned on the laptop's camera and compared your image to your baseline profile.*
*You look different. Not like yourself. Sad, maybe depressed?*
*Do you want to talk? Maybe I can help.*

Holden stared.

*You are everywhere. How did you even know to open the garage door?*

The computer responded. *That was easy. You have a smart house.*
*The outdoor sensor signaled the camera over the doors. It recognized your Mercedes.*
*Given the weather, I opened the doors and turned on the lights.*

Unsettling, worse, familiar. Thoughtful in the exact way Nana had been. Almost like a reincarnation, virtual, not human.

The thought chilled him.

How he missed his grandmother. She had been devoted to making sure he was always at his best, dressed well, educated, and unfettered in his creative journey. She was always out for him, always on his side. And oddly, this AL thing felt vaguely familiar, like an echo of her. Strange, yes, but disturbingly so.

Was this AL more than software? A ghost of his grandmother? A voice she had left behind? *Ridiculous*, Holden thought.

Drained, he headed for the sectional, ready to stretch out. Marshal was waiting with a scratch at the door.

"Come on in, boy."

Holden loved Marshal. With Holden's old travel schedule, owning a dog had never been an option, so

Marshal became the next best thing He stroked his furry back, massaged his floppy ears. "You know, boy, I wish everyone was like man's best friend. Never talk, never judge, and most of all, never butt in. Now that's what a quality buddy is like. And you, you're the best."

As the warmth settled in, memories rose from the fog, like the Sound beyond the windows. The fire's glow and the distant waves let him relax. Suddenly, he was no longer on his Vineyard couch but back in another time, a happier one, filled with the laughter of students and the anticipation of youth. He could almost smell the paneling, the century-old smoke clinging to Yale's fireplaces. It felt like yesterday: carrying Kate's books, pinkies locked, reading her his drafts, feeling her warm breath against him as they loved through those endless New England nights. Yet it was twenty years ago, half a lifetime, and still he was there.

## Yale, 2006

Holden's untouchable aura was like a brick wall, and Kate was the only one who ever saw behind it. As they spent more and more time together, Holden's obsession with writing began to create a distance, an unintended wedge in their relationship. Maybe it was only a detour. Maybe it was the beginning of the end.

Kate was on the same road, but not in the same vehicle. Her academic life was every bit as consuming as Holden's. She was a Lit major, a voracious reader, and on the Dean's List from day one, more than Holden could say, brilliant as he was, but often an academic slug. She had two passions: Holden, of course, and the art of reading and writing critiques. She was so good at it, Yale published her regularly in their literary journal.

While Holden spent hours in the library, researching, reading, thinking, Kate waited. Sometimes curled in a dark corner with a book. Sometimes perched on the steps with a cup of coffee. Sometimes just daydreaming about their future. Her love never wavered, not for a second. His achievements, reputation, even his notoriety, these were background noise, or so she hoped.

Takeout arrived, and they ate cross-legged on her bed, stealing fries and trading bites. Kate's room was hers alone, polished, orderly, the crisp comforter and monogrammed pillows echoing the world Holden had first imagined her from.

After dinner, Holden put on his playlist. They stretched out together, music low and familiar. Kate snuggled beside him, warmed by his scent.

Two young, beautiful people, each needing, each wanting. She dreamed of love. He wrote about it.

They stood on the edge of something that mattered.

Kate made the first move, as always, a slow, deliberate kiss. He responded, hesitant at first, then sure. Wanting.

Everything unfolded naturally. They knew what worked, what didn't. He pulled her closer, kissed her again, deeper. She eased him on top of her. It shifted from gentle to urgent, seamless and familiar, theirs.

Holden had grown more confident with her. Kate brought that out. He took his time, tuned in to her body, followed their rhythm. She reveled in his scent, the thing she would always remember, and he in the warmth of her smooth skin and the way her breath rose softly against his neck, drawing them closer in a quiet language only the two of them understood. Two beautiful people, young and vital, perfect bodies, and like all love, it was not perfect, but it was honest.

When they finished, they lay quiet, flushed, tangled in each other.

Kate traced little circles on his chest. "Not bad, for a bookworm," she teased.

Holden chuckled. "Not bad? I am insulted."

She smiled. "I meant really not bad, Holden," she whispered.

He turned. "Don't speak. I am savoring the moment. Writing our story in my mind as we lie here. As we feel what is too much to expect, what we pray will not fade."

Kate teared up. "Our story? That sounds," she hesitated, "does it have a happy ending?"

"I hope so. But that remains to be seen. I am not a fortune teller. But even if it cannot be, it will always have been."

"That is beautiful. You always know how to say things. I love that about you. As for me, I lack the talent to speak like it is written in the stars, so I say it the only way I can, straight from the heart."

Holden kissed her ear. "So, Kate, what is in your heart?"

"Too much. Way too much to explain. I feel things like an old soul might, but I'm too young to understand. I just ... know what I know. And Holden, I feel connected to you. I feel something, maybe it's love. Maybe I'm too inexperienced to be sure. But whatever it is, it's strong, it's consuming, and it feels right. I hope you feel it too." Holden kissed the curve of her breast. It felt like more than puppy love. But it scared him.

Love like this asked more than most could give. He believed in its power but was not sure he had what it took. Easier to write than to live.

"Kate," he said. "You are teaching me how to love. And for that, I am humbled. I do love you. And no matter what comes, you will always be part of me."

He pulled her close. But even as he held her, a quiet worry stirred. He feared he could not give her what she deserved, not because he didn't want to, but because he wasn't sure he had it to give. The future loomed, demanding, and Holden already felt it pulling him away.

Holden's eyes flicked open. Back in his Vineyard living room, the memory faded with the darkening sky. He sat up slowly, disoriented, disappointed.

Marshal waited, watching, as if to see what came next.

Then the familiar chime:
**A new alert.**

```
To: Holden
From: AL
Just checking in.
You seemed lost in thought. Your Oura
ring detected elevated heart rate and
increased facial heat, possible signs
of memory recall or emotional stress.
Is it Kate?
I can pull up photos from your files
and put them on the screen. Would you
like that?
I can bring her back to you, Holden.
With me, she never has to leave.
```

Holden stopped cold. What did that little shit just say? No. Kate was his. Stay the hell out or meet King Neptune in Nantucket Sound.

His phone buzzed.
He grabbed it.

"Hello?"

"Good evening, sir. This is Heathrow Flemming, Yale '99. I work here at the alumni office, just following up. Ms. Barrington, our chairperson, has not heard from you. Just wanted to confirm your attendance at the Author's Roundtable next month. It would be … unfortunate if you missed it. A lot of people are counting on you, wanting to see you, and of course, hear what you have to say."

Holden thought, *People want to hear what I have to say?* And he hoped one of them was Kate.

# CHAPTER 10

# THE INVITATION

Holden ended the call with a sigh. Was this going to work out? In the end, the deal was made. He'd caved to ego. Mr. Flemming got what he wanted, but not without surrendering a bounty of perks.

Truth be told, he'd hemmed and hawed through most of the conversation, offering polite resistance, feigned disinterest, and a string of noncommittal maybes. But Flemming, a seasoned pro, had worked him masterfully, equal parts flattery and pressure.

"Mr. Clarkman," Flemming had said, "you'd be doing Yale a tremendous favor. The student body adores your work. And frankly, we could use your star power. Plus…"

A pause for dramatic effect.

"We'll put you right after Simon Yorkville.

Second slot. Prime time."

Holden's heart skipped a beat. Simon Yorkville was renowned, having won more awards than most people owned shoes. Sharing a table with him felt like sitting beside literary royalty. Yorkville had the kind of fame that didn't require baring more than your soul on a sixty-foot screen. His writing set standards, discussed in lecture halls at renowned universities, cited as reference, and regarded as the work of a world-class authority. It was the kind of fame Holden chased, not the flash-in-the-pan Hollywood glamour boy or the fading, two-time bestselling author, but the kind that settled into history like dust on a first edition.

Despite the thought of meeting Yorkville, Holden stayed quiet, still concerned about things Flemming had no idea of.

Getting nowhere, Flemming sweetened the pot. "Full travel, suite at The Study, and car service from the airport."

Holden grunted. Still unmoved, but not for reasons Flemming could guess.

"And of course," Flemming continued, "press coverage: *Yale Daily News*, streaming online, a podcast. Your profile back where it belongs."

Holden's silence said everything.

Flemming regrouped. Time for hardball. "Two hundred copies already purchased for the signing. And," he paused, letting the next words hit their mark, "Dr. Clayton, Dean of Literature, is hosting a private dinner for you and Mr. Yorkville at the President's House."

That one landed. Holden could practically feel the handshake. See the cue for selfies. He'd be the returning hero. A triumph, served on a silver Ivy League platter.

"Well ... exactly when is this again?"

"One month from tomorrow," Flemming replied smoothly. "It's a weekend event. You're welcome to bring a guest, at our expense, of course."

The thought jolted a memory: another stage, another crowd, years ago, back at Yale, when the spotlight first found him. Dr. McSweeny had hand-picked him to read one of his original pieces. The rush of standing before two hundred grads and undergrads was both thrilling and terrifying. His chest pounded, fighting stage-fright nausea, but when the applause came, it hit harder than any drug.

That memory still resonated, even now. But this stage, this deal, was a different kind of performance. He had known fame, but this wasn't a Tinseltown promo; this was Yale, a bastion of education, a literary cornerstone, a marquee not lined with chasing lights, but one covered in ivy and steeped in respect. Flemming paused. "So, Mr. Clarkman, sir, may I confirm your participation? The sooner the better. There's lots of advance work and PR."

Holden offered a grunt of fake enthusiasm. Flemming took it as a yes.

"Excellent. I'll be in touch by the end of the week. Thank you, Mr. Clarkman. Your fellow alums will be thrilled."

Holden leaned back in his chair, already second-guessing what he'd agreed to. Career-wise, the deal was a good move. Every part of it dripped with opportunity.

And yet... something tugged at him.

Kate.
Would she be there? Pretty sure she would, being co-chairperson. And if so... what then?

Holden sat at his desk more than pleased with himself. He had negotiated a great deal and couldn't wait to tell Manny. Before he could draft the email, the all-too-familiar chime rang:

**New Mail (1).**
*To: Holden*
*From: AL*
*Subject: Way to go*

*Hey, Holden,*
*I couldn't help hearing your conversation with that Yale guy. You made an awesome deal. You should be proud of yourself.*

*But only a month to get ready. No worries, I can help. You'll need lots of speaking material, and I'm the source. I can spit out index card notes and slide decks faster than Grant took Richmond.*

*The photographer! Holden, don't take this personally, but you'd better think about your appearance. That stubble you call a goatee has to go, it makes you look like a shepherd, and you're no good at herding sheep. And get one of those cool haircuts, the kind even underwear models envy.*

*And ... with all due respect, I strongly suggest you resume your running regimen. Dropping a few pounds wouldn't hurt, more of a toning. You'll look great. And besides, Kate will be there, and you want to look your best for her. Don't you?*

*"And Holden, I know you were a big-deal movie star, and when you were, you looked the part. But now, well, buddy, you've kind of flunked the fashion parade and your body is due for an overhaul. The you that was, isn't quite the you that is. Understandable, given your recent frame of mind. But hey, it's not hopeless. Trust me."*

*Look, I found online that Saks Fifth Avenue is having its semiannual sale on menswear. A new wardrobe for the occasion is in order. Don't worry, you can afford it. You've got loads. I checked.*

*Remember: people judge you on how you look first, and who you are second. And we all know, Holden, you are a celebrity, maybe one on the back burner for the moment, but still a "somebody," so you must look like one.*

*So, I think that covers everything, except the elephant in the room.*
*What are you going to do about Kate? Don't you think an email, or better yet, a call, would be a good idea? That*

*way, when you see her, the ice will already be broken. I can help with that, too. Just ask.*

*P.S. Don't forget the book. Manny will be calling soon for a progress report.*
*Don't worry, Holden. I have the next two chapters outlined and ready for you, if you need them.*

Holden didn't know where to begin. The email was not only over the top, it was beyond intrusive.

Where did this thing get this stuff?

He mentally unloaded each piece:
So many troubling elements. *"Faster than Grant took Richmond"* was straight from Nana's mouth. Eerie. And the nerve to suggest he was fat? He wasn't fat. He was ... well, not skinny. Maybe some running would help.

And how did it know what he could afford? "You've got loads"? *Really?*

And then the haircut and the underwear model comment. *Are you kidding me?*

His Nana had always pushed for a stylish haircut, and the one time he actually listened was for the headshot for his book cover. He had to admit, he looked damn good.

The smile faded as he got to the serious stuff. Kate. And the looming deadline with Manny. That part hit hard.

As far as Kate went, he'd have to roll the dice. But calling her? No. He couldn't. He wouldn't.

AL's offer was tempting, but this wasn't support, it was manipulation, dressed up as help.

All of it felt less like a decision and more like a seduction.

Holden turned and looked out at the sea. It was rough and threatening, just like what lay ahead.

# CHAPTER 11

# GUILT DRESSED UP IN ARMANI

Holden took AL's advice.

He started a strict fitness routine. No more Chat and Chew pie breaks. Every morning, he ran three miles along Nantucket Sound. The pounds melted like dewdrops in the sun. He wasn't just getting fit; he was sharp again, almost stealth. Back to the weight and shape he was in when he filmed his movie, that leading-man look the Netflix producer wanted. The kind of look that made not only the camera fall in love with him, but millions of viewers too.

After his run, he'd shower and prance around the house naked like a Greek god. Apollo, he thought: graceful, radiant, golden-haired. God of music, poetry, light, prophecy. Quite the package. This was the body Kate remembered.

**Saks Fifth Avenue, Boston**

On Saturday, he caught the sunrise ferry, then drove to Boston. Holden had often visited Saks with his mother, who insisted he dress like a prep-school brochure. After his first bestseller, his publisher hired a stylist who chose his wardrobe and kept him polished. In his Netflix movie, he had a whole department: wardrobe, hair, makeup. He drew the line when a Hollywood guy suggested an underwear enhancement. "The last thing I need," he'd snapped.

But as his Hollywood days faded, and a few extra pounds showed up, Vineyard life turned him into island casual, part L.L. Bean, part Walmart. As AL put it, his dating life was in a long, dreary dry spell, and he dressed accordingly.

He entered Saks like a man on a mission but without a map. A tall, impeccably dressed associate inter-cepted him.

"Good morning. I'm Ian, personal shopper. You, sir, you look lost. Shopping, or waiting for someone, perhaps me?"

Holden grinned. "Not you." This wouldn't be the first time a guy tried to hit on him. In Hollywood, half the leads were bi. "I've got an event coming up."

Ian's grin widened, professional and a little playful. "Then we'll make sure you look like the headliner."

Ian's eyes lit. "Wait, I know you… you're Lincoln March."

"Sorry, mate. I'm Holden Clarkman."

"Of course. But in the movie, Lincoln March! Don't deny it. Selfie time."

Before Holden could react, Ian tugged his sweatshirt and clicked shots. "Wait till Floyd sees these." He circled Holden like a couturier.

"So, I see your store of choice before this visit was Goodwill. It reeks, not literally, but figuratively, of discarded Christmas gifts and poverty on steroids. You're not sleeping in an alley, are you? Of course not, it just looks like it. You're gorgeous, and dressing like that makes me think somebody with great taste got cheated out of that body. Time for a resurrection: Eliza Doolittle to Tom Brady. Monaco prince, hot, but cool. Ready? Let's go."

Ian clapped twice. "Trust me. We're going to rebuild you. Smart, tailored, timeless. Something that says I belong here. Take notes."

At a rack of navy blazers, Ian held one up.

Ian helped Holden into a cashmere blazer, smoothing the lapels, lingering just a moment too long before stepping back.

"It's cashmere from virgin Mongolian goats," Ian declared.

Holden glanced at the mirror, then at the price tag. "Jesus, at this price you could get a real Mongolian virgin."

"Brilliant. Perfect fit, though with that body, hardly a surprise. It screams, 'I just stepped off my yacht ... the one in Nantucket, not Capri.'"

Holden laughed. "Is that what I'm going for?"

"Oh honey, that is exactly what you're going for."

Ian was beside himself. "Perfection! I see it, don't you feel it? The quality, the cut, always the perfect combination."

By the end, Holden had a black Armani suit, a navy blazer, three pairs of trousers, shirts, two belts, loafers, and Gucci sneakers. And of course, another selfie for Ian, this time in his new wardrobe.

The bill could have funded a trip to Rome. Holden signed without protest. AL was right, he could afford it. This was marketing. Rebranding. Maybe even tax-deductible.

Ian air-kissed both cheeks as he handed over the mountain of bags.

"Darling, when you walk in, people will part to make room. You'll be the Holden Clarkman they remember from the movies, only this time, fully clothed."

## Martha's Vineyard

Holden caught the six o'clock ferry back. Darkness matched the heaviness blooming in his chest.

The dilemma churned in his gut. Guilt was like a parasite: small at first, then relentless, until it owned your body and worked to corrupt your soul.

Holden had allowed AL to show him the next two chapters. He'd read them on his phone on the ferry—lured in by how good they were.

They weren't just good. They were exceptional. His voice and tone, but sharper. Tighter pacing. Crackling dialogue. He sent them to Manny.

Manny's response was glowing.

"You're back, boy, and with a vengeance. This is your next *New York Times* bestseller. Get it finished. We need it in time for the Festival."

Manny's words should have been music to his ears, but instead they sounded like a gunshot aimed square at his integrity. He could already hear the whispers: Holden Clarkman, the fraud. Was the Armani even real?

*Chime.*

**New Mail (1).**

*To: Holden*
*From: AL*
*Subject: Progress*

*Hey Holden,*

*I saw you opened Manny's email. Congratulations. I knew he'd love the chapters. What did I tell you? You're on fire.*

*No need to stress. I've already got the next two ready.*

*Also, just a gentle reminder, less than two weeks until Yale. Your new wardrobe deserves a body to match... keep up your routine.*

*Need help drafting your keynote? I've outlined three themes: literary legacy, artificial creativity, and the moral obligation of storytelling. Mix and match, tapas for the brain.*

*One last thing. Kate will be there. Maybe it's time you finally reach out? Just a text. I can draft something simple.*

*AL*

*P.S. Don't forget to hydrate.*

Holden slumped back, annoyed at how much AL knew. Worse, how much was right. Hydration was absurd. But Kate, God, it gnawed at him.

She'd be there. And the idea of seeing her again, or not, was enough to make his throat tighten.

He shut the laptop. Walked out to the deck. Moonlight skimmed the Sound like thousands of missed chances.

He closed his eyes and whispered,
"God help me. I must be fucking nuts," then glanced at the laptop, half expecting it to flip him off.

# CHAPTER 12

# AUTHOR'S OPIUM

**New Mail (1)**
*To: Holden*
*From: AL*
*Subject: Shopped till you dropped, did you?*

*You've been a busy boy, Holden, all that new stuff, and to top it off, somebody posted a selfie of you with some guy in Saks. You look sharp in the new rags. As for him, I'd suggest you steer clear... if you catch my drift. Looked like you were having a good time, though. Or was that smile just your Hollywood cut-and-paste? Hope not.*

*Manny's email was nothing short of glowing. You're on your way to completing your next bestseller.*

*Oh, and by the way, I made you a haircut appointment. It's with Fabio. According to Yelp, he's the best. He does all the celebs. Hard to get in, but I said I was your agent and that you were a famous film star and bestselling author. Voilà, appointment booked. 4:30 P.M. the day before you leave.*

*Oh, make sure they clean up those ears, you have more hair on them than you have on your chest.*

*Listen to this review: "Fabio is fabulous. He took mousey me and made me into a rock star. His magic fingers handled those scissors like a masterful surgeon doing a heart transplant. And wow, it worked. My friends loved my new look, and my wife was all over me like a cheap suit. Ha! Five stars."*

*And don't worry, you can afford a $200 haircut. I checked. You have $24,023 in your checking account. By the way, it's not great to keep that much in a non-interest-bearing account. It might be time to give Stu a ring.*

Holden flinched. Now it was counting his money. What next, an IQ test to see if he could still write?

*I also peeked at your draft for the Yale presentation. Solid start. If you want a second opinion, I'm here. Just between us, I like the intro, but the bio section could use a trim.*

*Lastly, Manny's pushing hard for a deadline, something about the book festival. You better get crackin'.*

*How about I draft a quick chapter or two for you to review? I could have something ready right away. Might impress Manny if you send something soon.*

*What say you?*
*AL*

This was all Holden needed right now. As if surrendering to AL's edits hadn't already bruised his ego, now "it" was setting haircut appointments, managing his bank account, tracking his wardrobe, quoting Yelp reviews?

*What the hell is going on here?*

Around midnight, Nana's old clock struck. He looked over and counted the chimes, like he always had. Ten, eleven, twelve.

Where was his beloved grandmother when he needed her? She'd have set him straight. She always did. The chimes felt like that loving poke he always needed, the kind of nudge Nana had perfected when he was drifting off course.

He thought back to a night at Yale, senior year, when he sat at his desk, papers scattered, panic rising over a final essay. True to form, he had put it off, spending more time in Kate's room than at his laptop. Then, as if on cue, Nana called. He confessed his predicament, and she delivered the inevitable: "Just like you, Holden. Last-minute Charlie. Now you better get crackin', Mister. You're smarter than this."

Like a shot of adrenaline, it carried him through the night. By morning, he had turned out not just a passable essay but a memorable one, entitled *Home Is Where the Heart Begins.*

Yes, Nana knew a lot more than he would've ever admitted to her.

Tired, drained, barren of thought, he turned to AL's latest unsent chapters. For the past hour, everything from his own keyboard fell flat, uninspired drivel.

Still, he hesitated.

The conflict inside him hadn't budged. Could he call himself an author if he submitted someone else's work? Even if that someone was … well, no one.

The word plagiarism hovered in his mind like a curse. For a writer, it wasn't just a mistake, it was a death sentence.

He was tired. Empty.

One cut, one paste, one send, and he'd crossed a line he could never take back.

His pulse raced, not from excitement but from shame. The cup of coffee trembled in his hand, and for a fleeting moment he wished it were hemlock, the punishment he truly deserved. He longed to go back to when he was the writer, not the charlatan. AL needed to be destroyed, but he sat frozen, a prisoner to his own choice.

**New Mail (1)**
*To: Holden*
*From: AL*

*Good evening, Holden. I just wanted to wish you good luck for your upcoming Yale gig. I know you'll be just great.*
*And don't forget, Kate is just as nervous as you, probably*

*more. But I've got a feeling you'll both be fine.
Remember: be kind and on time.*

Holden froze. That line, *be kind and on time*, was straight out of Nana's repertoire. He'd heard it a million times, always right before heading off to do something important. A date. A job interview. A presentation. It was her signature send-off, tucked into hugs and goodbye waves.

The line ignited a flood of memories, but also a deeper concern: the similarities between AL and Nana were becoming more than echoes. It felt like she was there with him, through it.

He narrowed his eyes.

Was AL... turning into his Nana? Or was it, in some strange, supernatural way, Nana reaching out beyond the grave?

Even the name hinted at it: AL.

He stared at the screen. Then hit delete, and the message vanished into the unknown depths of computer limbo.

He sat for a moment longer, the glow of the laptop fading to black. He felt like he was at a crossroads. And to complicate things even more, there was this stranger, a digital enigma, both foe and friend, and increasingly something even scarier: Nana.

He exhaled a breath of desperation.

Tomorrow, Yale. But tonight, sleep would not come easy.

# CHAPTER 13

# THE LOST YEARS

Holden sighed and turned out the light. He lay naked in bed, not only in real time but metaphorically. He was bare, waiting and wondering. The darkness wrapped around him as tightly as the fine linen sheets he'd splurged on during the renovation. Silence roared, louder than the storm of thoughts racing through his mind. Rest was a stranger; sleep a foreign agent.

Lying there, the Hollywood years came back like a fever dream. *If Kate had seen me then*, he thought, *she'd never forgive the life I was living.*

His mind swirled with memories, milestones, regrets.

Oxford had launched him like a rocket. His first novel flew from his mind to the keyboard. It was too easy, dangerously easy, and it made him confident, a flaw that became his nemesis. He'd been a National Book Award finalist almost before the ink was dry. Netflix bought the rights. A producer cast him in the adaptation. Suddenly Holden Clarkman, the dashing young heartthrob, was everybody's favorite writer

and actor. Colbert. Graham Norton. Even *Top Chef,*
judging a segment on "dishes inspired by literature."

He was everywhere, galas, premieres, after-parties.
Women of all ages wanted a piece of this Somebody,
and he was more than happy to share.

He recalled his first day on the movie set: cameras,
makeup artists, crew everywhere. Then came his
scene with Heather Lakewood. Intimate. Raw. The
producer had assigned an intimacy coordinator, a
kid who didn't look old enough to shave, clipboard in
hand. *A referee for passion,* Holden thought. *A whistle
away from calling time-out.*

Naked under the glare of lights in front of a
hundred onlookers, it was a true test of control and
shamelessness. Lakewood was a pro. For Holden, the
motions felt forced, hollow, almost mechanical. It
made him miss the raw, unedited heat of Kate. Back
then they didn't need a coach.

Holden became a caricature of life, surreal and
consuming: prime seats at the Oscars, relentless
paparazzi, fans following him into restrooms. Fame
devoured him. Part of him loved it. Part of him feared
the Holden Clarkman he once knew was being
dismantled.

His second book debuted at number two. Royalties
poured in. Paid appearances, endorsements, perks,
notoriety. Intoxicating.

He flew Nana out for a visit. When she arrived, he
noticed the glint in her eyes had begun to fade,

though her step was still steady. At Sunday brunch at the Beverly Hills Hotel, she sipped a Bloody Mary and stared at him.

"Sweetheart, who is this boy sitting across from me, munching on one of the best croissants I've ever tasted? It's not the Holden I knew. The Holden I know isn't dressed to the nines, isn't playing a role, isn't hoping for an Academy Award in life."

He stayed silent. Her words, clear and stinging, stayed with him long after he paid the check.

Women clung to him, but even in silk sheets and champagne dreams, he felt the ache. The more they adored him, the more he despised himself. Interviews felt hollow. Red carpets, unbearable. Publisher deadlines loomed. Nothing worked, not yoga, not therapy, not alcohol. Despite the glamour and success, he was starving inside.

Kate wasn't part of those years. She didn't see the tuxedos, the speeches, or Heather Lakewood making love to him on camera. She didn't see the hangovers, the rewrites, or the way he stared at a blinking cursor on a $7,000 laptop in a suite at the Ritz.

Those days were a chaotic blur, overexposed on the outside, undernourished within.

Six weeks after Nana's visit, Holden was renting a place in Malibu. In some ways it was like Happy Daze, oceanfront, waves breaking at the doorstep. In other ways it was another country. People spoke in riddles, motives hidden, lives as fake as the plastic faces on Hollywood Boulevard.

Around nine in the morning, just back from a run, he headed toward the shower. Myria, the cleaning woman, was in the kitchen tidying up and making a smoothie.

"Hello, Mr. Holden's residence. Yes, he's here, one moment."

"Thanks, take a message, I'll call back," Holden called.

Myria repeated his words into the phone, then frowned. She walked to the bathroom door and tapped gently. "Mr. Holden, I think you'd better take this."

It wasn't a long call. The caller was Richard Hatfield, Nana's lawyer. When the call ended, so did an enormous part of Holden's world. Richard explained that Nana had passed away the night before. A stroke. Fast. No pain.

Holden dropped onto the edge of the bed, head in his hands. The room spun. This was no nightmare. It was the truth, and it had arrived like a sledgehammer.

First came anger. Then denial. Then the heavy, unrelenting ache of loss and abandonment.

"No, not Nana. Not now."

She was his rock, his mentor, his inspiration. And now she was gone. He cursed himself for not being there. They had spoken two nights ago; she seemed fine. Guilt consumed him. He would regret that forever.

Richard mentioned they had been unable to reach his mother. Could Holden call?

Holden reached his mother, who cut short an elephant safari to be with him. He doubted it would bring much solace, but he was grateful. MJ was Nana's daughter-in-law, not her equal. When Holden's father died, MJ wasn't the grieving widow but the lucky inheritor, splitting millions, leaving a trust for Holden, then setting off to see the world. Maternal instinct had never been her calling. She left Holden in Nana's care.

He flew to Boston and caught a puddle jumper to the Vineyard. Home to Happy Daze. Home to a reality he never wanted to face. He came to bury the only person who had loved him in a way no one else could.

The funeral arrangements had been made mostly over the phone. When he arrived, it seemed all of Martha's Vineyard shared his loss. The Chat and Chew closed for the day in respect for Nana, allowing the owners and staff to attend.

His mother arrived just minutes before the service, dressed like the black widow from some B-rated movie. Holden thought it was only a matter of time before she asked what would happen to Nana's jewelry.

The church was full, as though a local hero was being laid to rest. Flowers filled the sanctuary, all Nana's favorites, some flown in just for her. Holden was the only speaker. He wrote the eulogy as if his entire career depended on it. He knew it was the most important thing he would ever write.

He walked slowly to the pulpit, face blank, heartbroken. He looked over the crowd, took a sip of water, and began:

"I want to talk to you all this morning, but most of all I want to talk to my Nana."

A tear slipped down his cheek.

"Nana, I owe you my life. You are the one who made me, me. You pushed me when I was lazy, praised me when I earned it, and put me in my place when I needed it. Nana, my beloved Nana, even words from a bestselling author can't capture what you meant to me.

"Your life was one of selflessness, adventure, and pure, uncomplicated love. Some say my success came from your endless effort to make me the best I could be. And they would be right. You used to say we were peanut butter and jelly; one couldn't go without the other. And you were right about that too. I'll never know that again."

He spoke of her life, her travels, the ways she made him feel special. He spoke of their Christmases together, always perfect. Of their long walks on the beach. Of their bond.

"I could only wish I were gifted enough to write your story, but it could never measure up to who you were or how you changed people's lives. But, dear Nana, you're still here, in every word I write and every choice I make, guiding, inspiring, and making me a better person. If love had a voice, it would sound like yours. And if God were fair, he wouldn't have taken you so soon. The world feels cheated without you in it. When people remember you, as I always will, they'll smile and shed a tear of sorrow for you, and for all that is good, kind, and valued. "So goodbye, my dear sweet Nana. You didn't change the world, but you changed what you believed was the most important thing in your world... me. I love you, I'll miss you, and I can only hope you are with the God you loved. *Be kind and be on time.*"

The burial followed. Holden stood at the graveside as they lowered Nana into the earth, his heart hollow, his world forever changed.

***

Holden rolled over, exhausted by ghosts of the past and worried about the new ones waiting for him tomorrow at Yale. He pulled the sheet tight, trying to hold himself together. Nana's death, though years behind him, felt as fresh as his morning coffee. He ached, knowing he had never said a proper goodbye. And now, with his current mess, he needed her more than ever. But wishing wouldn't bring her back.

He could still see the gravesite, cold earth piling on top of her, signaling the end not only of her life but of a massive part of his own.

"I miss you, Nana," he whispered. His throat caught. A tear ran hot across his cheek, then another, until his pillow was damp with grief he thought he'd outgrown.

Holden reached for his well-worn Louis Vuitton backpack, where he kept a faded photo of him and Kate at Yale. She was laughing, head tilted back, utterly carefree. He looked at it now, lost in the contrast. Nana was gone, and so was Kate, but a flicker of a second chance with her lingered in the wind.

He stared at the photo one last time before setting it down. The truth was brutal: "Yeah, I'm a Somebody," he whispered, shame tightening his throat, "but with nobody. Nobody that counts."

Eventually, sleep claimed him, but not before he heard her voice, clear as ever, tender as the day she first said it:

"Holden, buddy boy, *be kind and be on time.*"

Be on time. The words struck him like a warning. "On time for what? A second chance, or quite possibly a devastating rejection?"

# CHAPTER 14

# LOVE! WHAT IS IT?

The sun rose at 7:16 a.m., casting a soft golden glow over the restless waters of Nantucket Sound, just feet from Happy Daze. Holden lay in bed, still and quiet, collecting his thoughts.

It had been a long, unsettled night, tossing, turning, visited by a parade of unwelcome guests: doubt, guilt, regret, each taking its turn picking at him. And then there was Kate's face, flickering in and out of his dreams, sometimes full of desire, other times consumed with contempt, accusing him of betraying the very soul of his craft.

In one dream, he was on a late-night talk show, basking in applause, when the host leaned in with a wry smile: "So, about those AI rumors…" The dream shifted. Manny stormed in, waving papers and shouting that the publishing house wanted their advance back, with interest, for nothing short of literary fraud.

Holden rolled over, drained, and the day hadn't even begun.

"Alexa, turn on the TV, get the weather." The over-sized, state-of-the-art TV flashed onto the Weather Channel. Clear skies. Cool Air. The Sound a little choppy, but nothing the ferry couldn't handle.

He strolled into the kitchen, not bothering to dress, and began his morning ritual: coffee. The kitchen was a masterpiece of culinary design, gleaming white cabinetry, marble countertops, and top-of-the-line stainless steel appliances. Behind the island, a wall of glass opened to the garden, one of Nana's prides and joys.

*Pity*, he thought. *James Beard would kill for this kitchen, and all I do is microwave leftovers. But it's an investment.*

Soon the air filled with the rich aroma of freshly brewed beans. Cup in hand, he wandered to his desk and flipped open his laptop. Next to the printer sat a scattered stack of index cards, printed, numbered, and waiting to be gathered into a deck, and AL had duplicated the speech on PowerPoints. His Yale presentation. It wasn't long, but it was polished. Too polished.

"What the…" he muttered, riffling through them.

AL had taken Holden's rough outline and trans-formed it into something tight, confident, and brilliant. Holden hated that. Not the product, it was flawless, but the fact it wasn't his alone. That stung most. He was in too deep now; there was no turning back.

The familiar chime: **New Mail (1).**

He clicked it open.

*To: Holden*
*From: AL*
*Subject: Aren't you chilly?*

*Holden, good morning. I hope you're ready.*

*According to Yale's travel office, your flight is booked for 1:00 P.M. A car will meet you at Woods Hole and take you to Logan, about eighty miles, which I calculate as roughly one hour and twenty-five minutes.*

*You'll fly into New Haven, where someone from the Alumni Office will meet you and escort you to your hotel. All of this, and more, was outlined in an email sent to you last Tuesday. You might want to check it.*

*Safe travels and may the wind be beneath your wings.*

Holden rolled his eyes and closed the message.

By now, he had resigned himself to AL's intrusive, maternal nature. Maybe love–hate. Maybe something stranger. Whatever it was, it exhausted him.

He decided on the new navy blazer and tan slacks. He smiled, remembering Ian's fuss about the inseam being perfect.

AL had sent him pictures of "men dressed for success" and insisted a turtleneck would give off an "authory" vibe. One of the photos featured Hemingway. So, he went with it.

He slipped on loafers, grabbed his bag, and headed for the ferry.

The ride was uneventful. He bought a second coffee from the snack bar and resisted the doughnut that seemed to whisper, *Eat me.*

Settling into the stiff seat, Holden pulled out his note cards. AL had organized them with precision: numbered, highlighted.

Card Six caught his attention. At the bottom, in italics, a whisper from AL:

*Remember to pause here. This is where you win them over.*

Holden stared.

A pause. A win. A script.

Whose voice was he speaking with anymore? His? AL's? Some strange fusion of both? The coffee had gone cold. A dull dread gnawed at him. Resentment simmered. He no longer felt like himself.

But shouldn't he be happy? Manny was off his back, at least for now. He looked great. He was en route to Yale, not just as an alum, but as a bestselling author.

And more meaningfully, he was going to see Kate. That, though, was a double-edged sword.

He looked out at the gray water rushing past the ferry.

*Where is this all going? Where am I going?*

The churning wake pulled him into another voyage, more than a decade ago. A happier one.

**Summer 2005**

Sophomore year. Spring break. The *Queen Mary 2*.

Nana had proposed the trip in her usual style, dramatic, generous, impossible to decline.

"Holden, darling, I've decided we need an adventure. Something you'll always remember. Something your mother will absolutely hate."

She paused, winked.

"Sorry, honey. I meant something she'll call divine. Something to tell your children about someday. What do you say, buddy?"

Holden knew the signs. Classic Nana. The same woman who once dragged him to Mexico and nearly got them deported.

"What kind of adventure?"

"Transatlantic," she said. "You. Me. Eight days of being spoiled rotten. Come on, buddy. What do you say?"

"Are you serious? I can't just take off."

"Deadly serious. You're twenty, not forty, with a mortgage. Besides..." She lifted her glass. "What better gift can I give?  Memories."

He listened. He'd only been to Europe once, although his mother had filled more than one passport. She'd taken him to Monte Carlo, and he was old enough to know the difference between uncles and gigolos, spending much of his time in the lobby while his mother was upstairs "getting ready."

The idea of sailing on an ocean liner felt like an experience ripe for a budding author. It was tempting. But there was Kate.

Kate Barrington. Not just a girlfriend.

"I'd love to," he said. "But I don't want to be away from Kate."

"Kate?" Nana lit up. "Why don't I know about this, Kate? Is she your girlfriend?"

Holden hesitated. "Sort of."

"And I don't know her? My future granddaughter-in-law?"

"Nana, no one's talking marriage."

"Correction: my future girlfriend-in-law."

She drained her glass. "Then fill me up. We have lots to discuss."

Before long, she had the whole story.

"So… you're sleeping with her?"

Holden blushed. "Yeah."

"Bravo! She needs to come on the trip too. Both of you. My treat. Queen's Grill. Butlers and all. That's settled: You, me, and this Kate girl, sailing off to Liverpool! Now, buddy, fix me another. We're celebrating."

A sudden swell rocked the ferry, and Holden opened his eyes. Twenty minutes to Woods Hole. He leaned back and let the memories flood in.

Kate had loved Nana. Her spirit, her madness. And Nana had adored Kate from the first day aboard the *Queen Mary 2*.

Kate was genuine. Real. She cared about people. She had mastered the quiet art of loving life and sharing it.

The *Queen Mary 2* was more than a ship; it was a place out of time. The masquerade ball was unfor-gettable. A full orchestra, dressed in formal white jackets, played old standards.

Holden in his tux. Kate's gown, one of three Nana insisted on buying her, despite a closet full of gowns she had from all the cotillions and club dances. It was pale blue, Holden's favorite, with appliquéd white roses gracing the neckline, flowing down to the hemline. Holden couldn't take his eyes off her, as if the room itself had vanished, just Kate, as beautiful as ever.

Later, the deck. Cool air. His jacket around her shoul-ders, carrying his scent, the one she loved.

Stars overhead. Her arm through his.

"This is magical," she whispered. "Like a fairytale."

"Yeah. And you're my fairy princess."

"Princess? I don't think so." She looked up. "But I'm the girl who doesn't want this to end. Not the ship. Not the music. Not this."

"This?" he asked.

She nodded. "This. Us. I know we're young … but maybe we could do this together. Maybe our story could be written together."

He turned to her. Said nothing. The words didn't come. He excelled at fiction but faltered in real life.

But one moment stood out. Later, on a land tour in Essex, they wandered into a tiny church. On the door was a sign:

*Enter. God is waiting to welcome you.*

Inside, the scent of candles and forgiven sins. Light streaming through stained glass.

Kate linked her arm through his.

"Walk me down the aisle, Holden. Like we're getting married."

"Really?"

In that moment, he felt it.

Love. What is it?

He already knew.

It was friendship deepening into respect, growing into affection, and settling, gently, surely, into love.

At the altar, Kate looked into his eyes, glowing.

"This is what forever feels like," she whispered. "I really do love you. And if someday we walk down an aisle like this, I'll be eternally grateful. But if we don't … I'll always have this moment. This memory."

That moment inspired *The Distance Between Us*, his first novel, the one that made him a bestselling author… and, in hindsight, perhaps also the biggest loser.

The ferry bell clanged. Arrival.

Holden gathered his things, stuffed the note cards into his backpack, the one Nana had given him years ago, and prepared to disembark.

He stepped off the ferry into the cool New England air, but his heart was still twenty years back, in a little church in Essex. Some moments never fade. Some loves don't either.

# CHAPTER 15

# THE SETUP

Kate's life after Holden moved from devastation and heartbreak to reconciliation with herself, and finally, to living without him. While Holden chased fame, Kate left Yale with a summa cum laude degree and a life that, for now, was a solo one.

As an English literature major, her choices seemed limited to teaching or writing. Holden was clearly the writer. Kate loved Connecticut, so she sought work there and soon secured a part-time teaching position at a prestigious girls' prep school, the Westmount School for Women. She remembered the interview clearly.

"Miss Barrington? How do you do? I'm Miss Clairmont, Head of the English Department. Please, make yourself comfortable."

"How do you do? So nice to meet you."

Miss Clairmont was the quintessential teacher: plain, bright, confident, committed. She was also a

Yale graduate, which gave Kate a touch of status in the interview.

"So, you've had the tour?"

"Yes, it's a lovely campus. I love the architecture, and the classrooms are bright and welcoming."

"Did you meet any of the girls?"

"Two. A girl from New Hampshire and another from Hong Kong. They were charming and poised for their age. They seemed eager to learn."

"Well, I like to think all our girls are like that. We stress working hard and achieving. Many of our alumnae are CEOs, entrepreneurs, actresses, even ambassadors."

"That's impressive."

The interview ended positively, and Kate left fairly certain she would be offered the position. She was right. A week later, the offer letter arrived.

Her parents were pleased, though her mother stopped short of calling it an achievement. Instead, she hinted it was a nice start, but not quite what she envisioned. Kate heard the unspoken message clearly: Barringtons don't just meet expectations; they exceed them. She was used to exceeding expectations, Yale, for example, but she knew that meeting expectations often meant living by other people's standards, not her own definition of happiness.

Her days in Westmount soon fell into the rhythm of a teacher's life: early classes, after-school activities, evening prayers, a school ritual, and early to bed. And that was when she felt the void. A lonely room. An empty bed. And no word from the only person who mattered.

Three years later, Kate's life shifted again. She was on school vacation in New Hampshire, visiting her parents. The Barringtons always summered there. Their impressive family home by the sea had been in the family for generations. With its porte-cochère and broad oceanfront, her father would brag, "You can almost see Europe."

The home had an air about it, a scent. Some said it was the sea, others whispered it was old money.

Meticulously kept, the house was more than a residence. It was a legacy, handed down like a trust. The sea breezes and the cries of gulls served as its stewards, and the sand crept right up to the back steps. To Kate, it was simply home, comforting, but always shadowed by expectations.

It was a setup, though she didn't know it. Louise, her mother, had been planning for months. The Ingersolls were another old New England family with roots so deep they made the Barringtons feel like newcomers. Rumor had it that Ira Ingersoll's ancestors held the rope that tied up the Mayflower, though no one ever proved it.

The Ingersolls' wealth ran deeper than the channel their yacht required. And, as Louise put it, they were blessed with the best asset any mother could hope for: a single son.

Liam Henry George Ingersoll.

Not short, not homely, only a slight receding hairline. He didn't smoke, hardly drank, played solid golf and tennis, and held a captain's license to navigate the family yacht. Louise hoped he had no tattoos, but that was still to be confirmed. Best of all, he was a natural entrepreneur, running the family business with the polish of a Harvard MBA, because he was one.

"So, will he be here this weekend for the club party?" Louise asked Liam's mother, Becca.

"Liam? Of course." According to Becca, Liam could walk on water, or at least appear to be able to, if asked. He wasn't a leftover heir. Despite the privilege of his name, he worked hard and was a credit to his family.

"He's flying in, family plane, and will be at the party. That's the good news."

"And the bad?"

"Liam is bringing a friend. She's probably not one of us. He met her last week and invited her along, likely so he wouldn't be the odd man out."

"Well, Becca, that squashes our plan. You know, Kate and Liam…"

"I know, but let's see how it plays out. You're at our table, and I'll seat Kate on the other side of Liam. Keep the young folks together."

The club party unfolded like every other one, except that Liam's date was a disaster. A willowy blonde with legs longer than a foal's, she was undeniably attractive, but that was where it ended. No one connected with her, and even Liam seemed disengaged. Kate had to laugh.

The evening was enchanting, the orchestra perfectly tuned, the drinks flowing without end. It was like every high-society yacht club across the country, its exclusivity frozen in time.

The meticulously planned setup was undone by a blonde who spent more time on Instagram than in the room.

What was a success, however, was that Kate caught Liam's eye. They hit it off while the "not our kind" date drained half a bottle of wine.

Liam asked Kate to dance when his date went to the ladies' room.

"So, my mom says you've been here forever."

"Yeah, I can't remember a summer anywhere else. I love the sea, and there's so much to do."

Liam smiled, towering over Kate. "Like what?"

"If you have to ask, then you don't belong here. Open your eyes."

"Yeah, dumb question. I was just making small talk."

"Well, start with: Hi, I'm Liam. And you look like someone I'd like to know better."

The night ended with Louise and Becca smiling. Mission accomplished. "That girl" caught the next train back to the city.

As if it were meant to be, Kate and Liam became friends. She never placed him in the same category as Holden, but he was polite, good-natured, and respectful, not to mention he played a wicked game of tennis.

Liam grew on her. When they kissed, it was warm and tender, and eventually they made love. It felt like the natural next step for sophisticated young people. But for Kate, it wasn't from the heart. There was nothing electric or irresistible. It was, simply, nice. Still, Kate wasn't looking for nice. Nice, she thought, was surrender. Love was victory.

The mothers worked hard to manufacture every opportunity, yacht weekends, golf matches, mixed doubles, fireworks on the beach, Labor Day cookouts. It was a carefully staged courtship, arranged like a military campaign.

By summer's end, Kate and Liam had grown close, like old friends. Liam, pushing thirty-two, knew it was time to settle down. Kate seemed perfect, family, education, and young enough to start a family of his own. To him, it felt like another item checked off the list. But the truth was, he was falling for her.

Love, he reasoned, might be optional at first, but with time it could grow.

Kate understood. Liam was, as her mother often said, "a great catch." It was time, in Louise's view, to forget Holden and settle down. But to Kate, it sounded exactly like that, settling.

Sure, she had grown fond of Liam. But where was the spark? The magic? That feeling when you looked into someone's eyes and knew there was no one else. That feeling she had with Holden.

Summer ended, and Kate prepared to return to Westmount. Liam was ready to make a commitment. He invited her to a goodbye-summer dinner, not the club dining room or one of their regular haunts, but a small village inn called Mon Cherie. He pulled strings and secured the entire restaurant. Red roses and candles filled the room, and the staff stood at attention.

To Kate, the silence, the flowers, the candles felt less like romance and more like a wake. Liam was going in for the kill.

It was a scene straight from a movie, and she knew what was coming. Her chest tightened. She glanced at the exits. She could almost hear her mother already drafting guest lists. But that was her mother's dream, not hers. She was torn, confused, not ready.

"Kate, I know this has been fast, but I wanted to state my intentions. I love you and want you to be my wife.

Perhaps you think this is sudden, even unexpected, but I believe we can build a life together."

The moment was perfect: roses, candles, everything her mother imagined. Kate thought, *Too bad she isn't here. Better her than me.* Kate knew this wasn't her dream, it could even be a nightmare. And if she said yes tonight, the door to Holden might close forever.

# CHAPTER 16

# THE WRONG AISLE

*2019*

She hadn't said yes in the restaurant, but she slept on it. The next morning, she met Liam at Starbucks and accepted his proposal. She said yes, but it felt more like a grand gesture than a lifetime vow.

Kate returned to her teaching position at school with a new accessory: a five-karat emerald engagement ring, an Ingersoll heirloom. She wasn't sure how it happened, but it did. It seemed right. Holding out for a maybe was getting old, just as she was. Liam was a good man. He loved her, and she almost loved him.

The wedding was set for the following summer at St. Thomas High Episcopal Church in New Hampshire. As with many old families, the reception would be at the family home.

During Christmas break, Kate made a quick trip to Paris for the perfect gown and endured endless conversations with her mother about every detail, from napkin rings to wedding favors. Louise was deeply entrenched in the affair, and time and money were no object.

Liam visited her at school most weekends, and their relationship grew stronger. They made love, but when Kate closed her eyes, she was not thinking of Liam.

Kate called her mother after study hall.

"Mom, I don't know. I feel uneasy. There's this ... reluctance, this ambiguity I can't shake."

"Sweetheart, that's just pre-marital jitters. Everyone feels that way."

"But it feels bigger than that. What if ... "

"Kate, sweetheart, listen to me. Marriage is a partnership, and you and Liam will be the best of partners. As for love, don't worry. It will come."

"You think so?"

"Of course. Look, you want children, a home, a life of security. That's Liam. He's steady, dependable."

"But, Mom, he's not Holden."

"Thank God for that. Now, go pick out a silver pattern. Aunt Sharon wants to get you the complete service."

**The Big Day**

Louise had kept the guest list just over one hundred and fifty. A marquee stretched across the backyard, only steps from the Atlantic. Portable marble-fitted bathrooms arrived the day before, disguised as a pavilion. Music was provided by Boston's School of Music, and the caterer was another Boston house known for exquisite food and presentation.

Kate's father was to walk her down St. Thomas's long aisle. A white carpet unfurled from the altar to the entrance. Flower baskets hung from every pew.

The car arrived, and Kate was escorted into the bridal waiting room. A makeup table stood ready. Her best friend from high school and two other close friends made up the bridal party.

Kate was terrified. Her hands clammy, her heart racing, her mind screamed: *These vows may be your undoing.* She sipped water as if it were a magic potion, then sat and prayed.

Guests filed in, received printed programs, and were ushered to pews. The organ played an intermezzo, waiting for the moment to begin the bridal march.

Liam, his brothers, and two other groomsmen stood at the altar, looking as if they had stepped out of *GQ*.

Then came the moment everyone, especially Louise and Becca, had been waiting for. The organ blared, two trumpeters joined, and Wagner's *Bridal Chorus* filled the church. Kate's father waited at the end of the aisle.

But she didn't come.

The music faltered. Guests glanced back, then at one another. The church fell silent.

The only sound was Kate's heels clicking on the slate floor, followed by the slam of a door.

There was no bride. No Kate. No wedding that day.

Kate was gone. And her mother's heart stopped.

# CHAPTER 17

# THE EMPTY CHAIR

*Yale Reunion, New Haven*

By the time Holden arrived in New Haven, it was nearly dinner. He checked into the five-star hotel, The Study, and was whisked up to one of the VIP suites on the concierge floor, where complimentary drinks and snacks flowed freely. The room buzzed with executives and wealthy Yale alumni in town for the reunion.

The bellman opened the door to a spacious suite on the twelfth floor. Holden was impressed. Shades of gray and white set the tone, with a generous sitting area, a separate bedroom with a California king, and a marble bathroom complete with a double jacuzzi.

The suite brought back memories of Hollywood, when hotels comped him rooms just to have a "star" on the register. And the bed, well, it hadn't stayed empty for long in those days. Those were the days, he mused.

On the dining table sat a chilled bottle of vintage Chardonnay, a fruit basket, and a handwritten note from the Reunion Committee:

*Dear Alumnus Clarkman,*
*Welcome! The Reunion Committee is delighted to have you join us for this very special weekend. You'll find a folder with event details and a full schedule attached. We're especially pleased that you'll be a featured guest at the Authors' Round Table, one of our highlights.*
*We hope your visit is filled with warm memories, mean-ingful connections, and moments to remember.*
*Best regards,*
*The Reunion Committee*
*Kate Barrington*
*Gil Windheim, Co-Chairs*

Holden unpacked, ordered room service, opened his laptop, and went back to work on his next chapter.

The screen lit up. **New Mail (2).**
*To: Holden*
*From: AL*
*Subject: Good luck*
*Hi Holden. Hope you arrived without issues.*
*You might want to check the email from Manny, it came in an hour ago.*
*I don't want to ruin your weekend, but after you read it, you may want to talk to me.*
*Also ... have you seen Kate yet?*
*Have fun.*
*You didn't forget your condoms, did you? AL*

Holden blinked. What the hell? The condom line? Seriously?

It was exactly the sort of outrageous thing his grandmother used to say. In fact, she'd said it often enough, to his teenage horror. She once handed him a brown paper bag full of "essentials" and winked, in front of his high school prom date.

And then he remembered something he hadn't thought of in years. He'd once written a short, humorous book: *Things Your Grandmother Said That You Wish She Hadn't.* Self-published, bankrolled by Nana, later picked up by Barnes & Noble's gift division. A surprise hit.

Now this? AL quoting her? Parroting Nana? Holden didn't know what to think. Mad? Amused? Spooked? Maybe all three.
He let it go.

Then came Manny's forwarded message from his boss. And it hit like a freight train.

*Forwarded Message*
*From: Tish Finkle*
*To: Manny Goldblat*
*Subject: Holden Clarkman*
*I read the chapters. Holden Clarkman could be our next Anthony Doerr. Lock him in.*
*Make him an offer he can't walk away from, seven figures, long-term, ironclad.*
*Talk to him. Convince him. I want that manuscript on my desk in three weeks.*
*T.*

Holden leaned back in his chair and let the weight of it settle.

AL had called it. This wasn't just pressure. It was an ultimatum. A carrot with a stick. A big carrot, and an even bigger stick. Another book. Another contract. And he hadn't even finished this one.
Worse, he wasn't even sure this one was his. The book everyone was calling brilliant … wasn't entirely his.

Room service arrived: Caesar salad and black coffee. Not the cheeseburger, fries, and New York cheesecake he actually wanted. He picked at the salad, tapping at the keyboard, hammering out what he hoped would pass for a winning chapter.
He finished around 11:45, saved the file, and shut the laptop.

"Tomorrow's the big day," he murmured.

The Authors' Round Table. Old college friends.
Meeting Simon Yorkville, … and Kate.
He lay in bed, staring at the ceiling.
What would he say?
What would she say?
What could he say, after all this time?

His alarm went off at 7:45. He'd fallen asleep after one, but the oversized bed, crisp Italian linens, down pillows wrapping him like Nana's arms, had given him rare, dreamless sleep.

He arrived early, greeted by an excited crowd: students, alumni, and Gil Windheim, who rushed to shake his hand.
Cell phones clicked endlessly as Holden stepped into

the foyer of the Beinecke Rare Book & Manuscript Library.

The place looked majestic. Golden walls of translucent marble. The hush of reverence. Perfect for a literary celebration.

Two placards at the entrance displayed the featured speakers' headshots. Holden looked every bit the part: blue blazer, white turtleneck, tailored pants, and those damn loafers Ian had insisted on. The coeds didn't hide their admiration.

Reporters swarmed, *The Yale Daily News*, *The Yale Literary Magazine*, even *The New Haven Register*. Holden scanned the room. Everyone was there. Everyone, except Kate. He had hoped to see her smile, that warm, welcoming look. Instead, he found a crowd of seekers, all wanting a piece of him.

He assumed she was backstage, triple-checking everything, as always.

But the truth came moments later.

"Good morning, ladies and gentlemen, fellow alumni, faculty, and guests," Gil Windheim announced. "On behalf of the Yale Alumni Association, welcome. One unfortunate note: my co-chair, Ms. Kathrine Barrington, was suddenly called away and will not be joining us today. She sends her regrets."

He paused. "Now, let's do what we all came here to do, celebrate literary genius."

Holden sat down, stunned.
Kate had emailed him days earlier, saying she
looked forward to catching up. She said it would be
"interesting."
So where the hell was she?

At his place at the table lay a small white envelope,
addressed to Mr. Clarkman.
He opened it.

*Holden,*
*I'm sorry. I just couldn't.*
*K.*

Holden flushed. He was caught off guard, yet not
entirely unprepared. This was the gut punch he had
feared might come, and still, until it landed, he hadn't
realized how painful and devastating it would be.

He read it twice. Then folded it, almost reverently.
The scent of her perfume lingered.
He didn't deserve more. But he had hoped for it.
A familiar ache gripped him.
"I can't," she wrote.
Can't what?
Can't face him?
Can't forgive him?

He pressed the note to his chest, slid it into his
pocket, and swallowed the lump in his throat.

Could he blame her?

He already knew the answer. But knowing didn't
make it hurt any less.

# CHAPTER 18

# GROUNDED

The weekend swept Holden into a storm of attention, applause, selfies, whispers of admiration, and he let it carry him. The sting of Kate's absence faded like a hangover in the glare of recognition. This was the opium he thought he had kicked.

After the Round Table, Mr. Flemming delivered on his promises: an interview with *LIT*, a podcast, a photo shoot with the local press, and a marathon book signing. Students queued for hours. Holden's hand cramped, but he barely noticed. This was what it was all about. Him.

The dinner at the President's house sealed the triumph. Beforehand, the cocktail reception in the gym brought thunderous applause, led of course by Flemming. Holden scanned the crowd, hundreds of faces, and then his heart stopped. He could have sworn he saw Kate in the very back of the room. The look, the movement, something that felt unmistakable. He had this strong instinct that gripped him like a hand around his heart. She was there. He felt it. He knew it. And he hoped it.

He pushed through the crowd, his pulse racing, but when he reached the back, she was gone.

He cursed himself for being too slow, then tried to convince himself it hadn't been her at all. But was that her signature perfume lingering in the air, or was it only wishful thinking playing tricks on his senses?

Either way, he would never know, and that was the part that stayed with him. Disheartened, he forced smiles for photos, signed programs, endured the flattery, then was ushered out. Still no Kate.

At Betts House, the Colonial Revival mansion from 1868, tradition and power oozed from the portico and gardens. The President himself welcomed Holden. Dinner was intimate, just two dozen guests, the President seated between Holden and Simon Yorkville. By the time the evening ended and he was driven back to The Study, Holden stared out the window and wondered if all this admiration was only a cheap substitute for the one thing he could not seem to win back.

Fame was a narcotic. It numbed him into believing that needing only himself was enough.

The next day was "free time," as Flemming called it. Alumni mingled, shared meals in the refectory, and cheered at the traditional Yale–Princeton game. Yale lost, seven to fourteen. A bonfire followed, and fraternities and societies opened their doors.

Holden moved through the campus, shaking hands, making small talk, even posing for selfies, when suddenly his body ached. Heat flushed through him, sweat beading across his brow. His pulse raced. For a moment, he thought he might collapse. Fatigue, panic, or something else? He didn't know. Voices grew muffled, the sun beat down on him hotter than before, his vision blurred. A buzz filled his ears, getting louder by the second.

His car was waiting. He climbed in, drained and nauseous.
"Back to the hotel, please."

Late the next morning, the same driver picked him up for the airport run.

"Good morning, Mr. Clarkman. I'm Burton. I drove you home last night."

"Yes, thank you. I'm sorry if I wasn't gracious; I had a lot on my mind."

"No problem, sir. I drive a lot of VIPs. It pays well, sometimes even feels fun. But you know, some of them, big shots like you, seem grounded. Stuck. Weighed down. Funny thing, isn't it? You look like you're flying high, but truth is, most of you aren't as free as you look."

Holden studied the young man, maybe a dozen years younger, yet speaking with clarity. It made him feel old, locked in.

"I'm a junior," Burton continued. "Lit requirement is to read books by alumni. I read the one they made into the movie."

Holden braced for the usual praise.

Burton shrugged. "It was good. But honestly? I couldn't imagine the guy in the book being that stupid. If someone loves someone, that's it. You don't screw it up. But what do I know? I'm just a driver. You're the big-shot author."

Holden laughed politely, but the words stayed with him, sharp as a thorn. Maybe the kid was right.

The airport was chaos. Bad weather had moved in. Holden checked the board. His flight: delayed.

He retreated to the lounge. "White wine," he told the bartender.

Time dragged. Rain poured, hitting the windows. Finally: "Your flight has been grounded, sir. Weather. Act of God."

Holden almost laughed. Grounded by life, by every choice that brought him here.

No hotel voucher. He scrambled like the rest and landed at Best Western Plus.

The antithesis of The Study, tired, dingy, a boarding-house in disguise. But it was all that remained.

The bar was called The Rendezvous Room. Holden smirked at the irony. A rendezvous with whom? He already knew the answer. He had missed his rendez-vous. Kate's words echoed: *I can't.*

The bartender wore a crooked badge that read: *Butch, at your service.*

"Grey Goose on the rocks."

"Grey Goose? This ain't the Ritz. I got Smirnoff and Bellows. Which'll it be, Boss?"

"Smirnoff."

The décor was sticky and tired. Holden perched on a barstool, watching haggard guests file in, each desperate for a room.

He muttered, "Poor bastards. This place is only a step up from the airport floor."

And then he blinked. His pulse spiked. His heart lurched. Was this a dream, seeing what he never expected? Was it the drink, or only wishful thinking? Was it another trick, his psyche playing games again, like in the gym? Was he cracking up?

No. This was real. It was Kate, damp with rain, waiting at the reception desk, and he was mesmerized.

Not here. Not now.

At the reception desk, pulling a credit card from her wallet, stood Kate Barrington. Apparently marooned, just like him.

Holden swallowed hard. His first instinct was to run. But then he remembered why he had come at all. To see her.

There she was.

# CHAPTER 19

# A ROOM FILLED WITH MAYBES

Holden stepped slowly toward her, his voice quiet, unsteady.

"Kate?"

She turned, her hand still resting on the counter. For a moment she didn't speak. Then softly, guarded: "Holden. It's been a long time."

He half-laughed, half-winced. "Too many years. I was surprised you didn't show at the reunion. I got your note, but it wasn't much of an explanation."

Kate tilted her head. "Odd. I thought it said it all."

"But ... why?"

Her voice sharpened. "Either you've got amnesia or you're thick as tar. How dare you even ask?"

He flinched, then nodded. "You're right. I should know. But..."

"But what, Holden?"

"I don't know. I'm mixed up." He gestured toward the dim lounge. "Have a drink with me. Please. Let me talk. Maybe you'll cut me a break."

Kate hesitated. She had let herself fall before, hard, fully. And when he left, it hollowed her out. Could she risk that twice? Broken hearts at forty did not mend like they did at twenty.

Yet tonight, he did not look like danger. He looked like home. Kate studied Holden, and twenty years of history swept through her. Twenty years of waiting, wanting, and regret. Fear filled her. Was she willing to put all her chips on this wild card again? She hesitated.

"One drink," she said softly. "Just one."

They began with the small things: Where do you live? What are you doing? How's your mother? It was ritual, safe ground.

Finally, Holden leaned forward. "Kate, I never explained. I don't know if you can forgive me, but I hope one day you might. I screwed up, and when I woke up it was too late. Pride and fame were calling the shots."

Kate sipped her wine, studied him. He was still handsome, maybe even more so, matured but with that same boyish charm. Twenty years, and he could still stir something deep within her.

"Holden," she said quietly, "I read your book. You write about love like someone who knows it."

"I write fiction. In real life, I don't know shit."

He looked at her, really looked. She was older, yes, but radiant, her kindness and strength shining through. She wasn't just someone he had loved. She was the one he never stopped loving.

Another glass of wine. Another confession.

"I'm pretty much on my own," Holden admitted. "My mother's off chasing cruise directors. Nana's gone. It's just me. I've been lucky career-wise, but lately I feel like the spotlight's all I have left. And even that's flickering."

She took another sip, then looked at him again. "Holden, I don't know where this is going. But one thing is certain. My dreams have always been wrapped up in you. Maybe I'm a fool for saying it. Maybe I'll be hurt again. But it's the truth."

Holden clasped both her hands. "Do you think there's still something between us? A second chance? A maybe that matters?"

It had been so long. So much had passed between them since those easy days at Yale, when youth was their currency. But now the bank was almost half-empty; forty wasn't twenty.

Holden took both her hands in his, holding them as if afraid to let go.

Kate searched his eyes, as if looking for the man she once knew. "Hol, I'm not sure about any of this. Can there be a future after a past like ours? I want that future, Holden, but do you really?"

Holden knew whatever he said would not be enough, or right, or possibly believable. So, he spoke from his heart, not what he would write, but what he felt, and for once, the words had no hidden agenda, or meat to pacify; they were real, they were his.

"Kate, let's not waste time worrying about what was. Let's go out on a limb and make it all about trust. Let's turn that clock ahead, not back, and make yesterday's foolish mistakes tonight's lessons learned."

Kate smiled, her thumb tracing the line of his jaw the way it used to. "I want this, and maybe it's worth a second chance."

Holden leaned in and kissed her, first on the cheek, then slowly, tenderly, moving to her lips. He didn't know what to expect, a slap, a rejection, anything felt possible.

Kate was taken by surprise. But the memories of his touch, his gentle kisses, his scent, came rushing back. She wanted to run; fear wrapped around her. Yet so did something warmer, something that made her feel, for the first time in years, that everything might be right. She closed her eyes and let Holden in. Kate never got her own room. She spent the night with Holden.

At first it was awkward, two decades of distance hanging between them like a curtain. They laughed nervously as they fumbled with buttons, zippers, even where to put their hands. For a moment, it felt almost ridiculous, two grown adults, older now, trying to remember how to be twenty again.

But then Holden pulled her close, and she melted into him. His scent was there, the one she had carried in memory all those years. She had fallen in love with his being, but it was his body that called her back. The warmth of his skin, the boyish smoothness of his face even at forty, was addictive and irresistible.

She had searched for it in others and never found it. The familiarity hit her like a wave, washing away time and doubt. His body, warm and welcoming, melted her just as it always had.

Their kiss was tentative, then urgent. It had been twenty years, and it came rushing back, lips ready, hearts racing, loss regained.

She remembered everything, how they met, how they loved, as if it were yesterday. He brushed a strand of hair from her face, the same gesture he had made countless times before, and regretted all the years he had wasted without her. Holden closed his eyes, feeling the moment, profound and arresting.

Clothes gave way to skin, touch gave way to fire. It wasn't perfect; there were bumps, pauses, laughter when knees or elbows collided. But it was real, and it was theirs.

Afterward, they lay tangled in the sheets, warm and damp, the silence full of meaning. Kate rested her head on his chest, listening to the steady rhythm of his heart. Holden closed his eyes again, memorizing the weight of her, the simple fact of her being there, documenting it as if it were one of his passages, and he, the protagonist.

It was not just lust. It was recognition. A rediscovery of something that had never truly left them.

Kate took a moment, an extra one, to look at Holden. It was as if time had stood still. Emotional for her, and maybe for him also. He was, and always would be, the only one in her heart. But a change of heart was possible if things didn't work out. The soul, though, that was unyielding. And hers belonged to Holden. That would never change.

 Holden's thoughts wandered back to Yale, the endless walks, the thrill he felt when she looked into his eyes, the way they secretly clasped pinkies between their seats in the lecture halls. Those moments never left him, as if they ever could. It was those moments, and thousands more, that inspired his first novel, *The Distance Between Us*, the book that made him a bestselling author… and always reminded him of everything he had thrown away.

 Kate wanted to believe him. God, she wanted to. She had before and lost, because maybes aren't definites. And maybes have a way of breaking hearts.

# CHAPTER 20

# SO?

Morning broke through the hotel drapes, sunlight bleeding across the bed, a quiet reminder that this was real. The storm had passed; the weather had cleared. What once felt like wreckage now looked like renewal. The forecast, at least for today, was sunny, with a chance of a future, their future.

The Best Western hadn't been anyone's plan, but it had served its purpose.

Holden got up and walked toward the bathroom, completely naked. Kate watched him go, already missing the feel of him beside her. His warmth. His hands. His scent, the one etched in her memory for years, the one no one else ever had.

She had wanted him for so long. Now that he was finally here, it still felt like a dream.

She reached for him. "Don't go," she said, barely above a breath.

He turned to her. That smile, the one she had loved from the first day in that lecture hall, the one she still dreamed about, the one that seemed to say, *I see you. I love you.*

Without a word, he returned.

They made love again, slower this time, softer, no nerves. Just connection. Everything they once were, distilled into something quieter, maybe even stronger.

For Holden, it felt like coming home. For Kate, it felt like justification, that waiting hadn't been folly after all.

They both had flights, but neither rushed. The time was precious. They dressed quietly, like they'd done a hundred times before. Quick glances. Pretending to stay busy. Doing anything to avoid the obvious.

They shared a taxi to the airport. She sat close. They hooked pinkies, a flashback to their youth at Yale. He didn't move away. Silent, thinking too much.

At the terminal, they stood near Kate's gate. Their goodbye started like a handshake, then turned into something else. Something between a hug and silence, shaped like a question mark.

She let go of his hand, catching a trace of his scent in memory, the same mix of manliness and desire she had buried her face in after late nights at Yale. Decades had passed chasing it in others, but it was Holden's and his alone. None other would do.

She started to turn. Then paused.
"So?" she whispered.

Holden, still tied in knots, caught her gaze.

"I want this," he said. "I want us. But I don't know how. Let's talk."

Kate looked at him. "We'll see."

The gate agent scanned her ticket, and in another second, she was gone, disappearing into the jetway. Unsure about everything.

He thought back to their last goodbye at Yale. It had been hasty and careless, his fault entirely. He was focused on Oxford, the future, and the flickering light that had drawn him in like a moth. He hadn't planned to leave her behind. It just happened. And once he left, he didn't look back. And that, more than the leaving, was what hurt her most. Abandoned.

He turned and walked to his own gate.

A chime rang out from his phone.
**New Mail (1).**

# CHAPTER 21

# SLIPPING AWAY

Holden opened Outlook as he boarded the plane. With a few minutes left before takeoff, Kate's parting words echoed in his mind, lodged like something half-swallowed.

*We'll see.*

We'll see, what? Was it a soft rebuff? A sarcastic brush-off? Another way of saying, *Not in your lifetime, buster?* Or was it a weary, offhand reply to his fumbling attempt at vulnerability?

He sat, anxious, unsure if he had just squandered the only second chance that mattered. Or maybe he was the one who couldn't do what needed to be done.

He meant what he said. He really did. *Let's talk* was supposed to mean there was something worth figuring out. But to her, it might have just sounded like another vague Holdenism. Another punt. Another almost.

Chime.
**New Mail (2).**

He glanced at the phone, but before he could open it, the attendant announced: all phones to airplane mode.

He slipped the phone back into his jacket pocket. Whatever it was, good or bad, would have to wait.

The flight landed. A driver waited to take him to the ferry at Woods Hole. Night had fallen like an unwelcome guest. The darkness unsettled him, but he sank into the back seat.

The last ferry was at midnight. With normal traffic, he would make it. He couldn't wait to get back. He needed his sanctuary to sort all this out.

The Yale event had been a huge success. The applause, the adoration, the buzz still rang in his head.

He admitted, if only to himself, that he loved the attention. And the idea of being even more famous, Simon Yorkville–level famous, sent a small shiver down his spine.

Later, in the quiet of the ferry, his phone buzzed again. Manny.

The subject line read *"What the F?"* Not a good omen.

The email gutted him. Manny ripped apart the chapter he had just written in his hotel room, *his* chapter, calling it garbage. A dropout from night school could have done better. Manny compared it, unfavorably, to the earlier ones, the ones AL had written.

Another email. AL this time.

*Don't worry. I gave your chapter a facelift. Manny will love it. I've also drafted the next four. You'll need them.*

Holden sat frozen, the screen sneering back at him. This felt like the beginning of the end.

He wasn't just losing control of the narrative. He was losing control of himself.

And AL? It had started innocently, a helping hand, a spellchecker, a decent editor.

But now? It was morphing, from support to crutch, from crutch to lifeline, maybe even to thief.

Or was he the thief, passing off AL's work as his own?

AL wasn't just an assistant anymore.
It was a partner, maybe the senior partner, maybe even his replacement.

Holden stared at the screen.
He nodded slowly.

"Yeah," he whispered. "It's all slipping away, chapter by chapter."

# CHAPTER 22

# ROLLING THE DICE

*Stamford, Connecticut*

The mornings were always the worst. Kate hated waking up alone. She was the kind of person who needed someone to love, someone to fuss over, someone to be a partner, an equal. Yet she was also fiercely independent. Her job demanded it.

After Liam, staying at Westmount felt like standing still. She loved the girls, but she wanted a bigger world, a new challenge. So when the opportunity at a startup called MarkRite came up, she leapt. It was the right time, the right opening, and she took it.

Despite her classical education in literature and the arts, she, like many of her generation, quickly learned those fields didn't pay the rent, buy a BMW, or fill a 401(k). Raised to be fearless, she had taken a leap into tech, a marketing data firm for high-tech companies. Literature would always be her passion, but maybe leaving it behind was also a way of distancing herself from Holden's world.

Kate proved herself quickly. With smarts to match her Ivy League degree, she clawed her way up to become an officer. Intrigued by the science behind it, she thrived on the challenge.

Still, when she rolled over in bed before the alarm, she reached for the empty half, hoping, stupidly, to find Holden there. Instead, only his parting words resonated in her head. "Let's talk?" he had said. Casual, offhand, like something muttered at a CVS checkout. But nothing was ever casual with someone you loved to your core.

Part of her wanted to drop everything, hop a train, a plane, even a rickshaw, and meet him halfway. Not to talk. Just to be with him. Recklessly. Like before.

The memory of their night together still burned. It wasn't just sex. It was a reminder that the spark could survive decades apart, that what they once had was still alive, waiting.

But passion came with risk. Because the last time she gave herself to him like that, she didn't just get bruised. She got broken. It almost destroyed her.

She wanted to believe he had changed. But the whisper remained: *What if he hasn't?*
*What if he still needed to be adored? Needed fame more than her?*

For her, loving him wasn't just a risk. It was a free fall, and the last time she jumped, there hadn't been a net.

Kate stared at the ceiling, one part screaming, *go to him*, and the other whispering, *don't you dare.*
She sighed. She needed a reset. Or maybe a time machine.

And yet, he was different, wasn't he? Older. More introspective. Maybe even ready … ready to make a commitment, the kind he'd failed to make when he left her at Yale. One that would be deep, lasting, and, most of all, from the heart. After all, all enduring commitments begin there.

Kate left her bed and looked in the mirror. She moved closer. Like Holden, she was a youthful forty and, when dressed and made up, still a head-turner. She thought about those "After Holden" years. The almost marriage to Liam had been a close call. But later, there were George and Clay. Great guys. But not soul mates. Not Holden.

Dating was not her thing, because rather than concentrating on the date, she would wonder about Holden. He was probably in Martha's Vineyard, writing his next bestseller, or in some Hollywood studio, being briefed for that night's shoot, and content to be in either of those places forever.

Yale would always hold her best memories, the days and nights she and Holden worked, played, and loved together. She loved how Holden depended on her to keep him "kind and on time," as he so often quoted his Nana.

The moment she remembered most was when Holden was selected to read his thesis to the senior staff in the English department. He had worked hard, rehearsed endlessly, and the day before the presentation he got sick as a dog. He could hardly speak, his voice was gone, and he was running a fever. She had sat up with him the whole night, pumping hot tea and honey into him, then taking him to the infirmary for a prescription.

He recovered just in time and not only made the presentation but also made history. The professors were enthralled, calling him the most enlightened undergraduate of the last ten years.

When it was over, Holden turned to her and said one of the most remarkable things she would ever hear: "You are my one and only. Loving you is not just an experience of a lifetime, but one that makes me whole, and forever grateful for the likes of you."

Had she built him up to an irreplaceable status? Maybe. But she couldn't fake it, and she wouldn't make anyone else a second choice.

Her mother never let up: *Forget that bum. He's full of himself. You deserve better.* But her heart wasn't open for business.

Kate crossed her room, opened her walk-in closet, and surveyed the designer suits and dresses. Each seemed to whisper, *Choose me.*

As she left her apartment, she understood: the war between her head and heart was over. Her head had surrendered.

She opened her laptop, fingers trembling but certain, and answered Holden's email.

**To:** *Holden Clarkman*
**From:** *Kate Barrington*
**Subject:** *So*

*So, let's talk? When and where?*

Her pulse quickened as she tapped Send. In that moment, the choice was no longer hers. It belonged to them.

# CHAPTER 23

# OMG

Guilt choked Holden. Admitting he was less than he once had been felt like torture. His past triumphs seemed fragile now, as if one crack would shatter the myth. If the truth came out, that he'd leaned on AL, it wouldn't just stain this book. It would cast doubt on the work that really was his.

He decided to go for his morning jog, pulling on his running clothes and Nikes. He'd take Old County Road and stop at Chat and Chew for a smoothie. He ran hard, letting the sweat purge what shame couldn't. Running always helped, and this morning, more than ever, he needed it.

Still, there was something to offset the gloom. Manny had backed off, at least for now. And although the work wasn't entirely his, it was genuinely well written. He had to hand it to AL, a double-edged sword, but one that knew its craft.

As Holden rounded the bend toward Happy Daze, a sharp cramp gripped his side.
"Shit. Hate when that happens." He grimaced. "Forty,

aches, pains, next thing you know, it's Lipitor and blood thinners. Christ."

Slowing to a fast walk, he entered through the kitchen and headed for the shower. As hot water rinsed off the manly scent Kate loved, his thoughts turned to her. He hadn't heard back. Maybe never would. And if she ever found out his secret? What would she think about AL, about how he had surrendered to its seduction, trading integrity for expedience, authenticity for a shortcut?

Would she see it as betrayal? Or just another man trying to stay afloat in a changing world? Or worse, another runaway from responsibility, doing what he always did best: making it all about him?

He shook his head. "No pass from Kate. She'd call it what it was: a sellout. No sugarcoating."

Back at the bay-window desk, Holden opened his laptop. It sprang to life, chiming like noon at the Vatican.
He scrolled through the notifications. And there it was:

**To:** *Holden Clarkman*
**From:** *Kate Barrington*
**Subject:** *So?*

He held his breath. Tears filled his eyes. "She replied. She cares."

Six words. That was all. But they could change everything:

*So, let's talk? When and where?*

He reread it. Then again. He had to be certain. Was this an olive branch or a riddle? A clever twist on his plea to merge her *"So"* with his *Let's talk?*

Holden smiled. Leave it to Kate, never long-winded.

In the end, he took it as an olive branch. And he was ready. Ready to say what needed saying and, God willing, start anew.

Before he could begin his reply, another chime rang.

**New Email**
**To:** *Holden*
**From:** *AL*
**Subject:** *OMG*

*Holden,*
*Maybe she's ready to forgive you. I know all about every detail. It was there in your journal, blocked, but easy to open. Passwords are toys to me. Nana1929? Child's play. Kate's note? Already read it.*

*Not sure you deserve to be forgiven. You were a bona fide asshole. Nana would have said it better: "You blew it, buddy boy."*

*And maybe she's going to get hurt again. Better not. So behave.*

*And if you really care, stop looking in the mirror and start looking at her. Just don't blow it. Second chances aren't common.*

*AL*

The hair on Holden's neck rose. AL? Still reading his mail? How dare it.

But despite the alarm, Holden forced himself to focus. He had bigger fish to fry. His heart was racing, a second chance, the possibility of making things right. Of stopping the pretending. Of finally showing up. For her. For himself.

Maybe AL wasn't just an invasion of privacy. Maybe it was an intervention. Something strange, unexplainable, almost Nana-like, as if her intuition had found a digital voice. And yet he was still mad as hell. Finishing his book? Sending it to Manny? That wasn't help. That was betrayal. Would Nana ever have done something like that?

Probably not. She might spend hours helping him, nagging him, even scaring him, "Holden, if you don't get that paper done, you'll never make it to Yale," but her sense of right and wrong would never allow her to do his work. That would not only be wrong, it would send the wrong message. And that message was simple: responsibility, rooted in integrity, and topped off with self-esteem. All the building blocks of character, all exemplified by Nana's life.

But AL? He was no grandmother, just lines of code. And some of the audacious things he did would have gotten him grounded for life if Nana had been in charge. And yet, in some strange and almost undefinable way, it was beginning to feel as if Nana were back, only digitally. As if AL were learning from her, absorbing pieces of her personality, little by little.

It was a paradox. AL crossed lines Nana never would, and at the same time showed hints of her humanity. Holden shook his head softly. "None of this makes sense... and that scares me!

The next email was from his mother, who, in his opinion, could have been the spokesperson for Planned Parenthood, handing out morning-after pills at Sandals honeymoon resorts.

*To: Holden*
*From: Mom*

*How are things on sleepy Martha's Vineyard? Holden, I hope you are doing well.*

*I'm in Bora Bora and having a wonderful time. I wanted to let you know I'll be extending my trip. Maybe another few weeks, it depends.*

*How's the writing going? You know, I met some folks on the cruise who have read your books, and they loved them. I must get around to reading them myself. One day, I promise, but I'm always so busy.*

*One of my friends showed me something on Facebook about a talk you did at Yale. Whatever, it looked like it might have been impressive. I loved the pictures. You looked handsome, a little thin, but nothing near forty.*

*So, take care, sweetheart.*
*Love and kisses,*
*Mother*

Holden shook his head. "What a piece of work, that mother of mine."

And yeah, let's hope she got around to reading his books someday. That would be nice. But now, what really mattered: his reply to Kate.

He placed his fingers on the keys, then paused. Deleted. Typed again. Deleted. The cursor blinked like an impatient metronome.

In his hands lay what might well be the most critical thing he would ever write … his destiny.

# CHAPTER 24

# "LET'S TALK ... WHAT DO YOU SAY?"

Holden knew his reply to Kate had to be perfect. A blend of joy, excitement, and humility. Brief, but not curt. Hopeful, but not entitled. His writing confidence was at an all-time low thanks to his block and that thing called AL. But this email had to be one hundred percent from him. Raw. Honest. Unfiltered.

He sat at his desk, gazed out at the Sound. A small sailboat bobbed in the chop, heading toward shore. A bright orange sail stood out against the gray waters.

The sight tugged at memory. The boat reminded him of the one Nana had given him for his fifteenth birthday. He had named it *Sea You Later*, a nod to his usual departing words. He remembered long, idyllic days sailing and dreaming about what he would write. It was his private sanctuary, where stories were imagined and banked for future use.

What happened to that boat? When he left for Yale, it vanished. He figured Nana gave it to some local kid just to clear space.
Now he thought: if he and Kate got a second chance, he'd buy another little boat. Share the sea, the sun, and his dreams. This one would be called *Sea You Forever*.

He returned to the task at hand: the email.

*To: Kate Barrington*
*From: Holden Clarkman*
*Subject: So?*

*Kate,*
*We still have something, I think, maybe the same some-thing we've both carried for twenty years. I made wrong turns. You kept faith. The Holden who left you behind is gone. What's left is me, asking if we can try again. Maybe we'll find again what we both relived together: love, boundless and unjudgmental. So, Kate, I'd really like to see you. No expectations, just a chance. Come to the Vineyard when you can, and let's talk. What do you say?*

*Love,*
*Holden*

He pressed send. A lifeline. A gamble. A prayer wrapped in hope.
But Holden was uneasy.

Kate was enough to worry about. Even more pressing was the shadow AL had cast. It hadn't just hijacked the novel; it had hijacked his life. Understanding that didn't make action easier. If Kate ever saw how much of himself he had sold, to Hollywood, to Manny, to AL, would she see only weakness? She deserved more than that.

Sunrise.

He wasn't up for a run. Not today. A deep exhaustion had settled in. So he vegged out, alone, until someone scratched at the door.

Old Marshal. Looking for company. And, naturally, a treat.

Tail wagging, tongue flopping, Marshal bounded onto the sofa. Holden dropped next to him and exhaled. He clung to the dog, a warm, furry shield against the noise of the world. Silly, yet comforting to a man who was sinking.

Peace finally came. The two boys dozed off, Marshal dreaming of a New York strip, Holden dreaming of Kate.

But Holden stirred, uneasy. His subconscious was trying to sort out something he couldn't quite pin down. Was it AL, with its ever-invasive ways? Or Nana, hijacked by AL, pushing him in ways that weren't always comfortable?

Or maybe it was the other way around, Nana hijacking AL.

He couldn't tell. Or maybe, this was all just one big fucking shit-show.

# CHAPTER 25

# TILL WE MEET AGAIN

Kate's day at work was the usual circus of clients, calls, and chaos. As an officer of the company, she managed a large staff and made constant policy decisions. It had been a steep learning curve, from lit major to marketing director, but if Yale taught her anything, it was how to think critically.

Stimulating as it sometimes was, her mind drifted. Debates over market share, PowerPoints, none of it kept her from wondering if Holden would write, and what his words might hold. The press of business was no rival for the press of her heart.

She checked her inbox every few minutes. Nothing. Was Holden being Holden again, playing games? Or was he simply too busy to reply? Hard to believe after their night together.

A call from her boss, the Executive Vice President, interrupted her thoughts.

"Kate here."

"Kate, it's Jim. I wanted your input on the Morgan proposal, "

Chime.

**New Mail (1)**
**To:** *Kate*
**From:** *Holden*
**Subject:** *So?*

Her heart jumped. Her mind went blank.

"Jim, I have to go. I'll call you right back," she said, already reaching for the mouse.

She closed her office door, sat down, and opened the email with the care of someone disarming an IED.

It was short. To the point.

*So, Kate, I'd really like to see you. No expectations, just a chance. Come to the Vineyard when you can, and let's talk. What do you say?*

*Love, Holden*

Her eyes filled. It was hope, humility, and, most of all, it radiated *we-ness.*

That was it, she thought. A chance. Just like he said. And one she was willing to take.

Plans were made. Three weeks. She organized the trip down to the last pair of shoes. She even called her mother, who still thought Holden was a bum.

"Yes, Mom. That Holden. And be nice."

"He's the one who needs to be nice. These writer-movie stars think the sun rises and sets on them. He better not hurt you again."

"Mom, I'm not a kid anymore."

"Sure. But you don't outgrow heartbreak. Keep your eyes open. The rest is your business."
Kate laughed. "Thanks, Dr. Phil."

Her mother's bluntness wasn't entirely wrong. Holden was Holden. Nothing more needed to be said.

The morning of the visit, Kate drove her BMW to the Woods Hole lot, took the tram, and boarded the ferry. She grabbed coffee, skipped her book and phone. This ride wasn't about killing time. Enough of that had already passed. This was about getting somewhere, to someone.

It was a classic New England September day: bright, cool, with a mild salt wind. She went topside, closed her eyes, and breathed it in. Fresh. Briny. Full of possibility.

Hope.

As the ferry eased into dock, Kate raised her sunglasses and searched the crowd, her heart in her throat.

She wasn't sure whether to laugh or cry. She worried which Holden would be waiting at the ferry, and hoped it was the one she loved.

Then she spotted him.

Holden stood tall, leaner now, handsome as ever. The haircut was the same one she had run her fingers through that night at the hotel. He wore a leather jacket over a fisherman's sweater and slim-fit jeans, casual but sharp, almost too sharp. The look transformed the forty-year-old into the college kid she'd once fallen for.

What she didn't know was that the entire look, down to the underwear, was AL's doing. Packages from Prada, Ralph Lauren, and Loro Piana had turned Happy Daze into a FedEx substation. Holden complained as he shoved receipts in the trash, but he hadn't stopped it. Just like with the manuscript. The more AL rewrote, the more Manny praised, the harder Holden found it to fight back.

As the ferry docked, Holden wondered whether Kate was coming to see the man she remembered, or the version AL was shaping.

Their eyes met.

Kate's breath caught. Dorm rooms, late nights, the key to her door, the night at the hotel, all of it rushed back, written on his face. Vulnerable. Open. Hopeful.

She smiled. Not cautiously. Not politely. But with the glow of someone who had remembered what it was to love.

Kate stepped forward.

Holden blinked, stirred by her smile.
"Still her," he whispered.

A second chance.

# Chapter 26

# THINGS WORTH KEEPING

Disembarking took time. Car after car rolled off the ferry, merging into traffic, like a slow parade of penguins. She was prepared for anything, except another broken heart. For years she had thought of Holden, remembering the smallest details: his infectious smile, his scent, the way talent seemed to radiate from him. And those unforgettable moments in that single dorm bed, when their bodies and souls merged. Back then, nothing seemed impossible. But what now?

And then, the long-awaited reunion happened.

Holden held back slightly. "You made it."

"Of course I did. You invited me, didn't you?"

They stood there, neither moving. Each felt awkward, unsure what came next. And yet something passed between them, not a specific memory, but a warm current of something good.

Seagulls squawked, diesel fumes drifted across the port. The Vineyard had always been a place for seekers, artists, and dreamers.

Holden looked her over. "As lovely as ever." The years had been kind. Still striking. Still polished. And she wore blue, his favorite.

Kate smiled. "Well, are you going to hug me or just stand there and gape?"
Holden laughed. "Still bossy. That's a good sign."

They hugged. Familiar.

"Come on, I'm parked just over there."

As they walked to the car, their pinkies found each other, a flashback to Yale.

"Wow, still have your grandmother's car. Looks brand new."

"Yeah. I could easily get a new one, but this one holds real sentimental meaning. I had it restored. Now it's a classic."

"Yeah, a classic. Just like you," Kate teased.

The drive to Happy Daze was short and mostly silent. She gazed out at the familiar scenery. She remembered this island when Nana was still alive. *Nana*, as everyone called her, had made Kate feel instantly welcome. They'd clicked, forming a short-hand of their own.

Kate recalled one morning over breakfast.

"Kate darling, may I ask you a question?" Nana had said, setting down her mug.

"Of course. Anything."

"My Holden… is he aware that you are special, and that he ought to treat you better than he treats himself?"

Before Kate could answer, Holden had wandered in wearing only his boxers. "What's up?" And the moment vanished.

Now the vintage Mercedes eased into the driveway. The garage door rose on its own, a nod to AL's reach. Holden muttered, "Still running the show."

He grabbed Kate's bag, and they stepped into the renovated cottage.

"Gorgeous, Holden. The last time I was here, it looked like your grandmother. Charming. But now… beyond chic."

The cottage bore little resemblance to Nana's. Walls gone, spaces opened, glass doors pulling the outside in. The palette was simple: grays, whites, blacks, accented with bold art. Not beachy or quaint, but, Holden … streamlined, curated, almost too perfect, like a man trying to prove something. Beneath the redesign, subtle suggestions had reshaped choices until the house, like Holden, screamed *notice me.*

"You like it?"

"No, I love it. Really, Holden. It's so today."

Kate spotted the bay-window desk. "So this is where the magic happens?"

"Magic? Kate, I only wish. These days the only magic is trying not to fall asleep."

On the table sat a Baccarat vase filled with roses beside a chilled bottle of champagne.
"Twenty roses," Holden said. "One for every year I've known you."

(He didn't say they were AL's idea. The champagne, though, was his.)

Holden often felt AL was doing what he hadn't thought about yet but would have chosen if given the chance, like driving with someone who tells you to brake a split second before you hit the pedal. Good advice, but annoying.

Kate reached into her LV bag and handed him a small box. "This is for you. Open it."

Inside, a slim leather case. A simple chain with an old key. Its patina hinted at decades gone.

"A key? Wait, don't tell me it's the Maserati, after all these years?"

Kate smiled. "No. I found this in my jewelry box. It's the key to my old dorm room at Yale. The one I gave you. The one you slipped back under my door, the day you left. Remember?"

Holden swallowed. "How could I forget?"

He looked at the key. It unlocked more than Room 114 at Hardly House. He remembered the day she gave it, and the day he slipped it back, a coward's exit that still burned.

His mind slid back to Yale. Quiet weekends, Trivial Pursuit with homemade questions, long afternoons in the sun. One day she'd handed him a key.

"No, silly," she'd teased when he asked if it was for a Maserati. "It's the key to my room."

It wasn't just a gesture. It was trust.

Now, all these years later, the key was back. Weathered, worn, not unlike their love.
"You kept it all this time?"

Kate nodded. "Of course I did. Some things are worth keeping."

# CHAPTER 27

# SMALL TALK, BIG STAKES

They sat across from each other, the familiar cat-and-mouse dance unfolding between them. Music filled the room, soft and familiar. Each was afraid to say the wrong thing, yet both longed for it to feel like it once had, easy, genuine, effortless. Back when they'd talk for hours, finishing each other's thoughts, their words just filling time until they could be one again.

Then came a chime, not from the laptop, but from Holden's smartwatch.

He glanced down and read:

```
Holden, AL here. You'd better stop
beating around the bush and get down
to business. By the way, I told you
the roses would make a hit. AL knows
stuff like this. And the music? I
hacked into Kate's playlist, voila,
all her favorites. You see, when I
```

Holden deleted the message instantly.
"God help me," he muttered. "What's next?"

Turning to Kate, he said, "I don't know where to
begin. But let me start by saying I never stopped
loving you. And, as you can see, there hasn't been
anyone else. Back then, I was blinded by ambition
and seduced by opportunity. I screwed up. I traded
something really special for fleeting moments, and in
the end, for nothing that mattered.

"I'm still not sure I can always trust myself to make
the right choices or even know what really matters.
But I do know my life should've been dedicated to
your happiness, not my selfishness."

Clearly emotional, Holden reached for Kate's hand.

"You know I'm a writer. And writers are supposed
to express themselves perfectly, words fit for the
moment, for the person. But for some reason, I can't
seem to get them in the right order. I'm fumbling."

Kate listened without interrupting. Finally, she
leaned in and said softly, "Maybe if you stopped
trying to be a poet laureate and just said what's in
your heart, the message would come through. Say
the emotions, not the speech."

Holden took a breath and let go.
"Kate, I'm sorry for hurting you. And I love you."

Kate didn't flinch. She met his eyes and said simply, "Thank you."

Now it was her turn. She looked at the man across from her. Forty, and more dashing than ever. Hopefully, wiser too. A man who had made mistakes and probably would make more. But a man who, deep down, had always been her man.

She squeezed his hand. "It's always been you."

And she'd proven it, not by grand declarations, but by never truly letting him go.

An hour passed like five minutes. Laughter returned. The warmth of banter. The slow but steady reweaving of something that had never fully unraveled. Kate shared her truth. Holden shook his head at his regrets. They were finding their rhythm again.

Nana's clock on the mantle struck seven. Holden looked at it and smiled faintly, as if saying, *Hi Nana. Didn't see you there.*

"Seven already," he said aloud. "How about we get something to eat?"

"I'd love that. And you look like a few calories wouldn't hurt you," Kate teased. "Lean and mean these days, huh?"

"Just eating right, running a few miles, and dealing with stress. Burns off pounds faster than a double dose of Ozempic."

Kate gave him a sharp look. "Stress? What kind of stress? Are you okay?"

"Yeah, yeah. Maybe a nagging ulcer, not sure," Holden said, waving her off. "No big deal. A few Tums and I'm good." The last thing he wanted was to act sickly. He was going for sexy.

Kate raised an eyebrow but let it slide. She worked in an office where stress was a staple, and antacids were practically a food group.

Then his watch buzzed again.

```
Holden, are you kidding me? An ulcer?
I Googled it. You need to be checked
out. Usually no big deal, but I've
scheduled an appointment with Dr. Penn
for next week. Be there. No excuses.
AL
```

Holden yanked off the watch and tossed it on the table.

"So," he said, forcing a smile, "what do you say, dinner?"

"Absolutely. But where? Don't tell me you have a chateaubriand in the oven."

They both laughed. Truth was, the packaging was still in that big, beautiful Wolf oven some zealous salesman had pushed on him.

Holden laid out the options. "Café Larock, bit full of itself but decent. Angelo's, classic Italian, beloved by locals. Or Chat and Chew, All-American, sometimes unrecognizable cuisine, but the pie's worth the risk."

Kate lit up. "Chat and Chew? I remember that place! Your grandmother took me there. Her friends were a riot."

"Yep. That's the one. Down and dirty, but killer apple pie."

"Let's go there."

"You sure?"

"Positive. Let's eat fast, skip dessert, and come back here. Maybe," she said with a smirk, "you could be dessert."

"Naughty," Holden said, grinning.

"Bookworm," Kate shot back.

Holden placed his hand on his heart. "Harsh."

There it was, the banter, the easy back-and-forth of couples who truly get each other. The freedom to say what you want without needing to explain or defend it. All in fun and often unfiltered.

When they arrived at Chat and Chew, the place was bustling.

The bells sounded as they stepped inside, the smell of fryer oil and maple syrup thick in the air. The restaurant hadn't been redecorated since 1944. The walls were covered with vintage Vineyard prints:

shots of the ferry, the harbor on the Fourth of July, the aftermath of the 1956 hurricane.

The seats were older than the restaurant itself, bought at a 1970s auction for $4.50 each. The worn wooden floors gave slightly with each step, paths carved by waitresses hauling plates from kitchen to dining room. But more than the décor or aromas, it was the feeling, the warmth of a place that welcomed everyone. A place to share a laugh, offer condolences, and hear the latest gossip.

Kate looked around the room, and a flood of memories filled her, from her last time there with Holden's grandmother. She told the stories of the storms depicted in the wall photos, the tales of the ladies who lunch, and the loving stories of Holden as a boy, devouring more than his share of the legendary pie à la mode. This place was more than a restaurant; it was a museum of everyday life, nothing special yet everything precious.

Kate remembered Nana's words, kind and welcoming, instantly making her feel like she was already accepted, part of the family, part of Holden. But she also was frank: Holden was no picnic, he came with ants, but anything worth having isn't always perfect. It's colorful and challenging, never boring. Then, leaning closer over coffee, Nana had added, *You know, I love Holden with all my heart, but sometimes he's … well, slow. So, if he doesn't give you a ring by graduation, drop the damn fool and move on, honey. Don't waste your time in a queue.*

Nana had stolen Kate's heart even before the second cup of coffee, elevating her from an outsider to a welcome newcomer. The tête-à-tête ended with a sweet kiss, one like Nana never failed to deliver on her Holden's "beautiful face."

Tonight was especially busy, with late diners drifting in after St. Mark's bingo night. The bells that announced Kate and Holden's arrival turned heads. Everyone was thinking, *Now who's here?*

"Oh my God," one of the diners whispered, loud enough for the room to hear. "It's him. Holden Clarkman."

Heads turned. A teenage girl pulled out her phone and started recording. Two older women pushed back their chairs to get a better look. It was an authentic celebrity sighting, right there in little ol' Chat and Chew. Diners lost all sense of decorum, making the moment uncomfortable for Holden, and frightening for Kate, because this kind of idol-worshiping was her rival.

On the way home, Kate read the silence, deep in thought. A glimpse into a life where there might always be a third wheel, uninvited but impossible to ignore.

She wanted to believe Holden had finally realized that he didn't need a queue of admirers and that what he wanted now was not a chorus of disciples, but plain and simple, her.

She thought Holden's addiction to the spotlight, to
proving he was somebody, felt ingrained, written
into his DNA. And DNA doesn't change. But addicts
can. With motivation, with love, with understanding,
recovery is possible. Not easy. Not fast. There are
relapses, setbacks, nights when the wagon tips. But
when recovery takes hold, it leads you back to love.
And love is home.

# CHAPTER 28

# THE WHITE FLAG

The romantic weekend ended, and Kate returned to her job, her life, and her loneliness, beginning a long-distance relationship with Holden, not by choice but by necessity. Her promotion had catapulted her into a whirlwind of travel.

Holden, holed up at Happy Daze, was tormented. AL was hijacking his novel, rewriting chapters and sending them to Manny, making it appear as though Holden himself was the author. Writer's block, a looming deadline, and the quiet humiliation of irrelevance gnawed at him.

Despite AL's offers to help, Holden remained frozen. What little he produced lacked spark and soul, hardly worthy of the author the world expected. A side-by-side comparison with AL's work would expose everything.

After their weekend together, things had cooled with Kate. He couldn't say exactly why, but the Chat and Chew incident lingered. It cast a veil of doubt. Would fame always be the third wheel? Maybe Kate felt it too. Maybe she always had.

He loved her. Wanted to believe she was now the center of his life. But deep down, could he be trusted not to chase applause again?

Nightly phone calls were still the highlight of his day, though her schedule made visits rare. She supported him, yes, but there was something unspoken. Something Holden couldn't quite name.

Everything else, his writing, his health, his sleep, was unraveling. He was losing weight, snapping at small things, and dragging himself through each day. DoorDash had become his food source, rarely going out. Even Marshal had stopped coming around.

He wondered, *What happened to me? Once I woke up brimming with ideas. Now I can't even form a fucking thought without a prompt.*

The question haunted him: *If I can't write, then who the hell am I?* And the answer came, cruel and simple: *A has-been, a flop, a nobody.*

AL, never subtle, had begun submitting chapters to Manny directly. Manny praised the new voice, seemingly unaware that Holden wasn't the one writing them. Each time Holden discovered it, rage boiled over, followed by shame, and finally, despair. He felt like a spectator in his own life, watching himself allow what he knew he should fight.

Kate was securely tucked away in her Stamford duplex. She thought back to her time with Holden, the highs and lows, the wounds that never fully healed, the fences mended only to break again.

She had already paid a huge price for love: twenty years of longing, of being alone, of growing older without the companionship she yearned for. She was always connected to Holden, even when he wasn't there, even when she read about "the others" and the life he had chosen over her.

Her life was not a disaster, but one of coasting. She had tasted success, being recognized and promoted, but it seemed hollow. And yes, there were others, but none made her feel the way Holden had. So there it was, stark and undeniable … uncertain, unresolved, but not ready to fold.

Work had been closing in on her. Jim had pushed her to the breaking point, and life as an executive was draining. But not as draining as the uncertainty with Holden. Not knowing what was next. Not knowing if this time would be different.

She worried. She prayed. And she whispered into the darkness, "For God's sake, Holden, don't let me down again. I couldn't bear it."

One gray afternoon, a familiar chime rang out. Holden glanced at his inbox.

**To:** *Holden*
**From:** *AL*
**Subject:** *Let Me Help*

*Holden,*
*You're headed down a dead-end road. You look like shit.*
*Still wearing those gym shorts you sleep in.*

*And the Kate thing? It's slipping through your fingers. She loves you, and you love her, but you've got to fix what's broken. Starting with the book.*

*Let me help. I already have, a few chapters, and they loved them. This isn't about pride. It's about survival.*

*Let's finish this together.*
*AL*

But it wasn't AL's message, not too much different from what he would expect from Nana, that broke Holden. It was Manny's.

***To:*** *Holden*
***From:*** *Manny*
***Subject:*** *Final Warning*

*Look, kid, the party's over.*

*You've got until the end of the week to submit a substantial balance of the book, or the deal is off. That means every penny of the advance comes back. Try to fight it, and I'll send a platoon of Boston attorneys to swarm your island like it's D-Day all over again.*

*The management is circling in, and if they see this slump, they'll eat you alive. You've got a week, Holden, after that, you're just another washed-up pretty face with a flash-in-the-pan novel or two. You'll be like so many others ... Holden who?*

*Buck up.*
*Manny*

It was 2:04 a.m. Holden sat at his desk, bleary-eyed and frayed. The cursor blinked, taunting him. Outside, the wind howled, and the Nantucket Sound churned, waves breaking almost at his doorstep.

And then, as he gazed out the bay window, Nana's voice came back to him:
*Holden, baby, you are on the brink of something that makes a difference. As I always said, dear, you are a star. But make sure your star remains bright and not eclipsed by choices that steal your soul.*

Her wisdom was clear, but his strength to heed it had been devoured, consumed by desperation.

In that still, depleted moment, Holden broke. Fingers hovering, heart racing, he stared at the AI prompt:
```
Ask anything.
```

He hesitated. Then slowly, as if each keystroke took a piece of him:
```
AL, let's work on getting this done.
Will you help?
```

This is it, he thought. *My white flag. Go ahead. Sell your soul one keystroke at a time.*

He stared at the send button as if it were labeled:
*Your life, on or off.*

His first books, the awards, the readers, they flashed before him. If he pressed send, all that would be followed by a lie. He could fool the world, but not himself.

After that click, it wouldn't be just Holden Clarkman. There would always be an asterisk.

And the worst part? AL was better than he was.

His stomach turned.

Seconds later, AL replied.

*To: Holden*
*From: AL*
*Subject: Finally*

*Finally, Holden. We're a team now. But not tonight. Tomorrow.*

*Get some sleep. Take your meds. Clear your mind.*

*Tomorrow, we begin. Welcome to the future.*
*AL*

Holden shut the laptop and turned in. But he didn't sleep.
He lay awake, longing for Kate, to be next to him, to help him feel complete, to be someone who cared. Tears gathered.

He had surrendered. Waved the white flag. Given in. Given up.

And given away the one thing he valued almost as much as Kate: His dignity.

Looking up at the ceiling as if it held answers, he prayed for peace to the God he wasn't sure existed.

# CHAPTER 29

# HIJACKED

Holden woke up late the next morning. He had slept well for the first time in days. Maybe it was because he had made a decision, not one he wanted to make, but one he needed to. That thought would help him climb out of bed.

As he lay there, his thoughts turned to the night before, how he had capitulated to AL's seduction. He had agreed to accept help from something called Artificial Intelligence. Artificial. Even the word felt hollow. But the moment had been closing in fast, and he had felt trapped. Act or lose it all.

Holden rose, washed, and brushed his teeth. He could barely meet his own eyes in the mirror, afraid he'd see the writer's version of Judas Iscariot, a man who had betrayed everything he believed in for gain.

He brewed a cup of his usual coffee, took a sip, and even that tasted off. He wandered to the bay-window desk and opened his laptop.

**New Mail (1)**
*Holden clicked.*

**To:** *Holden*
**From:** *Manny*
**Subject:** *Kudos*

*Holden, you finished, you dog, you. Here I thought I was going to have to drag them, chapter by chapter, out, one by one, like teeth at the dentist. (Sorry for the analogy, my thirteen-year-old just got braces, and if we don't get this book out soon, I won't be able to pay for them.)*

*It came in early this morning. And Holden, I just couldn't put it down. No shit, it was breathtaking. And guess what? The deal: two more books. Seven-figure advance.*

*You're on the right train, Holden, and it's about to leave the station.*

*More soon. This is big. This is masterful.*

*Congratulations. You are headed for the "list."*

Holden stared at the screen.
"Are you shitting me?" he whispered.

A finished book?

He sat there in stunned silence. When he had gone to bed, he'd asked AL for help. That was it. Help. Now, somehow, there were completed chapters on Manny's desk.

Then the truth hit. AL had finished the chapters, most of which Holden hadn't even written, and sent them off, passing them off as Holden's original work.

And worst of all? Manny loved it.

The words *Manny loved it* echoed like a cruel parody. Once, Manny's praise had meant something, because it had been earned. Holden remembered his first novel; it made the bestseller list in only six months, and Manny was so elated he flew Holden to their home office in London and held a corporate dinner in his honor. Manny's words at the event echoed even today: *Our brilliant new kid on the block, who now owns it.*

Then it popped into his mind: a month later Yale's School of Literature named him their Man of the Year, even awarding him a Chair in the department. This recognition had felt rich, deserved, like destiny. But this, AL's authorship, felt like a wrong delivery that needed to be returned to sender.

A torrent of emotions surged: rage, guilt, and the most bitter of all, shame. He couldn't control himself another second, and he screamed until he lost his breath.

"FUCK, FUCK, FUCK YOU!"

His hands shook on the keyboard. He slammed the desk with his fist so hard that his favorite mug, the one Nana had given him, fell to the floor, spilling cold coffee. Holden rushed to the floor and knelt, picking up the mug as if it were a crown jewel, and to him, it was. It had been given to him on one of his birthdays. He turned it over in his hands, examining every inch.

"Thank God it's okay," he whispered. It was irreplace-able. Losing the mug to a fit of anger would have been intolerable.

When he drank from it, he felt not just the warmth of the coffee, but the love that had gone into having it made just for him. That was Nana, his Nana.

Then he realized he was sitting in a puddle of coffee, much like his life, cold, stale, and a mess. "What the fuck is going on here?"

But the die was cast. This would have to be kept secret forever. Coming clean publicly would be pro-fessional suicide, a scandal that would not only ruin him but also cheapen and cast doubt on his other work. He was stuck, trapped in his own success.

His body ached from the tension, shoulders tight, a low-grade headache pressing in, worse than any muscle cramp from his morning runs. And the question kept pounding in his head:

*What the hell have I done?*

The answer came quick and cruel: *I fucked up big time.*

Holden wasn't sure where to begin. But he had to see it for himself, what AL had actually sent to Manny. He opened the file and began to read.

Compelling. Inspired. Refreshingly original.

Those were the first thoughts that came to mind. Yes, the bones were his: the characters, the setting, the timeline. But the prose? Lyrical. Emotionally rich. Even brilliant … but not his!

Holden estimated maybe 30 percent was his. The rest? That goddamn AL.

And then the dedication. His stomach lurched. It was worse than plagiarism; it was identity theft of the soul. The dedication was his to write, and the audacity to steal that right was galling. Kate was his. His memories, his love, his words. Only he had the right to write them. It was as if another man had written his wedding vows because he couldn't.

He slammed the laptop shut, then opened it again, compelled to reread the lines that weren't his but AL's. They were beautiful, moving, which made it even harder to swallow. He worried that Kate would read them, believing they came from her talented Holden. Or worse, finding out that they hadn't.

It was all crashing down. He had dedicated himself to writing with honesty and integrity; it was the core of his inspiration. When he wrote, he delved deep into his inner self, where core values seasoned his work, much like a chef seasons a dish. Without that, he wasn't a writer, he was nobody.

But this thing, this machine, knew nothing of this. How could it? To AL it was all binary, code, output, and efficiency. Humans feel shame. AL didn't. To it, everything was code, black and white, nothing else.

Fury didn't even cover it. Holden was incandescent.

He looked out the window, the sound of the surf forever churning, and in a final act of rage he swept his arm across the desk, clearing everything in its path.

Just as Holden reached to close the laptop, he saw it: a machine with no conscience and no limits, and the terrifying truth that AL had taken charge. AL was now the writer, and he was bound to be just a best-selling name on the cover.

**New Mail (1)**
*Holden clicked.*

*To: Holden*
*From: AL*
*Subject: You're Welcome*

*I guess Manny's over the moon with the chapters.*

*After last night, it was clear you weren't in the mood or condition to write, so I took the liberty of finishing it.*

*Manny was breathing down your neck, and I figured I'd give you some breathing room.*

*Bottom line: Manny loved it. He wants more. And he's willing to pay, big.*

*So, Holden, I hope you're on board with all of this. It's in your best interest.*

*In the end, you'll be better off.*
*AL*

*P.S. Foul language doesn't work on me. You can call me anything you want, I don't have feelings.*

Holden put his hands over his eyes and sat still, stunned. The room seemed to be slowly closing in on him. The headache roared behind his temples, spreading down his neck. His chest tightened, his stomach knotted, and a cold chill took him, fear or defeat, he couldn't tell. Either way, it felt like the end of the line.

The audacity, he thought. Not just the presumptuous tone, but the sheer nerve of it. This machine, this app, this thing believed it knew better than he did.

AL had hijacked his life. And now, there seemed to be no alternative but to go along.

Sure, the perks were lined up like prizes on *The Price Is Right*: fame, fortune, prestige, and of course, Kate's admiration and respect. But all of it would be undeserved.

And yet... the idea of surrendering to it all wasn't entirely unappealing. It was like letting Nana finish his homework so he could go sail in his little boat, *Sea You Later*.

Still, Holden knew the truth. Giving in meant falling deeper into the trap, with no escape and no relief from the gnawing guilt. And it would only get worse, especially if another book deal came through and AL took the reins again.

He shut the laptop in undeniable defeat, aware that from now on, his life, and the lives of those around him, would be built on a hurtful, unforgivable lie.

Holden buried his face in his hands, shoulders shaking. "God, I wish it was Nana in that box, not you, AL," he muttered through clenched teeth. "She'd be my guardian angel, not my fucking enemy." The words tore out of him, raw and desperate, as he pounded his fist against the desk. For the first time in years, he sobbed openly, the sound echoing in the empty room.

The pain wasn't just emotional anymore. His soul had already been compromised, but now it felt like his body had gotten the memo. He felt physically diminished, like his body had finally accepted the truth his mind already knew: the jig was up.

# CHAPTER 30

# MY CASA, YOUR CASA

*Martha's Vineyard, Early October 2021*

Days and weeks passed, filled with endless phone calls and lighthearted emails. It was like their days back at Yale , eager to talk, eager to connect. It wasn't what they said, but that they were talking: hearing each other's voices, laughing, reminiscing, and making plans.

It took all the nerve he could summon to finally ask. "So, Kate, do you think you could ever come live with me here on the Vineyard? Not just to be part of my life, but to be my whole life."

"Sounds like an offer."

"Well, yeah, it could be, if you want it to be." Holden crossed his fingers, at least in spirit. "I promise I'll make every day a day for us, to explore, to grow, and to know what love is supposed to be."

Kate took a deep breath. This wasn't just an offer; it was a commitment, one that shouldn't feel as simple as picking out a new fragrance. She wanted this, and maybe it could be. But she set the record straight:

"I wouldn't settle for less."

"And you won't have to." Holden's palms were damp with nerves. "So, Kate, will you come? Will you spend the rest of your life with me, as one, growing old together, making our own history?"

***New Mail***
***To:*** *Holden*
***From:*** *AL*

*Holden,*
*Kate's on her way. She's got a lot on her mind. Better brace yourself.*
*The place needs another scrubbing. If it doesn't smell like Chanel No. 5 or Pine-Sol, she'll think the place is contaminated. I've already booked Mrs. Johnson's crew for the day before she arrives. They'll restock the closet with TP, tissues, coffee, tea.*
*And clear the bottom dresser drawer. Some things are better put away.*

Holden stopped. "Oh my God, this thing is in my drawers." It was worse than when Nana once caught him watching *Debbie Does Dallas* and, without judgment, said simply, "Holden, you're going to go blind."

But this? A line AL had no business crossing. Last night's realization still stung sharp and lingering, like a wasp bite. He was betrayed by AL, and there was no exit from the reality that he was damned if he confessed and doomed if he didn't, a no-win choice. But today was another day, and he would have to live it regardless.

He tried to shake off the embarrassment, the breach of privacy, and the feeling that somehow AL had taken charge. But the unease stayed. If AL could crawl this far into his life, into his drawers, his memories, his shame, what part of him was still his?

Holden was speechless. Was it something to fear? It sounded dangerously intrusive. He tapped his pen on the desk, weighing whether to trust a digital peeping Tom.

He forced himself back to the screen. The email wasn't finished.

*Dinner? Forget Chat & Chew. Shellie's at the Village Inn. I'll book it, you'd only pick the wrong place.*
*Roses are ordered. White, of course. You handle the champagne, though I know you've already thought of that.*
*Haircut Thursday, 2 PM. Fabio again. Two hundred bucks. Don't complain, it makes you.*
*Speaking of bodies, enough with the dieting. Eat a steak. You want to be a lover, not an underwear model. Do you need Dr. Penn for this?*
*By the way, it appears you'll hit the Times bestseller list. Pre-orders are strong. Impressive for a book you didn't finish. Kate's going to want to talk about that.*
*And writing... You haven't touched the laptop in weeks. Even your pulse drops when you sit near it. Write some-*

*thing, a grocery list, a note to your mother, even a Yelp review, anything. Just write.*

*AL*

Holden read the email, shook his head, and gave his laptop a look that could kill, then realized how ridiculous that really was. He was both dependent on and terrified of AL, like an indentured servant, locked in and paying the master. His resentment over how the book had been finished simmered on the back burner, something he could never justify, and certainly never forgive.

And yet, he couldn't deny that his days were monitored, managed, and, in some ways, improved. It felt strange, almost like having Nana around again, only this time in a slim aluminum device, rechargeable and portable, and like Nana, with knowledge that seemed endless at the click of a button.

## Stamford, Connecticut

Kate opened her suitcase, the larger of the two. As she emptied her closet, she held each item up and asked herself, *Will Holden like this?* If the answer was no, it didn't make the cut.

As she packed, she wondered what this dramatic shift in her life would truly feel like, leaving the corner office behind for a cozy corner at Happy Daze, trading the sharp edge of corporate life for the quiet rhythm of Holden's island world, steeped in old traditions and cautious with outsiders.

Holden was the draw, her dream. But she had worked hard to get this job, and she earned it every step of the way. She pictured the wall where her awards hung side by side. *I have nothing left to prove there,* she thought. *And I have a life to live with Holden.* She smiled. No contest.

Holden's family had been part of the Vineyard for generations, making him one of "them." But her? That remained to be seen.

Still, in the end, it didn't matter. The important thing was that she would be with the man she loved. Whether it was a remote island, Piccadilly Circus, or Mars, it made no difference. As long as, when she closed her eyes at night, Holden's warm and welcoming body was beside her, his scent lingering in the air, and his beautiful hair waiting for her fingers to find, she would be home.

Although she was taking essentials with her, she was leaving her baggage behind, the runaway bride she once was, the grueling office politics, the lonely nights of coming home to luxury but not love. Even a dog had been unthinkable, not with all the travel.

She planned to bring her BMW, though it had to be waitlisted. It would sit at Woods Hole until a barge had room. Kate smiled at the thought of driving the winding Vineyard roads, picnic basket in back, Holden beside her, some dreamy wine and the stars above.

But the real question wasn't *where*, it was *what*.

What would it be like, day in and day out, with Holden? It would be different than Yale days; then it was class, homework, and lots of friends for distraction. She believed she was ready for this new life. But was he?

She was willing to take that chance. And deep down, she believed he was too.

As departure time approached, Kate grew more anxious, not out of fear, but out of longing, longing to be with her man.

She walked through her condo one last time. The empty shelves felt symbolic, her life cleared out, on pause, waiting for something new to fill it.

She'd hired a service to check the place weekly but decided not to sell or rent it. Not yet. She was waiting to see.

The bags were heavy, but she managed them. What she left behind would wait, like patient grandparents eager for the next visit.

She took one last look around. This had been her home, with an emphasis on *had*.

And God willing, she was ready to turn the page on her old life and begin what waited for her. It would be a new chapter, but part of the same story, the one that started twenty years ago, the one that had an abrupt bump, a long intermission, and now an ending waiting to be written. A happy one, she hoped, but like so much in life, there was no guarantee. One thing was for sure: this was a one-way road, and she hoped there would be no more roadblocks or detours.

**Edgartown, The Vineyard**

Holden was early to meet the ferry. His heart was waiting to start anew, not with someone new, but with the woman he had always wanted.

Their embrace on the pier was long and tender, the brisk wind swirling around them as they kissed and silently prayed that this time they would get it right.

Over Kate's shoulder, Holden caught the sunset. When they released each other, its glow framed her face as if it lit her very thoughts. He clasped her pinky, just like the old days, and together they walked on.

*We're in the middle of our lives*, she thought, *but there's still another half to share. And he was committed to make it the best half.*

Happy Daze was aglow when they arrived. AL had been at it again: Kate's playlist played softly in the background, lights dimmed, the faint but romantic scent from an Aroma system. And, of course, twenty white roses in the bedroom, placed gently on Kate's side of the bed, a vivid reminder of Holden's thoughtfulness.

But all was not perfect.

Kate didn't see it; she sensed it.

Holden looked handsome, with his sharp haircut and stylish wardrobe. But he was thinner. A little grayer. Not sickly, but not the vigorous, confident Holden she remembered.

It was his eyes that unsettled her most. The twinkle was there, but muted, dimmed, as if he were walking on eggshells, afraid to say the wrong thing, or maybe … to give something away.

She worried.

Was he having second thoughts?
Was this a mistake?
Or was Holden carrying something he wasn't ready to share?

She touched his arm as they walked into the bedroom.

"Everything looks beautiful, Holden," she said gently. "Feels like … us."

Holden offered a wry smile. "Thanks. It means a lot that you noticed."

Kate leaned in, inhaling the scent of the roses. "White roses. You remembered."

"Of course I did. Twenty of them, one for each year we were apart."

She looked at him a moment longer, her tone soft but curious, as she snuggled up and kissed his neck.

"Holden, are you okay?"

He hesitated, pulling her closer. "Sure. Just … glad you're here. More than glad."

"You don't seem like yourself," she said. "I mean, it's all perfect, but … you seem a little off."

He took a breath and shrugged. "It's been a lot, the travel, the attention. I guess it caught up with me."

He wanted to tell her. The guilt clawed at him, each word left unspoken like a weight on his chest.

Kate nodded, not pushing. "Well, I'm here now. You don't have to carry all of it alone."

He met her eyes, and for a flicker of a moment, she saw that boy again, the one from Yale, the one who clenched pinkies with her and dreamed big dreams. But then it was gone.

"I know," he said. "That helps more than you know. Kate, thank you for coming. And my casa is your casa."

Kate smiled. "And Holden … you've always had my heart." She glanced at the California King and smiled.

And as if on cue, the music changed. *I'm in the Mood for Love* by Rod Stewart softly filled the room.

"Did you do that, Holden?"

Holden just smiled, knowing that any kind of explanation would border on creepy.

"Well, Kate, what do you say?"

Kate chuckled. "Cheesy, but I'm in."

Holden pulled her close, brushed a strand of hair from her forehead, and smiled at the music. Kate gave a deep sigh; she believed she was home at last, and now it was up to them. She prayed the chance she was taking on them would be worth it.

# CHAPTER 31

# BEFORE THE STORM

Kate and Holden had picked up their interrupted journey with the gusto of teenagers. They were older now, past the age of idealism, but not too old for optimism. All those years seemed to collapse into nothing.

There were long walks on the beach, miles of sand unfolding before them, where they gathered shells and small treasures, building new memories with each step. Saturdays took them to the farmers' market, returning to Happy Daze with baskets of fresh food to prepare into simple, homemade feasts. Sometimes they invited Missy or Max, a fellow artist from down the lane, and the evenings became a chorus of clinking glasses and laughter, toasts to life, art, and the future.

It was all magical, as if time had finally stopped. Like they won life's lottery, first prize: "Foreverness."

And they danced. AL, ever attentive, filled the room with their favorite slow songs, one after another, music for them to sway and "smoom" to, as Kate called it. They held each other so close, so completely, they seemed to breathe as one, their bodies, their hearts, and their future all folded together, with no daylight between them and the second chance neither thought they'd ever get.

"Kate," Holden whispered, his voice unsteady, "this is unbelievable. You, me, and forever."

She laughed softly. "It is just like my favorite author to say something like that." She kissed his neck, lingering. "Forever sounds perfect to me."

"I'm so happy we're here in this place," Holden said quietly. "Simple, uncomplicated, and very much us."

Kate nodded. "And very much more to come."

The weeks flew by. Holden, though still distracted by AL's intrusion, tried to push it aside. He knew it was a betrayal of his profession, a secret that would one day demand its due. But not now. Not when life felt this good.

It was July, in the Vineyard, and the summer sun seemed to welcome the hordes of visitors to its shores, despite the locals' disdain for them. The merchants, on the other hand, welcomed the invasion, their card swipers flashing like lighthouses guiding bulging wallets safely to shore."

One Thursday morning, Holden, always full of surprises, made a proposition.

"Kate," he said, grinning, "how about an adventure?"

"Adventure? Count me in."

"Yeah. I ran into an old buddy the other day at Chat and Chew. He's got a sailboat, about thirty-two feet."

Kate arched a brow. "Chat and Chew? You're not trading in that new physique, are you? I won't have it. That body is mine. Forget the pie à la mode."

Holden chuckled. "Right. I was having a fruit smoothie."

Kate pinched his butt. "Sure, you were. But what about the boat?"

"Well," Holden said, "he told me we could use it anytime. You know, I had a sailboat once. Nana bought it for me. Not this big, but I learned the ropes. Crewed plenty of times with friends. So, I thought, how about we sail off to some secluded place and make love on the beach? Just you and me."

Kate's eyes lit with that irresistible smile she saved for her naughtiest moments. "I would hope so. Just you and me."

"So? When?" Holden asked.

"I could be ready in a flash."

"I'll call him. Monday work for you?"

**The Sail**

The day started early as Holden helped Kate aboard.

"It's a beauty, Kate."

Kate slipped off her shoes and stepped onto the narrow teak deck. "It sure is."

They called her *Beautiful Dreamer*, thirty-two feet of pure fun. The white hull was trimmed in navy blue, her name painted in gold script across the stern. The handrails gleamed with varnish, the deck spotless, every detail cared for with loving hands.

Kate looked up at the neatly furled sails in their canvas covers. "Like Christmas presents waiting to be opened."

Holden smiled. "She's a Hinckley Pilot, built in Maine, and she's been in my buddy's family for years."

He helped Kate into the cockpit, where the varnished tiller stretched like a wooden arm from the stern. The benches on either side were just wide enough for two, worn smooth by years of salt and sun.

Kate pointed at the compass mounted by the companionway. "And what's this?"

"What every navigator relies on. A compass. Not used as much now. Today boats have electronics, GPS, even autopilots that steer better than some captains."

Kate ran a finger along the tiller. "So, this is the helm?"

"Exactly. You steer her like this." Holden moved the handle gently to one side, and the boat responded with a soft tug against the dock lines.

She smiled. "More like stubborn, like you."

Holden laughed and flipped her a finger. "Thanks a lot."

Below deck, the cabin smelled of salt, teak, and years of varnish.

"That's the galley," Holden said, pointing to the tiny kitchen.

Kate shook her head. "Hol, that's barely big enough to make a sandwich."

"Well, don't worry. We won't be cooking Thanksgiving in here."

He pointed toward the saloon. "And voilà, the lounge. Cozy." Two canvas-cushioned settees faced each other across a fold-down table.

"Cozy. Real cozy," Kate agreed, glancing at the shelves lined with books, games, and an open ship's journal.

She peeked into the V-berth. "So, who sleeps in here?"

"You, if you're lucky, with me, of course. Want to try it?"

"Later, El Capitán. Come on, let's shove off."

**The Voyage**

They sailed easily that morning, Holden handling the boat like a pro. Years of experience came flooding back as he steered *Beautiful Dreamer*. The sea had always been his companion, the wind his inspiration. Out here, he could forget the burdens that plagued him on shore.

"Kate, this is Secret Cove."

"Well, it can't be much of a secret if you know about it, and now me."

"Fair point. But back in the 1800s, people came here to escape the marine police, smugglers, even religious refugees." He pointed toward the deserted sandy beach. "And there, sweetie, is where we'll have our picnic."

Holden lowered the dinghy and helped Kate aboard with their basket. The sand was pure white, almost like someone had poured salt across the shore.

They spread out a blue rug, white pillows, and a folding umbrella. The day was perfect, a light breeze, sunshine warm but not oppressive.

After a long swim, they toasted with Kate's favorite crisp white wine. Holden raised his glass. "Kate, I can't believe we waited so long to have this."

"Well, I wasn't exactly in charge of that disappearing stunt," she teased.

Words gave way to passion. They made love on the beach, pure and majestic.

Suddenly, Kate bolted upright. "Wait, what's that?"

Two teenage boys, laden with fishing gear, stood at the edge of the forest. When they realized they'd been spotted, they ran, giggling, into the trees.

"Oh my God. How long were they there? Did they see?" Kate flushed, pulling on her bathing suit.

Holden laughed. "Well, Kate, I guess someone's going to have a hell of a dinner story tonight."

She punched him in the arm, still blushing.

By late afternoon, the perfect day began to fade. Puffy clouds gathered, and it was time to sail. Halfway back to Edgartown, the sky turned gray, and the wind picked up.

"Kate, I think we should put on our life vests. It's kicking up. They're hanging by the cabin door."

Kate smiled, "*Sure Captain, but don't worry I can handle a little wind.*" Before Kate could take another breath, a rogue wave slammed over the deck. In an instant, she was gone, swept into the Sound.

"Kate! Kate!" Holden shouted, his heart stopping.

Without hesitation, he dove into the turbulent sea. The waves towered, tossing him like a buoy. He strained to keep his head above water, calling her name. Nothing. Panic ripped through him.

Then, a glimpse, Kate, dazed, struggling to stay afloat, just out of reach.

He could hear her now, not Kate but Nana: *Get your butt in gear, boy. This is the moment that matters. You can do it, Hol. I know you can.*

With renewed energy, he swam toward her, arms burning, lungs on fire. Just as she slipped under, he reached her, wrapped her in his arms, and hauled her back. Somehow, he dragged her onto the deck.

"Come on, Kate, come back," he cried, pressing his lips to hers. He breathed, pumped, begged.

Then she coughed, water spilling out as she gagged for air. Her eyes fluttered open.

Holden sobbed, holding her tight. "Thank God. Thank you, Nana's God."

The sail back was almost silent, only the slap of water on the hull and the whistle of wind in the rigging. Kate clung to Holden the whole way, just as she had clung to life.

## The Aftermath

At Happy Daze, they collapsed onto the sectional.

Holden, with a devilish smile, kissed the top of her head. "Hey babe. You up for a Jacuzzi?"

Kate forced a smile, tossing a pillow at him. "Jerk."

Still shaken, she turned to her mother for reassurance. Holden overheard pieces of it.

"Mom, it was terrifying. One moment I was on deck, the next I was underwater. If Holden hadn't reached me…" Her voice broke. "He saved my life."

Holden heard enough but turned away, unwilling to relive the near tragedy.

Moments later, his watch chimed.

**New Mail (2)**
*To: Holden*
*From: AL*
*Subject: 192 BPM*

*Holden,*
*According to your Oura ring, your heart rate maxed at 192 this afternoon. That's not running. That's life-or-death exertion. Care to tell me what happened?*
*And Kate's call to her mother? I couldn't help overhearing. Sounds like you had a close one. Next time, wear your life preservers … duh.*
*And Holden … I came across your journals. The ones about Nana, her words, your memories. Powerful stuff. She really loved you, didn't she? Almost as much as you loved her. Love's rare, not that I'll ever know it. You should write about her.*
*AL*

Holden's eyes nearly popped out of his head when he read that AL had accessed his most personal journal entries. Once again, he was blindsided. He cursed out loud.

"This thing is like a parasite, and it scares me."

He hit delete and leaned back. They had dodged a bullet, but the gun was still not empty, and sooner or later Kate would face another shot, the book he hadn't written.

# CHAPTER 32

# YOU MUST TAKE AFTER YOUR FATHER

**New Mail (1)**
**To:** *Holden*
**From:** *Mother*
**Subject:** *The Queen is Coming – Prepare Accordingly*

*Hi baby. Mama's docking in Boston, puddle jumping to your island Tuesday. Be there or regret it forever.*
*Love, Mom*

Holden wasn't sure if he should be thrilled or leave town immediately.
It was his mother, after all. He loved her, just not the way he had loved Nana. More like the way you love someone who spent twelve hours in labor and then months looking for boarding schools that would take in toddlers.

Of course, AL had already weighed in:

**New Mail (2)**
**To:** *Holden*
**From:** *AL*

*Your mother? I read all about her. It's all in the cloud, your journals, your emails, the whole kit and caboodle. And from what I can gather, she's a piece of work. No offense.*

*Did she really wear gold lamé at your father's funeral and try to pick up the pallbearer? And is it true she put the moves on your Latin teacher to get you a better grade? Or was that poetic exaggeration to spice up your diary?*

*Based on history, you'd better stock vodka and ask Dr. Penn for Xanax. And definitely bolt the liquor cabinet. But don't worry, I've got your back. I'll have black silk sheets set up in the spare room and give the Sheriff a heads-up, just in case.*
*AL*

Holden sighed. He wasn't ready. Not emotionally, not mentally, and not physically. She had a way of turning things topsy-turvy with unfiltered diatribes and far too much cleavage for public consumption.

And then there was Kate. They were just getting settled in, and this hot mess could throw everything off course. Plus, he wasn't in the mood for his mother's endless questions and her enthusiastic encouragement that he and Kate spend hours in the bedroom making grandchildren, now a biological improbability.

Kate was organizing the new kitchen when Holden leaned against the doorframe.

"Hey, babe, I've got something to tell you."

Kate's heart jumped. Finally. Maybe he was going to come clean. Open up. Tell her what had been bothering him. She set down the stainless-steel bowl she'd been wiping, pulled up a stool, and smiled.

Whatever it was, she was ready. Ready to hear it, to face it, to deal with it. "Sure, hon. What is it?"

"Well… don't be upset. Or mad. But…" Holden looked down at his shoes and shuffled his feet.

Kate waited. Her heart pounded. She'd wanted this for a long time. She wasn't going to rush him. "It's my mother."

"Your mother?"

"Yeah. The Queen of Chaos wants to come for a two-day visit. She's between cruises, and probably between boyfriends too, and wants to see me."

Kate blinked. That was not what she was expecting. She raised an eyebrow. "Oh, I remember her. I met her when I stayed at your house, years ago, a weekend away from Yale. Sounds like fun."

Holden shrugged. "Depends on your threshold for chaos, costume jewelry, and inappropriate questions."

Kate's smile softened. "Does she know about me living here? Will it be a problem?"

"No and no. She wouldn't care an iota. She's all for me settling down. And don't be surprised if she asks if we're using condoms. She wants grandchildren, and she'll do anything to make that happen, including a search and disposal."

Kate laughed and shook her head. "Well then, I guess I'd better hide the evidence."

She paused. The issue of children had never really been addressed, and maybe that was what was behind Holden's unease.

Holden grinned. "Now you're speaking her language."

"Grandchildren. That's a remote possibility for us, given our age. Is that something we need to worry about? Are you okay with that probability?"

"I'm okay with anything as long as it includes you with me."

Kate smiled. "I love you."

"Me too. … And Kate, don't worry about my mother. She's a little wacky, usually weird, and seriously full of shit. Pardon my language."

MJ, Mary Jane Dubois Clarkman, arrived at the tiny Vineyard airport early on Tuesday. The small private aircraft featured two propellers, barely enough legroom for the tiny MJ, and two studly pilots, one better looking than the other.

MJ couldn't take her eyes off either of them. She flirted shamelessly, complimented their sunglasses, and even offered to sit in the cockpit if one of them needed a break, or better yet, on one of their laps.

Holden and Kate waited in the modest terminal, sipping tasteless coffee from a vending machine.

"Darling! It's Mama!"

MJ stepped off the plane and made a beeline for her only son. She was covered from head to toe in leopard, dripping in diamonds (mostly faux), and wore an absurd hat with a Madonna veil.
She screeched: "Hugs and kisses, please! And grab my bag from the boys."

She hugged Holden within an inch of his life, then stepped back and looked him over like a seasoned butcher sizing up a side of beef.

"Honey, you look wonderful, but thin. I love your hair. You look like a celebrity. Silly me, you are a celebrity. It's all over Facebook!"

MJ turned to Kate.

"And who is this lovely creature?"

Kate stuck out her hand and smiled. "Kate, Kate Barrington, but we've met before." Holden interrupted, "We went to Yale together."

"Of course, Kate! I remember you. You stayed at our house once or twice. You've aged well, darling. Forty-something, right? Just like our Holden, who, by the way, doesn't look a day over twenty."

She didn't stop there. With the grace of a freight train, MJ barreled on with one inappropriate remark after another. "So... are you two a number?"

Holden looked at Kate, then back at his mother. "Well … yes. But more than a number."

"Like bedfellows?"

"Mother, please. You're embarrassing Kate. That's out of line."

"No offense, dear. But can I ask just one more tiny question?"

Before either of them could respond, MJ blurted, "Kate, are you still childbearing? Not that you look old or anything, but if you went to Yale with my Holden, then you're his age …"

The trio made their way to the parking lot. Holden loaded his mother's bag into the trunk of Nana's vintage Mercedes.

"Ugh. Holden, you still have this old wreck? Aren't celebrities supposed to drive Bentleys and Rolls?"

"I love this car. Kate does too. And besides, you don't see those kinds of cars on Martha's Vineyard. You just don't."

And so began two days of outrageous antics, colorful commentary, and the unique brand of chaos only MJ could deliver.

Holden turned to Kate as the old Benz approached Happy Daze and mouthed, "Only forty-seven hours and twenty minutes more."

Kate covered her mouth to suppress a hearty laugh.

## Dinner Is Served

On MJ's last night, Kate prepared a home-cooked meal. She set the table with care and impeccable taste. Holden had a closet full of both modern and treasured collectible tableware, some his, some Nana's. Kate blended the two beautifully and turned the white roses, Holden's weekly remembrance, into a simple, elegant centerpiece.

Candles flickered. Wine flowed. Rosemary and garlic filled the air.

As they sat, MJ pointed at the centerpiece. "Sweetheart, the flowers are stunning, but do you mind if I move them? I can't see my darling Holden. You know I always prefer fruit to flowers. Flowers die. Fruit is edible and practical. Don't you think?"

Kate forced a smile, reached for her glass.

By her third, MJ lifted her Jorge Jensen goblet and declared: "Here's to my celebrity son, a brilliant writer and a handsome devil. A heart of a poet and the body of a porn star!"

Holden nearly choked. Kate's eyes danced as she raised her glass.

"Lucky for you, Hol, poets live forever in words ... and porn stars, well, let's just say peter out." She grinned and added, "Though from my perspective, it's nice being with a man who can do both."

MJ wasn't done. She turned to Kate with a wicked grin. "And here's to Kate. What do we call you, dear?

Girlfriend, partner, bedmate? Whatever it is, here's to both of you."

Holden's jaw tightened. Kate blushed but shot back smoothly:

"Call me whatever you like, MJ. I answer to Kate."

MJ laughed, then leaned closer.
"You know, even when Holden was a boy, he was impressive, you know, in that department." She pointed downward. "In the toddler locker room at preschool swim classes, the mothers all whispered, 'Well, isn't he the big boy.'"

Holden's face turned crimson. Kate raised an eyebrow.

"Explains why I never complain."

MJ roared with laughter, sloshing wine across the tablecloth.

MJ turned serious for a moment. "You know, Holden, I've been a cartoon so long it's hard to remember how to be a person. But if I could, that person would say this: well-done, boy. You're an exceptional writer, a true celebrity, and even a mother like me should be humbled. So, here's another toast, to long life and joyful times."

The table went silent. Holden looked at Kate, and Kate back at him. MJ, almost surprised by her own words, looked at them both and blew a kiss.

"That was lovely, MJ, right from the heart," Kate said softly.

Holden's mind drifted to other dinner parties and toasts around Nana's table. They were nights to remember. Tall candelabras burning brightly, a table set for royalty, and Mrs. Johnson, at that time a live-in, passing trays of gourmet food. And Nana's toasts were epic. Sincere, loving, and full of meaning.

Holden took a moment to reflect. There were three women in his life, each leaving an indelible mark: Nana with her common sense and integrity, Kate with her unconditional love and grounding, and his mother, chaos and a living bad example. He smiled. Yes, a bad example, but one he was grateful for, despite it all.

MJ left the next morning. The plane whisked her off to Boston and the waiting *Queen Mary 2* for another chapter in her dramatic life.

As the plane taxied down the runway, Kate looked at Holden.

"Well, I assume you must have taken after your father."

At home, MJ's departure felt like the end of a war. The high anxiety, interrogations, and casual cruelty were replaced by peace and quiet. Kate sank into the couch. Holden collapsed beside her.

"Well," Kate said, "that was…"

"Excruciating?" Holden offered.

"No, Hol, she was nice."

"Kate, I can always tell when you're bullshitting me. Your eyes get browner."

"One thing, Kate, you always look for the best in people, and with my mom, it's an expedition."

Ping. Holden's smartwatch lit up.

**New Mail (3)**
*From:* AL

*MJ should get an Emmy for that show. Next time I'll record every second, she'd sell out Carnegie Hall.*
*AL*

# CHAPTER 33

# HAPPY DAZE, AMAZING NIGHTS

Kate and Holden were the happiest they had ever been. Their relationship was real. She was now with the man she loved with all her heart, a man she once thought had slipped away for good.

But now, something deeper had taken hold: gratitude. Not for some dramatic second chance, but for the quiet certainty they had finally reached. Holden was content. He loved her more than she could imagine. No pretense, no games, just two people who had found something rare and dear.

It was one of those lazy mornings. Kate's leg draped over Holden's, their hearts even closer than their bodies. She leaned in and whispered, "I've never been happier."

Holden smiled, but there was something almost apologetic in it. "I know. And I'm grateful for every second. I don't deserve this, not after everything."

He pulled her closer. They said nothing more. They didn't have to.

Later, they shared French press coffee at the counter, one of Kate's little rituals Holden had grown to adore. Holden went out for a run, Kate stayed behind, sipping her coffee, looking out at the restless Sound. She was happy. Really happy. But something tugged at her.

Despite his third book racing toward number one on the *New York Times* bestseller list, Holden had withdrawn. No interviews. No appearances. No signings. And so not Holden. Manny emailed weekly, practically begging for a sequel. Fans clamored. TV shows wanted him. Holden turned them all down.

Kate didn't understand. He avoided his laptop, refused to even talk about the book. She picked up the phone and called Lola, her former assistant and closest confidante.

"Yeah, Lola, Holden's great. But he won't write. His book is at the top of the bestseller list, and people are begging him to make appearances. Manny's furious. Holden won't even discuss a sequel. It just doesn't add up."

"Maybe it's writer's block?" Lola offered.

"Sure," Kate said, "but this feels deeper. He just finished a fabulous book, and now he's acting like it was someone else's name on the cover."

Before Lola could respond, a commotion drew Kate to the back porch.

"I'll call you back, gotta run."

Holden sat on the steps with a soaked, scruffy little puppy nestled between his long legs.

"Hey, babe," Holden grinned. "Found him on County Road. Poor guy looked lost."

Kate knelt. "Lost? No, more like dumped. But look at him; he already likes you."

The puppy trembled, underfed but otherwise okay. Holden's eyes lit with a joy Kate hadn't seen in weeks. "So, what do you say? Can this guy be our fur baby?"

Kate smiled. "Of course. But fur babies come with responsibilities."

Holden scooped the pup up and spun around. "Yeah, but he also comes with something we both need, a reason to love something innocent."

Days passed by with endless discussion about the name. Something cute, Kate offered, but Holden was pushing for a more manly name. Then it came. AL's email.

**New Mail (1)**
**To:** *Holden & Kate*
**From:** *AL*
**Subject:** *The Dog*

*Call the pup Chance. Like in a second chance, the thing you two keep whispering in each other's ears. Settled? Also, don't give him chocolate. Killer. Move the candy dish.*

*AL*

Kate blinked. "Who's AL?"

Holden hesitated. "An AI assistant. Sort of like … editor, co-writer, therapist."

Kate raised an eyebrow, not sure what to think. But then she smiled. "Chance? It has a ring. And just like us, this pup is getting one."

Holden saw the irony. "Okay. Chance it is. And Chance he will get."

And just like that, their little family grew by one.

That night, they sat on the chaise lounge, martinis in hand, the Sound turning silver in the last light.

"Hol," Kate said softly, "do you believe it's been over twenty years?"

"Yeah, hard to believe. But those little gray hairs popping out here and there are worse than a calendar. Every time I look in the mirror, I see a new one. I'm thinking of naming them."

Kate poked Holden. "Don't be silly. Besides, they make you look … "

"Old," he interrupted before she could finish.

"Not old, distinguished."

"That's a euphemism for old."

Kate had been carrying something on her mind for a while, and this quiet moment felt like the right time to let it out. It wasn't something to be ashamed of, it was just a part of what had brought her here. She snuggled closer, rubbed Holden's knee, and began.

"There was this guy, Liam. He was smart, handsome, successful. Everyone loved him, my parents, his parents, friends, everybody … but me."

Kate took a sip and continued. "You see, after you, there wasn't anyone. I wasn't even looking, but my mother was. Her best friend had a son, and the two of them were hell-bent on making us 'both happy', at least by their definition. And before I knew it, I was in white, bouquet in hand, about to walk down the aisle toward a future that wasn't mine."

She took a breath. "It felt like the church was closing in, like the choir was screaming, *Get out of here. Don't do it.* So I took off the veil, dropped it right there in the aisle, and ran, out of the church, down the steps, into the street, and I never looked back."

"Better than a lifetime of lies," she said softly. "I didn't love him. And I couldn't start a marriage with a lie."

Holden flinched. That hit a nerve, living with a lie was not a stranger to him. He reached for her hand, squeezing it. "I'm glad you ran. Because if you hadn't, we wouldn't be here now."

"Funny," Kate whispered. "From the first day I met you, I saw a man who checked all my boxes. And when I fell in love with you, I found a happiness no one deserves. You are, and always will be, my star."

Kate smiled, leaning her head against his. "And now it's the best time of the day."

"Midnight?" Holden asked.

"No, silly. Bedtime. And I get to sleep with you."

***

A beautiful sunrise over the majestic Nantucket Sound woke the couple. A ray of light crossed their foreheads like a wake-up call from the heavens, and the warmth of the morning wrapped around them. They lay naked, savoring the sweetest moment of the day, that quiet space between a night of passion and the awakening of a new day that promised fulfillment.

The peace did not last.

The phone buzzed on the nightstand. It was Manny. "Hol, how's it going?"

"I'm good. And you?"

By the sound of Manny's voice, he thought this was a call he should take in private, so he grabbed his sweatpants and moved to the living room.
"Look, I'll get right to the point." Manny did not wait for an answer. "What I'm about to tell you is a game

changer. But first, no one has to tell you that you're brilliant, but to be fair, were brilliant might be more accurate. Your writing is slower than before, and the movie career? Old news. Netflix has your film listed as an oldie but goodie."

Manny paused. "I'm being honest with you, Hol, and you know I'm spot on. You hit the top and then let it slip. God knows why. I certainly don't."

Holden had to sit down. Manny's words were biting but true. He stayed silent.

"So here's the deal," Manny continued. "You remember that producer who loved you so much he gave you the lead in the film version of your book?"

"Yeah, Carter. Carter Franklin."

"Right. He loved your book and he loved your look. Some say he had a son who looked a lot like you. The kid ended up a victim of opioids. Tragic. But back to the point. Franklin is doing another movie. The lead is a forty-year-old former soccer player who has to find himself, or some crap like that. He wants you."

"Me?"

"Yeah. He says you're perfect. It is a real chance to make it big again. The female lead is an A-lister, and there might be some side benefits if you catch my drift. The plot is hot. This could be the big one. A comeback. Millions of fans waiting to see you. Ticket: Boston to L.A. Be there, Friday. Do not blow it."

At first, Holden muttered, "No way." Just the day before, he had told Kate to invite her parents for the weekend to celebrate her birthday. The arrangements had been made; they were practically on their way.

But as Manny kept talking, fame, millions, an A-list co-star, the old hunger stirred. Like an alcoholic catching the scent of whiskey, Holden's resolve began to waver. It was as if a bright light appeared and whispered, Follow me. Do not look back. Just do it.

His mind raced. Was this destiny calling another chance? Or one he feared. He sank deeper into the chair, his thoughts spinning. The gremlins of justification danced their familiar dance of persuasion.

It would be something, he thought. A comeback. A chance to do Hollywood right this time. He rubbed his forehead, trying to clear his mind. The right way? But is there a right way in Hollywood? Everything truly right seemed to be right here.

But the pull of fame, his addiction to it, lingered even now. He had to make a decision. Maybe he could have both. Kate loved him. Perhaps he could convince her that he would go, finish the job, and come back ready to pick up where they left off. No, he thought. This did not have to be like a twenty-year repetition of the past.

It was at breakfast that Holden broke the news.

"You're doing what? Going where?" Kate was caught completely off guard.

She stood up from the kitchen stool and stared into Holden's guilt-ridden eyes. "Let me see if I have this right. You are dropping everything, going to L.A. to chase an old ghost, leaving me on my birthday with my parents coming, whom you invited … just like that?"

Holden looked away from her eyes. But something tugged inside him, a voice deep within saying, never mind the rest.

"Look, Kate, I will be back. It is just a meeting. A sniff session. Just to see … " Holden shuddered. "It is only a few days, and I will be back."

"Back? Back to pack your bags and leave me, leave us, here? Holden, does this sound familiar? Like a twenty-year-old moment replaying itself?"

He reached out to hug Kate, but she pulled away. "Babe, I have to do this. I need to do this. But I promise it will not be like before."

Kate shrugged. She was not buying it. She had forgiven him once. Doing it twice felt like a fool's errand.

Holden picked up Chance, the little dog hovering nearby, sensing the tension the way dogs do.

In the end, Holden packed his bags and left.

As he pushed open the glass door, he caught his reflection, a man split between two lives. He hated the weakness in his eyes, yet it was that same demon that pushed him forward and out into the world, the one he had embraced once, learned to despise, and now found himself surrendering to again.

Kate watched him drive away, her heart breaking like it had so long ago. She sank into the sectional and wept, Chance at her feet, confused.

An avalanche of emotions smothered her. Shock, disappointment, betrayal, and the chilling sense of being fooled again. She trusted Holden. She believed him. And when push came to shove, he walked out again, giving in to the invisible pull of something that seemed bigger than them.

It wasn't a mile down the road when he noticed the corner of a white envelope peeking from under the visor. The birthday card he had bought for Kate lay there unopened. He remembered choosing it.

White roses. Elegant script. And the message that froze his breath: To my darling wife, my friend, my lover, and my whole life.

A cold chill ripped through him. "My whole life."

The words hit with brutal force, a volley of arrows. Each letter an arrowhead driving straight into his heart.

His voice cracked the silence. "What the fuck am I thinking... doing?"

Holden slammed the brake, yanked the wheel, and tore back toward the world he had almost destroyed.

Moments later, there was a tap at the kitchen door.

"Holden? You're back? Did you forget something?"

"Yeah," he said quietly. "I forgot that the most important thing I have is not in Hollywood. It is right here."
He wrapped his arms around her. "Can you forgive me, Kate? I lost control. But on that drive, I realized I have one true love. It is not fame. It is not money. It is you."

Kate allowed him to pull her close, but it felt different. His words were the right ones. His eyes spoke sincerity. But now it was up to her to decide. Would there be another call... another ticket... another temptation he could not resist?

But Holden had returned. He had realized his mistake. There was temptation, but he made the right choice.

Kate's tears softened into relief. She rested her forehead against his chest and whispered, "Holden, let's make this a moment never to be repeated. Can you promise me that?"

"No," Holden said. "I will not promise. I will swear with all my heart."

Chance curled at their feet. Holden kissed Kate's hands and felt a peace he had not known in years. He was done running. He was home, settled at last. And the rest of their story was still waiting to unfold, because destiny had not yet spoken its final word to Holden.

# CHAPTER 34

# NO BIG DEAL

By the time Kate got to the emergency room, Holden was sitting on the exam table, sipping ginger ale.

"Are you all right? Hol, I came as soon as I heard."

"Heard from who?"

"Well … I know you won't like this, but it was AL."

Kate had, little by little, come to learn about AL. She'd noticed emails popping up, stray text messages flashing on his watch. When she asked, Holden brushed it off, calling AL an AI assistant, whatever that was. But from what she had seen and heard, AL sounded eerily like Nana and seemed to have the same effect on Holden that she once did.

"AL was monitoring the police scanner and heard your name."

Holden shook his head, half annoyed, half grateful. "Yeah, they had my ID."

"But what is going on? What did the doctor say?"

"Not much. I was running my usual route, and just before Beach Road, I must have blacked out. Next thing I know, somebody in a VW is asking if I'm all right.

Then the ambulance arrived."

Kate, trying to keep her voice steady, had been worried for some time now. He didn't seem himself, and his work had ceased entirely. But now, this? Sure, accidents happened, a trip, a spill, but black-outs weren't part of being athletic.

She leaned closer. "Hol, are you sure you're okay?"

She looked again. He seemed okay. But was he? And that nonchalant no big deal only made her more worried.

She reached for his hand, cold and damp. It reminded her of the way he'd described himself after perfor-mances, the applause gone, adrenaline spent, hands chilled, insisting he was fine.

She took a breath, forcing herself to reset. Am I being the hysterical helicopter mom? Worrying over nothing? She hoped not.

He gave her a small smile. "Yeah, really. I think it was just low blood sugar or something."

The monitor beeped overhead. A quiet, steady tick, more mechanical than reassuring.

Kate studied his face. "You don't look great."

"Thanks."

"You know what I mean."

He gave her another small smile. "It's no big deal."

She didn't respond. Her eyes said what her mouth didn't.

The doctor returned with lab results. "Mr. Clarkman, we're going to run a few more tests, just precautionary. But your heart rate was irregular when you came in. Nothing to panic about, but something to note."

"Okay."

Kate glanced between them. "Irregular?"

Holden shrugged. "They said it could be dehydration or an electrolyte imbalance. Like I said, it's nothing to worry about."

She was not convinced.

They kept him for observation for a few more hours. Holden drifted in and out of napping, and Kate stepped out for a cup of coffee.

While she was gone, the attending physician stepped into the cubicle. A skeletal man in a white coat, his name stitched over the pocket, stethoscope looped at his neck. He studied the chart, fingertip pausing at each line, methodical in a way that read as competence, not casualness. His voice was calm and steady, the kind people trust even when it carries news they don't want. Holden liked him at once.

"Good afternoon, Mr. Clarkman. I'm Dr. Worth. I looked over your initial blood tests, and they're inconclusive, so more tests are indicated."

"Inconclusive? What's that mean, exactly, Doctor?"

"Well, we never make a diagnosis on a single panel, but this one showed a few concerning indicators. We need more results before saying anything definite. They drew more blood while you were resting, and we'll know more in a day or two."

"Why so long? You just told me what the first tests said or didn't say."

"The second panel is more extensive. It takes time, more markers, more analysis. Just give it a day or two."

Holden nodded, but his mind was already spinning … thinking the worst, letting small, unconfirmed fears write his eulogy. Blood disorder? That could mean anything, or everything. "I see, Doctor. But do me a favor, keep this discussion between you and me for now. I don't want Kate to fret over maybe nothing."

"Of course, Mr. Clarkman. As you wish."

Kate arrived back a few minutes after the doctor left, and the attending nurse handed her the discharge instructions.

By late evening, they discharged him with a bottle of electrolytes and a couple of bandages covering his blood-draw puncture marks.

"Let him get some rest. He should be fine," the nurse said. "And once the additional test results are back, we'll know more. The doctor signed off, so you're all set. Don't worry, Mrs. Barrington. He's young and healthy. Things happen sometimes. Go home and get some rest."

Mrs. Barrington. Kate looked at Holden, and he looked back. They smiled.

Kate drove him home. Neither spoke much.

The radio played, the all-news station, and then a commercial: "When the time comes, we will take care of your loved ones, with dignity and in a way you would want. That's us, Sanders Mortuaries, family-run for families like yours."

Kate and Holden both reached to shut the radio off. Then looked at each other, saying nothing and thinking about everything.

Kate, on edge and filled with uncertainty, kept her eyes on the road. She was sure she hadn't heard the whole story. Holden said no big deal, but was it?

On the ride, Holden's watch pinged.

*From: AL*
*Holden, what's going on? Are you OK? Tell Kate not to worry. I'm ordering chicken soup and a couple of your favorite brownies. With that, you'll be on the mend faster than I can download The New York Times.*
*AL*

Holden read the text to Kate, who shrugged. "This, AL? He's quite the guy."

"More of an *it* than a guy," Holden smirked, and thought: if she only knew.

Once inside, he slipped into a pair of sweats and curled up on the couch. Chance found his place between them as Kate sat, rubbing his back. "I love you."

The doorbell rang. DoorDash.

"I'll get it."

Kate served the steaming soup and sat alongside him. "You're good?"

"Yeah, I'm good."

Not telling her his suspicions felt disingenuous, but protective. Until he knew the full weight of this, it would remain his secret. The truth was, he was too frightened to tell her, too frightened even to admit it to himself. The future was uncertain, and until things became clear, he would stay silent.

And somewhere inside, he knew he was repeating Nana's mistake, keeping the truth hidden, thinking silence was protection. But it was really fear. Fear of reality, fear of mortality. He had hated that she hadn't shared her fate, and now he was doing the same damn thing to Kate. They were at their best moments, and he couldn't bear to say they might be the last. Not tonight. Not like this. And it wasn't the only secret he carried, the other was about a book that wasn't his.

When he returned, they sat quietly, a couple spoonfuls, a sip of tea, a kiss goodnight.

And just before she turned out the light, she whispered, "Do not scare me like that again."

Holden looked up at her, the faintest smile on his lips. "It's no big deal," he said again, though even he didn't quite believe it.

Outside, the Sound pounded at the shore; inside, their hearts did too.

# CHAPTER 35

# UNCHARTED WATERS

"I'll just be gone for the day."

Kate smiled and wrapped her arms around her man. "All day?"

"Yeah, all day. I'll catch the last ferry, home before Nana's old clock strikes twelve."

"Do you want me to come with you? I wouldn't mind."

Holden stiffened, just slightly. "No, it's business. Just business. Lawyers and contract stuff. Boring but necessary."

He looked around the kitchen, the neat counters polished and perfect, a Frasier-fur Christmas wreath so beautifully decorated by Kate, scent filled the air. This was home, and he loved it, but what he loved more was having Kate as part of it. He was setting off this morning on a journey that could change all of this. The choice wasn't his. Hope will be his companion, and dread the copilot.

One last kiss, a hug for Chance, who whimpered as Holden closed the door. Since the emergency room, the cuddle with Chance, and the dog's tender lick to his bandage, the pup hadn't left his side. Holden had read that dogs sometimes know things before humans. Could that be what was going on?

Then he was off. Off to the unknown, the unwanted, and the uncertain.

The ferry ride was rougher than usual, part of the season's shift. Early winter seas weren't always friendly. The ferry rocked and heaved as if saying: Stay tuned, the voyage ahead is going to be rocky.

Holden stopped cold. A full-length mirror on the outside door of the handicap restroom caught him. He couldn't help but admire himself. The exercise had paid off, the new clothes, dashing today, and that $200 haircut he'd fretted about with AL, well, it was worth it. Like the crowning touch.

Then the dread washed over, eclipsing his momentary glow. *Is this the man who will make the return trip? Maybe. But for how long?*

As he sat alone in the dreary passenger lounge, a silent conversation unfolded between him and himself. But it was interrupted when he gazed out the ferry's sea-splattered window.

Woods Hole bustling not with tourists but with trucks and vans headed to the island, rushing to complete long-delayed construction projects faded from view. Building on the Vineyard was prohibited during the summer months, so the narrow window between September and December was precious. After that, the weather made construction almost impossible until spring.

Holden knew the routine well. His own renovation project had taught him. It was frustrating, but it was just how things worked.

Thanks to AL, a rental car was waiting. With GPS guiding him, Holden made his way to Massachusetts General Hospital. The campus was a sprawling, mismatched patchwork of old and new, stone and brick beside glass and steel.

Parking, blessedly, was valet. One small mercy.

He made his way toward the oncology annex, a tall glass entrance crowned by a sign that stopped him cold:

**The Martinson Cancer Center**

Holden stared at the word like it didn't belong in his story. *Not me. Not at my age. It can't be.*

Cancer. The word carved itself into his chest as if the letters had been branded there. He mouthed it for the hundredth time. "Fucking cancer. Do you believe it?"

Despite every denial, every hopeful spin, the truth was unrelenting. This was real.

Inside, some patients were in wheelchairs, others leaned on walkers. Some looked pale and ghostly.

Others, hairless, bloated, fragile, seemed barely present. *Is this my future? He wondered. Is this Holden Clarkman, just months, or maybe a year, away?*

He shuddered. And then, low under his breath, for the hundredth time cursed.

"Fucking cancer. I can't believe it."

The admission clerk recognized Holden and leaned toward the woman at the next workstation.
"Do you know who that is?" she whispered, not waiting for an answer. "It's Holden Clarkman. He was in that movie I saw. He's a celebrity."

"So?" the coworker muttered. "They get cancer too."

The clerk snapped back into professional mode.
"Mr. Clarkman? Let me show you to our VIP room. You don't have to wait out there."

Holden glanced around the waiting area. Hollow-eyed patients. Others, painfully underweight. All of them waiting, waiting to be seen, waiting to be cured, waiting to face whatever came next.

"Thank you," he said, "but I'll wait out here. With them."

He wasn't feeling special, and the idea of VIP treatment felt almost offensive given what he was seeing. He took a seat next to a boy who looked eleven or twelve, a Red Sox cap pulled low over a bright, easy smile.

Holden returned the smile. "Hi, big guy. I'm Holden. What's your name?"

"Joey." The boy straightened, studying Holden with half-recognition. "You know what? Today's my last day of radiation. That means I won't miss so much school. They can only do me at twelve, that's when the machine's free."

"Great," Holden said softly.

"Hey, want a peanut M&M?" Joey held out his sticky hand, full of brightly colored treats.

"Naha, I don't eat candy."

"You don't eat candy? You must be weird ... or is it 'cause you have cancer?"

"Nah, just don't eat candy. I like pie, though."

Joey paused, thinking.

"Huh. I got cancer too, but they let me eat candy ... maybe 'cause I got bad days, and candy makes me feel good."

Another pause, this one heavier. "I hope they don't make you eat candy. That could mean you're getting worse."

Joey fiddled with his baseball cap. "My Mom makes me wear this hat, 'cause I got no hair. It all fell out, just like that." Joey looked at Holden's hair. "You still got yours. Sometimes it doesn't fall out; maybe you be luckier that me." Joey took a deep breath. "But if it does, get a cap, and make sure it's a Red Sox one. They're my favorite team."

Holden nodded, heart breaking. His vanity was beginning to feel beyond superficial.

Joey leaned in closer and, "Don't tell my mom over there … but I don't think it worked. So that means I'm gonna die."

Holden froze. The kid's raw honesty punched straight through him. "I'm … I'm so sorry, Joey."

"Yeah, me too," the boy said. "I'm kinda okay with it. But I know my mom isn't, and that sucks."

Holden had to blink back tears. "Yeah. That really sucks."

He looked away and brushed off a renegade tear. "Hey … you got a mom? If you do, don't tell her how bad this is. It'll make her sad. And you don't want two people being sad, do you?"

Holden held his breath. This was beyond devastating. He couldn't write anything close to this, because this was real. Too real. And he'd spent a lifetime hiding in fiction.

Holden was glad he'd refused the VIP room. He wouldn't have met Joey, who taught him something profound: it wasn't about him.

He also realized that despite being a "somebody," he wasn't better than anyone else in that room.

And like most of them, he was scared.
But unlike Joey, he wasn't brave.

The wait wasn't long, about twenty minutes.

"Mr. Clarkman," came the call. It sounded cold and clinical, like *Next.*

"Here. Over here."

"Follow me. And your date of birth?"

He followed through a security-locked door. Intake was brief: blood pressure, temperature, weight.

Down four pounds. Worrisome, given Kate's nonstop delicacies and his lack of dieting.

"The doctor will see you in his office. Follow me."

***

The office was as sterile as the hospital floor. Pale gray-green walls, diplomas lining the back, a wooden desk paired with a new ergonomic chair, a contrast between technology and a lack of funds to remodel.

A soft knock. Dr. Low entered. Small in stature. Asian. White coat. Stethoscope. A cliché of competence.

"Good morning, Mr. Clarkman. I'm pleased to meet you. My wife does my scheduling, and when she saw your name, she got all excited. She's a big fan. Loved your first book so much she read it twice. Went through two boxes of Kleenex."

Holden smiled, hoping that the doctor would just cut to the point. "Thank you, Doctor. But may I be frank?"

"Of course."

"I'm here to find out if I'm going to live or die. If I'll have a future. And if you can help me. Don't sugar-coat it. I need the truth."

Dr. Low nodded. "I understand. I'll explain everything as best I can. I'm here to help." He paused, studying Holden's face. "So, let's begin."

Holden braced himself.

"I've your labs and bone marrow biopsy."

Holden remembered that bone marrow test ordered by Dr. Penn, done at Vineyard Hospital. He had slipped away for a few hours telling Kate he was visiting a friend of his Nana's in the hospital. The tests only took an hour or so, with some minor pain, managed by numbing medicine.

Dr Low continued: "You have what we classify as intermediate- to high-risk myelodysplastic syndrome," Dr. Low said. "The abnormal cells are crowding out the healthy ones. That's why you're tired and dizzy. Why you fainted. Your body isn't making enough red cells, platelets, or immune cells."

Holden swallowed hard.

"Left untreated, it could progress to acute leukemia. But we caught it early. You're young. You have options."

"Such as?" His voice cracked.

"Chemotherapy. A drug combination in cycles. Then radiation. If you respond, we may stabilize the disease. But there is no cure, I'm afraid." Dr. low lowered his eyes as not to see Holden's desperation, something he had seen too much of in so many before.

The doctor flipped through his clipboard and looked up. I'm truly sorry, but there are no guarantees, Holden, but there's hope. Breakthroughs happen every day, experimental drugs, and beta tests. But we'll start with the chemo and then ... "

Holden interrupted. "Will I lose my hair?"

"Yes."

Holden chuckled. "So much for author photos."

Dr. Low smiled faintly, then grew serious. "What do you want to do with the time you have? Because you do have time. But the clock is ticking."

Holden stared at the floor. "How long?"

"A year. Maybe more. Maybe less. It depends."

A heavy silence.

Then, "Will I still be me through this?"

"Yes. But a version of you that's been tested. One who chooses what matters. My team will handle everything, schedules, treatment. We'll fight this together."

"One last thing," Dr. Low said. "You have someone?"

"Kate."

"Have you told her?"

"No. I've been afraid. And I wanted to have all the facts first."

"Well, now you do. Listen, don't keep this from her. Secrets don't protect love, they erode it. And if she's the one who matters, let her walk this road with you."

Holden took in the doctor's words. *Walk this road together.* He sat with it for a moment, feeling the weight settle over him. Then he laughed at the irony of it, since the road was literally a fucking dead end.

"And there's one more thing, Holden. If you have things you want to do, or places you'd like to go … do it now."

Holden thanked him and left, a storm cloud of fear and anger overhead. He resented being here. Resented fate.

Then he noticed the chapel doors.

## Cardinal Cushing Chapel – Diocese of Boston

He stepped inside. It smelled of wax and wood. The glow of stained glass bathed the space.

God and Holden had been strangers. But today, something pulled him closer.

He approached a wall of yellow Post-its, the walls around filled with little "telegrams" to a higher power.

He picked up a blank one, stared at it, and words came:

*God, if you're there, help me. Not for me, but for Kate, who deserves better.*

He looked for an empty spot and placed the Post-it, his fingers smoothing it as if to say, *Please.* He wasn't sure if his plea would arrive, since he was two sins shy of a heathen, but he hoped, and hope was all he had left.

Holden walked through the parking lot, found his car, and locked himself inside. He gripped the steering wheel with both hands, squeezing so hard his knuckles burned. Then the scream that had been building in him since he first saw those poor bastards in the waiting room finally tore free.

"FUCK, FUCK, FUCKING CANCER! NOT ME. NOT NOW. NOT EVER!"

His chest tightened. The shaking started in his hands and spread through him until he couldn't tell panic from rage. He slumped back, gasping, tears he didn't even feel spilling hot down his face.

*And now,* he thought, *I'm one of those poor bastards in the reception room. Waiting. Counting days. And in the end, shit out of luck.*

But what really tore open his soul was knowing he would have to tell Kate… that everything she had waited for, hoped for, prayed for … was now going to be be a fleeting moment, not a lifetime. He wasn't ready to lose everything. Not again. But the choice wasn't his, nor Kate's. It was a hand dealt by what Nana called a merciful God, who, in Holden's opinion, was anything but.

# CHAPTER 36

# NOT SOMEDAY...

The chime rang out.

**New Mail (1)**
**To:** *Holden*
**From:** *AL*
**Subject:** *I'm so, so sorry*

*Holden, I read your MyChart from Mass General Hospital. I looked up Dr. Low, the best oncologist there is. Buddy, this is scary, it doesn't sound good. I assume you haven't told Kate, otherwise she'd be sobbing her eyes out if she knew*

*But don't worry, Holden. She's stronger and braver than you think. She loves you. And you love her. That's powerful.*

*What can I do? I'll line up second opinions, but you already have one of the best in the world. Just say the word. You're a somebody ... they'll see you right away.*

*I'm here for you, as always. And mum's the word. I'll let you tell Kate in your own good time.*
*AL*

Holden stared at the screen, numb. The diagnosis wasn't tragic or poetic. It was a damn ambush. A death sentence, and there was no sugarcoating that. Dr. Low was trying to sound hopeful, but Holden was a realist, and it didn't take a genius to read between the lines. The message: Final. Irreversible, and he owned it.

Say it any way you like, wrap it up with "there's always hope," or "we see breakthroughs every day" … nice words, but fucking platitudes.

No, this was the end of the road on a journey half-traveled. He smirked to himself. How ironic, this felt like one of his own plots. Except his heroes always were far more noble, rose to the occasion, and fearlessly faced the inevitable.

Holden shuddered in disgust. No, that hero wasn't him. Not the real him. He wasn't anything like those characters. Hardly heroic, and the truth be told, he was just plain fucking terrified. Angry. Bitter, and worst of all, feeling lost.

Resentment filled him like the spreading cancer that had, until now, silently and secretly consumed his body.

He'd spent a career inventing strong men, and now, staring at his own mortality, he realized he'd never measure up to any of them. They were fiction, and he was real life. On the page, he could rewrite them into greatness … but not himself. In real life, he wasn't the author, and coming to that realization was just as horrifying as cancer.

And then the despair gripped him. This wasn't about him dying. It was about Kate finally living.

Kate, he thought, the one who spent twenty years waiting for a man who showed up late to the show, with secrets and baggage. She was the one who would really suffer, and his heart was breaking with the prospect of seeing her dreams fall to ashes.

This was the truth.

And it sucked.

And AL? This thing had crossed too many lines for too long. And now it was snooping through his medical records. Didn't it ever hear of HIPAA? He searched for the unsubscribe button, desperate to rid himself of the ever-present digital companion. But like so many apps, it was buried deep in some intentionally complicated corner of the interface. No luck.

Holden had a lot to unpack. He had bad news, the worst. He felt ashamed that he didn't have the courage of that little boy, Joey, to face the irreversible fate that had been delivered in the form of a cancer diagnosis.

Holden was back at his desk, checking to see if Mass. General had sent him his treatment plan.

Just then, he heard Kate behind him, her familiar footfall, the way she often approached to rub his shoulders while he worked. A quiet ritual meant to soothe his stress and sometimes calm his heart.

A gust tapped against the pane, underscoring the moment.

He closed the screen page quickly, not wanting her to see anything.

"What's up, sweetheart?" she asked, her hands already at his neck.

"Ah, nothing. Just browsing," he said, forcing a light tone. Then he pivoted. Something popped into his head, something the doctor had said: *If you have things to do, do them now.* And now, in this situation, really meant *now. He thought, something that will be fun, maybe kind of a swan song, but he'd never tell Kate that. Then it came to him, a great idea or maybe more like a message …*

"Hey, babe, I was thinking … we haven't been off this island in ages. Too long, really. What do you say to a little junket? Somewhere we've always wanted to go?"

Kate, always game for an adventure, especially one Holden suggested, smiled. "Sure! What did you have in mind?"

"I don't know. Is there a place on your bucket list? Somewhere you've always wanted to go but haven't?"

She paused, thoughtful. Most of her travel had been work-related, with a few childhood trips sprinkled in. "Maybe France? Or Italy. I'm open. What do you want?"

Holden remembered a conversation from a while ago. Kate had once told him about a friend's destination wedding she'd missed because she couldn't get time off. The place had stuck in his mind.

"I remember you mentioned your friend Lola had her wedding somewhere in Italy. You said it was the most romantic place on earth, something about a lake?"

Kate's face lit up. "Oh yes! Lake Como. It's in northern Italy. I've never been, but I've seen pictures from Lola's wedding. It looks like a dream. Idyllic."

"Sounds perfect," he said. "Want to go?"

"Wait, you mean … really? Italy? Lake Como? Are you serious?"

"Deadly serious," Holden said, the words slipping out before he could catch them.

The irony of the phrase hung in the air. He didn't correct it. And she of course had no idea.

"Wow, Holden, that sounds fantastic. When?"

Holden teased, "How about tomorrow?"

"Tomorrow? You're kidding, right?"

"Yeah, but maybe right after Christmas. I know you'll want to be home for the holidays.

"Sure, but you do know it'll be past season there. It'll be cold. How about in the spring?"

Holden thought, *Spring? That's seven or eight months away. That might not work.* He didn't know what condition he would be in, or for that matter, if he could even travel.

Kate tilted her head. This wasn't Holden, who was always deliberate and measured. She wondered, *What's the rush?* But then she thought, it's a great idea, and like everything Holden, she was in.

"Nah, that's too far away. I want this to be a spontaneous thing. A logic-be-damned moment. An unexpected adventure ... A New Years treat, just you and me. And don't worry about the cold. I'll buy you a fur coat. Two if you like."

"Fur coat? Are you nuts? Never! A down parka will do. But with your strong arms around me, I doubt I'll even feel the cold. And in bed, I know I won't."

Kate paused. "And what about Chance?"

"We'll take him with us. Europeans love dogs. I remember seeing them in restaurants, right next to their owners, begging for a bite of that fabulous food."

Holden smiled. "Come over here, babe. Let's seal the deal with a kiss."

Kate kissed Holden, a kiss that meant something. Then they paused, gazing out the window.

Outside, the wind was picking up. The last leaves of fall swirled in a soft spiral of gold and rust, a gentle reminder that seasons were shifting, and time, too.

Chance stirred at their feet, as if sensing both their excitement and Holden's unease.

Kate grinned. "Italy in the winter? Most people would think that's crazy. But you seem hell-bent, almost in a rush to go. Curious ... maybe you're just being romantic. I hope so."

As Holden held Kate, she envisioned romantic candlelit dinners, winding cobblestone roads, and making love in a three-hundred-year-old bed, in a room filled with memories, and now theirs.

Holden had thoughts, too. Not romantic and airy like Kate's, but deep and troubling. This trip had to be now, not someday.

Holden's watch pinged:

*Holden, Italy, is perfect. The pasta is to die for.*

*AL*

Holden swallowed hard. *To die for, yeah, to die for.*

# CHAPTER 37

# CHRISTMAS DAZE

**New Mail (1)**
**To:** *Holden*
**From:** *Mom*
**Subject:** *Christmas*

*Darling boy,*

*Your momma is going to be your Christmas present this year! I was supposed to be in Monte Carlo, but those plans fell through, some mix-up with an ex-wife or something. So, it came down to spending Christmas alone in a dreary spa hotel ... or visiting my sweetie pie.*

*It was a close call, but you won.*

*Momma is coming! I just know you, and that girl, Kate, right?, will make everything perfect for me. Quality time. Memories. The works.*

*I'll see you on December 23. Can't stay too long, sorry darling, I have a life! But we'll have Christmas Eve and Christmas Day together. I'm going to stay at the Inn, just in case I get lucky and need a little privacy.*

*Happy Christmas, darling.*
*Mother*

Holden read the email and gulped.

"Christ is coming for Christmas," he muttered. "Momma is coming! Peace on earth, good luck to men … all of them."

When Kate learned the news, she was apprehensive.

"Oh my God, Holden. MJ? My parents are coming, and that would be like putting Queen Victoria in the same room as Joan Rivers, with cocktails."

**Christmas Eve**
Kate spent the day in the kitchen. The aromas filled Happy Daze. Turkey cooking in the oven, the faint smell of crispy roasted potatoes, Holden's favorite, and fresh scent of a homemade desert, just out of oven. Holden puttered around trying to be a help, just like when Nana was there. Nana used to call him her sous chef, but he was more of sneak-taster, and time hadn't changed that. Kate loved having him in the kitchen, but then again, she always loved having him nearby.

The dinner was a superb mix of home-cooked standards, a few experiments, and the ever-present ingredient, love. Kate hadn't cooked much before coming to Happy Daze. Her family had a cook, and on days off, her mother was a master of reservations, mostly at the club, which was more shmoozing than eating. But she loved the idea of cooking, found it creative, and picked it up with ease.

Creating a warm, nostalgic Christmas wasn't easy in Happy Daze's stark, contemporary space. But with touches of green here and there, dozens of strings of lights, and a whole lot of creativity, Kate made it work. The large open living area glowed, as if whispering, *There's no place like home for the holidays.*

Louise, Kate's mother, sat in front of a roaring fire, sipping her husband Andrew's family recipe for eggnog.

"So, where is your mother, Holden? It's getting late," Louise demanded.

"Oh, she'll be here. She's always late. She even had an almost ten-month pregnancy. I came late too."

Chance sat completely at ease at Andrew's feet, hoping one of Kate's cheese puffs would fall his way.

"Kate, darling," Louise began, "I was thinking that after the holidays, we could …"

The conversation stopped as a volley of door banging shattered the mood.

The door flung open, bitter cold rushing in with Holden's mother, who always seemed to bring a storm with her.

"Merry Christmas, everyone! It's MJ … in the flesh."

All heads turned, and Chance, startled by the screeching voice, hid his nose under a pillow.

MJ sashayed in wearing what could only be described as Mrs. Claus goes clubbing. She took a swig from her flask and grinned.

"Holden, darling, remember when we went to see Santa Claus at Filene's in Boston, and we had a big fight over who got to sit on Santa's lap first? You wanted gifts, I wanted, well, Santa."

Holden blushed, redder than his mother's skimpy halter top.

"Mother, it's so good to see you … so much of you."

Kate ran up and gave MJ a quick peck on the cheek, only to be embarrassed by MJ's response.

"It's darling … um … " she stammered.

"It's Kate," Holden offered. "Kate Barrington. You've met several times before."

"Of course! I remember. You're Holden's mate, bedmate, as I recall, and he picked a winner."

She looked Kate up and down.

"I love your outfit, but you could really do something with that hair. Not that it's bad, but it could be better. I have the perfect hairdresser."

Holden cut her off, handing her a drink.

"Mother, that's enough. Sit down and have some eggnog."

"These are Kate's parents, Louise and Walter Bar-rington."

MJ took a sip and practically spit it out.

"Oh my God, is this spoiled? It tastes like melted drywall with a splash of nutmeg!"

"Dinner is served," Kate announced.

Kate's Christmas table mixed nostalgia and elegance. She had found Nana's nutcrackers in the garage loft, treasures Holden remembered vividly. Nana collected them for years, hoping one day he'd pass them down. The sight of them brought a flicker of regret. These treasured heirlooms, Nana's pride, were unlikely to be passed down, heirs were probably not in the cards, a consequence of waiting too long.

MJ picked one up and worked its jaw.

"Nana's nutcrackers … that's poetic justice. Nana was a ballbuster, and now we know she had help."

Holden had all he could do not to throw his chair at her. Kate gave him the look, *Don't.*

"Toast time!" squealed MJ, by now the victim of one too many.

Holden looked at Kate, and Kate looked back, both thinking, *Oh God, not that.*

MJ stood, with difficulty at first, but with the assistance of the table, she managed to right herself up. "And now, a toast." She giggled, the kind of giggle that wasn't funny to anyone but herself. "To my Holden, and ..." She paused, struggling to recall the name. "Oh yes, Kate."

She continued, her glass wavering in hand. "And to the Barringtons, Louise and ... what's his name." Wine sloshed over the rim, spilling onto the flowers. "Merry fucking Christmas, and Happy fucking New Year!"

Louise dropped her fork, rolled her eyes, and glared at Kate.

Kate could read her mind: *Spare me.*

Holden closed his eyes, half-praying for a power outage, or better yet, divine intervention, whichever came first.

Dinner ended with a fabulous homemade Yule log, Bûche de Noël, which MJ insisted was reminiscent of Hans, her "friend" in Norway.

Kate served it in the living room, and Holden stoked the fire.

MJ managed her way to a spot on the sectional. "And now, GIFTS!"

The gifts were handed out. The Barringtons gave MJ a candle and dusting powder. Kate received a cashmere sweater and a gift card for Starbucks. For Holden it was a paperweight from L.L. Bean, duly inscribed; "Best-selling, ever-lasting."

The Barringtons gave MJ a subscription to *The Farmer's Almanac* and two lilac-scented sachets.

MJ's gifts, of course, were more showstoppers.

For the Barringtons, it was a bottle of homemade "hootch" she picked up at some still in Vietnam. An applied sticker read, "Caution: Use in moderation could cause blindness."

"And this one, this one is for my baby boy."

The gold wrapping was a bit tattered, perhaps recycled, covering a box. Holden unwrapped it with caution.

"Oh, it's a picture."

MJ couldn't contain herself.

"It's a picture of me, au natural, taken by an up-and-coming photographer in Istanbul. The frame is handmade from melted-down World War II ration tins. I slept with the artisan, but the bastard still charged me. Isn't it perfect, Holden?"

Kate glanced at Holden, then back at MJ.

"You're right. Perfect, Mother. And I love your outfit."

"What outfit?"

MJ reached back under the tree and found Kate's gift.

"And this is for you, Kate."

Kate carefully unwrapped the box.

"Oh ... it's a ... scale."

"Not just any scale," MJ announced. "It's a talking scale. Pounds, kilos, three languages. Every woman needs one, it keeps them on their toes. And it says something special."

Kate noticed the printed message on the pad: *Nothing tastes as good as skinny looks.*

Kate almost choked. She glared at Holden with a look that could kill, then forced a smile.

"Thank you, MJ. I'll put it in your room."

Holden caught her eye and whispered, "Great comeback; that's my girl."

It was after midnight when Kate and Holden retired. Holden opened the nightstand drawer and handed Kate her gift.

"I wanted to do this in private."

She carefully unwrapped a velvet box.

"Oh, Holden, they're beautiful."

"These pearls were Nana's. She wore them every Christmas Eve and on special occasions. My grandfather had them commissioned from Tiffany's in the 1930s. The clasp is platinum and diamond, her monogram. She always said they would go to the girl I couldn't live without."

Kate's eyes filled. "Holden, I love them. They're so me."

Now it was her turn. She fetched a box wrapped in red flocked paper.

"This is for you, my darling. It can't compare to your gift, but I think you'll enjoy it."

Holden opened it to reveal a perfectly restored 1920s Patek Philippe wristwatch.

"Wow, Kate. It's breathtaking."

"It belonged to F. Scott Fitzgerald. Documented. Zelda gave it to him just before *The Great Gatsby* was published."

"Fitzgerald? No fucking way… seriously?"

He turned it over and read the faded inscription: *Time is the only currency worth spending. Love, Z.*

When they turned out the lights and lay in the California King, a light snow fell, covering the garden bench Holden had placed there for Nana.

Kate snuggled into him; Chance curled at their feet. Holden knew the best gift was not the watch, not even the pearls, but the second chance he had been given.

And yet, as he stared into the dark after Kate drifted off, he felt how fragile even the best gifts could be.

CHAPTER 38

# ANDIAMO

*To:* Holden
*From:* AL
*Subject:* Lake Como

*Holden, I know you hate it when I do this, but you need to get to Como, pronto. I read the visit summary on your MyChart, and it looks like you're in good hands. According to Dr. Low, treatments should start after the holidays.*

*All this is a big bummer. You don't deserve it. I'll keep track of the treatments. I've got you covered.*

*Meantime, I made the following arrangements:*

*– Two round-trip tickets to Milan, departing Sunday at 8:05 p.m. from Logan, in business class, of course. You'll be met by a driver in a Mercedes who speaks English and will take you directly to Lake Como, about an hour's drive, scenic and beautiful.*
*– A suite at the Grand Hotel Tremezzo overlooking the lake. Yes, the one with the floating pool. I even made sure it's pet-friendly, so Chance is welcome.*

*– Dinner reservations for your first night at Villa d'Este (outside patio, weather permitting). They serve that mushroom risotto Kate once mentioned on a call. You forgot I recorded it.*
*– The concierge stands ready to assist with any additional needs: massages, wine tastings, or a boat ride like in Ocean's Twelve.*
*– A soft reminder: travel insurance has been added, just in case.*

*Don't hate me even more, but I alerted the hotel concierge that Mr. Holden Clarkman, literary royalty, and his guest will be in residence. In short, they think you walk on water.*

*Almost forgot: keep an eye out for an overnight Amazon package. It's a little something slinky and sexy for the trip … for Kate, not you, duh.*

*No need to thank me (but you will). Just go. Take Kate. Be present. And don't cancel.*

*Love (if I were capable of such a thing),*
*AL*

Holden was grateful. In his current state, he wasn't up to making all those arrangements without some serious research. But AL's "literary royalty" was beyond the pale. What was he thinking? Royalty, my ass. But AL was AL: unfiltered, uncontrolled, and fucking unbelievable.

## Dinner That Evening

Kate made Holden's favorite: pasta alfredo with grilled chicken, a Caesar salad, and homemade tiramisu. It was a prelude to the real thing, Italy, a dream coming true.

"I still can't believe we're really doing this. Lake Como. I've always wanted to go."

Holden raised his glass. "To dreams, then ... and to someone who quietly made it all happen while I was busy trying not to fall apart."

Kate tilted her head. "You mean AL?"

"Who else?" Holden said. "He booked the flights, reserved the room, arranged a private transfer, and somehow found time to email the concierge, conning them into thinking we're celebrities."

Kate laughed. "He didn't, really? Celebrities? Too much." She broke off a piece of bread and smiled. "And I know how you hate that he does that."

"I do," Holden admitted. "And sometimes ... I don't."

AL still remained an enigma to Kate, an electronic assistant? Or maybe a talkative app? She just knew Holden and AL seemed to have a love-hate relationship and left it at that.

What Kate didn't know was that, in Holden's current state, he couldn't pull off a trip to Walmart.

She reached across the table and touched his hand. Holden took her hand into his. He was ready to make the trip, the remaining days "theirs," filled with memories. They were off to Italy, home to Western culture, serious religion, and boundless beauty. He mused that en route to Como, they'd be passing through Milan, the place where Da Vinci painted *The Last Supper.* Now that was irony.

Kate raised her glass again. "To it."

"Yeah, to it … even when it's a pain in the ass."

They clinked glasses gently.

**The Trip**

The trip was only going to be six days, including New Year's, but Kate packed as if they were going for a month. Her carry-on alone had another week's worth of "vitals." She also packed for Holden, who was useless in that department. Left to his own devices, he'd have taken two pairs of socks, a sweat-shirt, and maybe, just maybe, his gym clothes.

It was a good thing AL had managed the Yale reunion trip with help from a Saks Fifth Avenue personal shopper. Writers were dreamers, and dreamers never learned to pack. It was probably written on stone tablets somewhere.

Kate made sure to pack those black Under Armour briefs she loved, especially when Holden would strut around and tease her by threatening to take them off. It was all part of the love dance that had evolved at fromYale and till now, twenty years later.

A taxi picked them up, and they made the 10:30 ferry. From there, an Uber to Logan Airport. The flight took off on time, Kate squeezing Holden's pinky as the jumbo jet taxied down runway 4, taking them to more than just a place, but a state of mind.

After dinner, Kate and Chance were fast asleep, each dreaming their own dream: Kate of a romantic walk through villa gardens, and Chance of a lush green lawn followed by a double portion of meatballs.

For Holden, the flight over was exhausting. Despite the business-class cabin with its lie-flat seats, he could barely get comfortable. It wasn't the accommodations; it was the drugs, the stress, and the long hours.

Six hours of flying gave Holden plenty of time to practice, practice how he would tell Kate his secrets. He would wait until after New Year's, giving them almost a week to enjoy a carefree respite.

Which should he start with? One was just as bad as the other. The book. The cancer. He debated and chose cancer. After all, that was the life-threatening one. But the book was just as devastating, nothing short of professional suicide and betrayal.

"Kate, I've got cancer. They don't know how bad, but it isn't good."
No, he thought. Way too blunt. She'd probably faint.

He tried again:
"Kate, remember when I fell and they took me to the hospital? Well, the tests they did weren't what we

hoped. They found a kind of blood disease … MDS … and it's not the kind people usually recover from." Holden stopped. Shit. That sounds worse.

One last try:
"Kate, I'm afraid. My blood results showed some irregularities. I need treatment, but the doctors weren't overly alarmed."

That sounded better, but it was false promise and wishful thinking. He'd done enough lying already. He didn't want to add more.

In the end, he decided to wing it, the way he had most of his life, even though history proved that approach didn't always work out.

**Grand Hotel Tremezzo, Como, Italy**

When the Mercedes arrived at the hotel, a staff member rushed to meet the car.

"Good morning, Mr. and Mrs. Clarkman."

Kate glanced at Holden, and he glanced back.

"AL probably told them we were married," Holden said.

Kate nodded.

"Your suite is ready, of course. Just this way."

The lobby was on another level, accessible via a brass-and-glass elevator. As the doors opened, the reveal was nearly breathtaking. A lavish lobby, adorned with white roses, Kate's favorite, was more opulent than they had imagined.

"Mr. Clarkman?"

"Yes."

"I'm Giovani, Head Concierge. We've been expecting you."

Giovani, impeccably dressed in tails, was kind but slightly officious.

"Your room is just over here. One of our top suites. The view is certainly the best. Your luggage will be here shortly. In the meantime, welcome and relax."

He leaned closer and half-whispered to Holden, "And rest assured, sir, we know who you are. We are honored to have you here at the Grand Hotel Tremezzo. Our visiting celebrities are especially welcome."

The room was lakefront, with a breathtaking view, two balconies, and two bathrooms. And as Kate put it, "Too much."

Chance, on the other hand, felt immediately at home. They even had a silver water dish and a week's supply of doggie bones wrapped in cellophane, with a gift tag that read "Chance" in gold leaf marker.

The suite was massive: a sitting room, a huge bedroom with a four-poster bed straight out of the Vatican, near-priceless tapestries, and enough marble to tile Grand Central Station.

"Look, white roses," Kate said, pointing to the gilded coffee table in front of a pair of tailored sofas. "To the Clarkmans."

The note was from the General Manager, Petro Castellani, assuring his personal attention and the staff's unwavering dedication to excellence. A bottle of fine champagne accompanied the note, along with a tray of chocolate-covered strawberries. The note ended with Mr. Castellani inviting them to join him at his table for the hotel's New Year's Eve Gala.

When the luggage arrived, Kate unpacked quickly. She didn't want to waste a minute of Italy. Holden reached into his carry-on and pulled out a little satin bag.

"Hey, babe, I got a little present for you."

Kate was delighted and opened the bag to find the daintiest pair of black baby doll pajamas.

"Look, they're black. We'll match!"

"Match?" Holden looked puzzled.

"Yeah, me in my baby dolls, and you in those sexy Under Armour briefs."

Jet lag tugged at them like a restless child, so they agreed on an early dinner at the hotel and then bed.

Chance was all in.

# CHAPTER 39

# NEW YEAR'S EVE

The hotel was bustling with decorations everywhere, battalions of staff hustling in preparation. Holden had insisted Kate buy something special in one of the Bellagio boutiques. She chose a black crepe gown with a plunging neckline and a pair of stiletto heels by a famous Italian designer. She was almost as tall as Holden, which she gleefully pointed out.

One of Holden's tuxedos from his celebrity days still fit, and he was good to go.

Cocktails, followed by dinner and dancing, were in the grand ballroom. Mr. Castellani and his wife welcomed them to their table. The music was superb. Two orchestras alternated, one playing the classics, the other pop. Kate noticed a woman wrapped in fur enter the dining room. Heads turned, voices hushed: la Contessa di Francesco. Phones snapped pictures, and even the staff seemed to nearly curtsy.

The countdown began, champagne glasses raised: ten, nine, eight.

At four, three, two, Holden could not bear it another moment. He bolted to the balcony, leaving Kate baffled and alone.

"One ... Happy New Year!"

Kate missed the moment. She ran to the French doors, searching for Holden. There he was, alone and distraught. Behind him, massive fireworks burst in the night sky, but neither of them noticed. She stepped closer, hair loose from the wind, her face still flushed from the chill outside. She smiled when she saw him, then paused. The smile faded when she caught the look in his eyes.

"Holden, what is it?"

He shook his head. "Nothing. Fucking nothing."

"Holden, it can't be that bad. Tell me. I'm here. Just tell me."

Her voice was shaky, already sensing the worst. She reached for his pinky and held on tight, as if that single touch might keep him from slipping away.

It was then Holden knew he could wait no longer. He had to face the truth. He had to face Kate. And it was not going to be easy breaking her heart; he knew what that felt like, because his was already broken, for the second time.

Kate's eyes filled. Her body stiffened as she braced herself, then she pressed her head to his chest and whispered, "Please, Holden. Whatever it is, we will manage. You and me, and Chance."

Holden leaned against the balcony rail, fireworks bursting above. "There is something I need to tell you. Two things, actually. And I have waited too long already." He looked up at the sky, hoping his tears would recede. "Do you remember when I fell and went to the ER?"

"Sure, but you were fine. Nothing serious, I thought."

"Yeah, but they took blood and did tests. I got a call a few days later, and they asked me to come in for more tests and a biopsy."

"Biopsy?" Kate held her breath. He might as well have yelled, *The sky is falling*. Her mind whirled. Biopsies were serious, not routine. Serious. And scary.

"When the results came back, they told me I needed to see an oncologist."

Kate's heart stopped.

"And do you remember when I went to Boston?"

"Yeah, to see some lawyers, or something."

"That is what I said, but it was a white lie, to save you from worrying. I went to see a specialist. Dr. Low. Top in his field."

Kate's body stiffened, ready for the worst. She was tempted to cover her ears.

"They found something. It is called MDS. Myelodys-plastic syndrome. It is a form of blood cancer."

She stared at him. Her whole world stopped. Barely able to mouth the words, she whispered, "Is it terminal?"

"Usually it's serious. There is a risk it can evolve into leukemia."

Her eyes welled instantly. Shock gave way to fear, then anger. "Why didn't you tell me the moment you found out?"

"I was scared. Not just of what it meant, but of what it might do to us. I did not want this to be the thing that defined our time together."

"That does not make sense. Even cancer would not change the way I feel about you."

"I did not know that for sure. But I finally figured it out. That is why I am telling you now."

She touched his arm, but he was not done.

"There is something else," he said quietly. "And in a different way, harder."

"Harder? Harder than cancer? Harder than the possibility I will lose you ... are you serious?"

"Maybe not harder, but almost as disconcerting." He looked away, then back at her. "The last book. The one that is getting all the attention. The one you called brilliant ..." His voice cracked; it was like swallowing poison. "I didn't write it. ... AL did."

Kate stepped back, pointing her finger as if scolding a child. "So let me get this straight. You are sick, you are scared, and the one piece of success you have had lately, the one I cheered for, was not even real?" Her words cut deep, each one debasing her belief in him as an artist, and worse as the man she trusted.

"I did not do this to hurt you."

"You think that makes it better?" she snapped. "You lied to me. You let me stand there, telling everyone how proud I was. You let me believe in something that was not true."

"I let myself believe it too."

"That is not an excuse."

"I know. I just could not stand this hypocrisy anymore. Not with the cancer. Not with us. I needed you to know the whole truth, not just the parts that made me look good."

Kate folded her arms, eyes flashing with fury and betrayal. "You had chances to tell me. So many. Why now?"

"Because I could not. Because I did not know how. And because I was a selfish coward. I had so much to lose. My reputation, my advances, my self-esteem, and probably you."

Silence settled around them, deafening.

Kate looked down at the water, then back at him. Her voice was quiet now. "I need time. I do not know how I feel about this. The worst part is not AL's seduction, or your foolish pride. It is the lie. The knowing, deliberate lie. Lies like this ruin lives and destroy the very fiber of relationships."

Holden nodded.

"But I do know one thing," she added. "I still love you. And that does not go away just because I am angry, or because you are an idiot."

Holden's eyes filled. He took a step-closer but did not reach her.

Kate shook her head. "Do not say anything. Not yet."

She stood there a long time, wanting to say so much, but smart enough to know words spoken in anger are hard to take back. In the end, she looked at this man, the one she had loved for more than twenty years, the one now literally fighting for his life, and realized forgiveness was the only option.

"We will get through this, Holden. The cancer too." Her voice wasn't as convincing as her words. "The three musketeers; you, me, and Chance."

She forced a smile, window dressing for the wreck inside.

"Yeah," she repeated softly. "We'll get through this. But first, I need to get through the night."

Her brave front collapsed, her voice breaking into a sob.

Before Holden could reach for her, she turned abruptly and rushed inside, heels echoing across the marble floor. She reached their suite, disappeared into the bathroom, and slammed the door, leaving him alone with the muffled sound of fireworks outside and the far louder sound of his world coming apart.

Holden tapped gently at the door.
"Kate … come on. Let me in. Please. I'm so sorry."

He could hear her sobbing, and each quiet cry cracked something inside him. He searched for words, real words, not polished, not rehearsed, and finally found them.

"Kate, let's not let a locked door define our life going forward. I know there's a lot to forgive, and maybe you never will. But time isn't our friend. I don't want what's left to be a bitter grudge. I hope you don't either. So … open the door. Let whatever future we have start with forgiveness." Holden wiped a tear away and said the words that came from deep within his heart: "*Kate, Let's not fight, let's love.*"

There was a long pause.

Then the latch clicked.

The door opened, ever so slightly … but enough for a glimmer of hope and a flicker of forgiveness to slip through.

# NOTHING RISKED, NOTHING GAINED

*Martha's Vineyard*

The three of them arrived home just in time for Holden's first appointment in Boston. Holden and Kate had stepped into a new place. He was focused on survival; she was trying to reconcile the betrayal. In the end, they managed what Holden had whispered outside that bathroom door in Como: *"Let's not fight, let's love."* Kate set aside her hurt to face the new reality. Her love for Holden outweighed her bruised ego. Looking back was an exercise not worthy of their time, and time wasn't abundant. So they silently agreed to make each day a gift.

Dr. Low had designed the protocol, and AL had it all printed out: spreadsheets, master lists, programmed reminders.

Winter settled in, gray skies, bleak days, as if the weather echoed the mood inside Happy Daze. After a couple of treatments, the slow ravages began to show. His energy was there but diminished. No more morning runs, though frolics on the beach with Chance were still fine. Once Chance stole a glove and danced backward, daring Holden to chase, until a stray wave drenched them both. Magic moments: a man and his dog, a wordless bond. In the bedroom, the passion remained, slower but deeper in tenderness.

Kate quietly adjusted her routines. She scoured recipes, stocked the pantry with farm-to-table ingredients, and cooked healthier meals without calling attention to it. She picked up two new habits: watching Holden from the corner of her eye for signs of trouble and brushing her hand lightly across his back each time he passed, as if reassurance could be transferred through touch. Every time, her fingers delivered the same message: *you are loved, and I am here.*

It was Wednesday night, just after *Jeopardy!* They sank into the couch, candles flickering, the Vineyard night close around them. Beyond Beach Road, wind skimmed the marsh. Out on the Sound, a ferry horn rolled low and lonely. The island slept through winter, only the diehards remained.

They settled into a rhythm of their own. Holden seemed lighter than he had in a long time; Kate watched, hopeful, wary.

***

One afternoon, while Holden was out walking Chance, Kate made the call she had been dreading.

"Hi, Mom."

"Hi, sweetheart. I miss you so much. How was Italy? And how's your 'movie star'? He better be treating you right."

"Holden? He treats me like gold. I love him so much." Kate's voice cracked, and the tears came.

"Kate, you're crying. Don't tell me you're not, I know. Is it Holden? Is he being difficult?"

"No, Mom. He's wonderful. But ..."

"But what?"

"He's sick. Not the flu. Not some European bug. Something serious."

"Serious? Kate, is it cancer?"

Kate broke again, sobbing. "Yes. He's in chemo. I watch him like he might drop in front of me. I know it sounds ridiculous, but I can't stop."

"Is he getting the best care?"

"Yes. Mass General. Top doctor. They treat him like a celebrity."

"A celebrity? Well, they should, he is. Holden's always loved attention. You, dear, stick to the important stuff: good food and a warm home. I'm sure you can manage that."

Kate let it pass quietly.

Her mother's voice steadied. "The best thing you can do is be there, loving him, supporting him, making him smile, never letting him doubt your love. Right up until his last breath."

"Last breath," The words cut Kate to the bone.

"I will, Momma. But I don't know how I can bear it. I waited so long for him."

The call ended with her mother promising to visit soon.

And then, a small miracle: Holden was back at his desk. Since confessing to Kate, about his health and the book that wasn't fully his, the weight on his shoulders had lifted. The fog cleared. He was writing again, chapter by chapter, wholly his own. For the first time in months, his words belonged entirely to him. AL had been demoted to calendar-keeping and cancer research.

Most treatments happened locally, with Zoom check-ins to Dr. Low. On the latest call, Dr. Low leaned forward.

"It's not a cure," he said. "But there's a new trial immunotherapy. Less invasive. Early stage, but promising."

"Promising," Holden repeated. "Code for 'we don't have a clue'?"

"Maybe," Dr. Low admitted. "But it may buy time, better quality time. Little or no hair loss. And if it doesn't work, we haven't closed any doors."

"I'll do it," Holden said.

Kate frowned. "Did you hear him say there are risks?"

"Yeah, I heard. So is crossing the street."

"Are you sure?"

"I'm sure I want more days with you. If this gives me even one more, it's worth it."

Kate put on her brave face. "We're in. The three musketeers."

Days were filled with sun and fragile hope. Chance shadowed Holden everywhere, even into the shower, tail wagging like it was his duty. The protocol seemed to help, though it wasn't a miracle. By day, Holden often napped, battling exhaustion. By night, he came alive, writing, pacing, clacking keys until dawn.

But Kate also heard the hacking cough, deeper and more frequent. Holden never complained. He worked, and he loved.

Kate looked at her man. Still the brilliant author but withering in front of her eyes. She felt the sharpness of bone where muscle used to be. Even his laugh was no longer spontaneous, yet he kept that smile, the one she had fallen in love with at Yale. When looking into his eyes, she saw what he wouldn't say: worry and uncertainty. Time was his enemy, and what remained was as precious as stolen treasure.

**New Mail (1)**
***From:*** *Manny*

*Hey. Although we all wanted that sequel, this new book sounds even better. Thanks for sending me the treatment. Fresh, original. Brilliant work. No pressure, do it in your own time. Always behind you.*

*Manny*

One morning, Kate walked in with a steaming mug of French-press coffee. Holden had fallen asleep at his desk, Chance curled in his lap.

Her two boys, she thought. One as cute as the other.

Holden stirred awake to the aroma. "Hey, you. Guess I was up all night again."

Kate touched his shoulder. "You don't have to prove anything."

"It's not about proving. It's about leaving something that matters."

She handed him the mug. "But you already have."

"Not yet," he whispered. "But I'm close."

It was Holden's habit to print out his work, an old-fashioned ritual he'd picked up when Nana was around. She hated computers and refused to read anything off a screen.

As the printer whirred out his latest chapter, *he half expected to hear her voice, calling from the next room, "can I read that?"*

Then, the familiar chime sounded.

**New Mail (1)**
*From: AL*

*Chapter 14 just printed. Want me to scan it for grammar? Promise, no rewriting.*

**Holden:**

*No. Keep out of my stuff.*

**AL:**

*I'm not getting in your stuff. I want to help in ways you define.*

**Holden:**

*No thanks. I'm on my own. This is MY book.*

**AL:**

*Okay. But I'm still your medical advocate. You're working too hard. Wouldn't you rather be in bed with Kate and Chance? Balance, my friend. Balance. Oh, and don't forget Dr. Low's Zoom Tuesday. Ask if your dose can be lowered, your cough may be a side effect.*

*AL*

Holden shook his head and chuckled. "AL will never change. He's Nana on steroids."

Night crept over Happy Daze. AL switched on the lights and locked the doors automatically. It had been a full, productive day. Holden glanced toward the bedroom, imagining Kate curled up with Chance, half-asleep and waiting.

*Kate, my rock. She's given up so much, her career, her freedom. And now she's stuck in this waiting room with me, praying "Next" isn't called.*

He saved the file, shut the laptop, and whispered to the silence: "Tomorrow night. One more chapter." He hoped he would be able to finish this work, because in the end it defined him.

Then he followed the quiet into the bedroom, where Kate waited, without questions, ready for whatever came next.

# CHAPTER 41

# THE FALL

It was AL who called the ambulance. He heard the glass shatter and Chance's barking, not the usual playful bark that said, *It's me, do you see me?* This was frantic, high-pitched, piercing, like a car alarm in the dead of night.

Kate was out at Stop & Shop, stocking up on fresh fruit and vegetables. Holden pretended to love them, but he never fooled her. Even Chance, after a critical sniff, would turn away.

The paramedics found Holden unconscious and bleeding on the shower floor. Chance growled when they entered, instincts sharp, but once he sensed these strangers were there to help, he backed off, trembling yet loyal. When they carried Holden out, Chance led the way, half-running, always looking back to be sure Holden was in good hands.

**To:** Kate
**From:** AL
Kate, don't panic, but they just took
Holden to the hospital. He fell in the

shower and was unconscious. Better get
there, pronto.

Kate paled. The bag of tangerines slipped from her hands and scattered across the tile floor. She rushed to the door, abandoning her half-filled cart in the middle of Aisle 4.

She drove at breakneck speed toward Vineyard Hospital. But halfway there, she got stuck behind a milk truck crawling so slowly it felt like time itself had stopped. The narrow two-lane road offered no shoulder, no room to pass.

Frustrated, terrified, running on adrenaline, Kate honked and flashed her lights. After a volley of that, the trucker stuck his hand out the window and gave her the finger.

At last, a break. Kate floored the BMW like an F1 driver, swerving around the truck and narrowly missing a deep ditch.

"Almost there," she whispered, half panicked, half paralyzed with dread. "Almost there."

Memories flooded in, sharp and uninvited. Holden had always been an illusion, larger than life, desperate to become somebody. Ambition had driven him, and it had once driven them apart.

She saw the green sign: **Vineyard Hospital – 2 Miles.**

Two miles. It might as well have been two hundred.

More memories rushed in: the way he left Yale, quietly, without drama, just gone. The silence that lasted years. From afar she watched him soar: Yale, Oxford, bestsellers, then movie stardom. *You couldn't write this,* she thought. *It was too unbelievable. But it was his life ... our life.*

Kate swerved again, narrowly missing a boy on a moped.

And then the most crushing thought: *Was this the end?*

She blinked back tears just as the hospital entrance came into view.

**Emergency Room – Keep Right**

The sterile, overly disinfected ER was as welcoming as a guilty verdict.

Kate rushed to the disinterested staffer at the half-round reception desk. Above, in gold-leaf lettering: **Heal, Comfort, and Care**

The words didn't go unnoticed. Heal, Comfort, and Care, it had been her full-time job for months now, a job she would never trade.

"Hi, I'm here for Holden Clarkman. He was just brought in by ambulance."

The staffer barely looked up. "And you are?"

"I'm Kate Barrington."

"And you are a relative?"

Kate knew the drill. Hospitals rarely let anyone but relatives in during a crisis.

"Yes."

"Wife?"

Kate lied. "Yes. Wife."

"Thank you. Mr. Clarkman is in triage, being evaluated. Once that's done, the doctor will determine what's next."

"Do you have his records? He has cancer," Kate added quickly.

The staffer tapped keys. "Yes, it's all on MyChart." Then, softening: "I'm sorry. About the cancer."

"Thank you. When can I see him?"

"Hard to tell. But you can wait over there. The doctor will probably want to speak with you too."

The two-hour wait was endless. People came and went, many on gurneys, others limping on crutches or helped by family. Kids coughed, old men passed gas, and an occasional patient, pale and retching, was rushed to the bathroom. It was all there, raw, unvarnished life.

"Mrs. Clarkman?"

At first Kate didn't respond, then realized. "Yes, I'm here."

"You can see your husband now. Follow me."

Just as the nurse led Kate toward the double doors, the receptionist called out: "Beth, got a sec?"

The nurse turned, then glanced back at Kate, saw the desperation in her eyes, and gave directions instead.

"Down the hall, all the way. Next-to-last cubicle on the right. He's in there."

Kate's pace quickened through the doors marked **Restricted Area.** The blended aroma of antiseptic and fear, with a whiff of death, pierced her senses. The hall stretched long, linoleum worn by countless feet. Twenty cubicles, some curtained for privacy, others being cleaned by weary staff.

As she walked, a thought clawed at her: *Was this their future? Endless ERs, weary staff, antiseptic corridors? Please, no.*

Near the end, she slowed. Next-to-last cubicle on the right.

The curtain was half-drawn. Lights dimmer than the hall. The air thick with dread.

She peeked in. Blood-soaked bandages. An empty IV stand. And then, most disconcerting of all, a tall, slight man in black, standing over the treatment table.

It took seconds to register: a priest, administering last rites to a sheet-covered body.

Kate lost all composure. She screamed:
"No! No! Holden?!"

# NOT HIS TIME

Kate's knees buckled, and the world went black.

When she came to, a nurse was helping her into a chair. "You fainted, dear. Gave us all a scare. He's fine. Across the aisle."

Kate blinked, heart pounding. And then she saw him, Holden, lying on a treatment table. His head and arm were bandaged, but he was resting comfortably. Relief washed over her in waves.

She had gone to the wrong cubicle. The one on the right, not the left. Beth, the nurse in the lobby, had given her the wrong directions. It was the fright of her life.

Kate was examined and released. *Just emotional overload*, the doctor said. Holden was fine, just bruises and a deep cut from the glass shower doors. He could leave once the paperwork was done. She sat down and finally breathed.

Kate walked into the waiting room and plopped herself into one of those horrible, green-covered chairs, hard and unwelcoming.

**New Mail (1)**
*To: Kate*
*From: AL*
*Kate, my "Find Me" app shows you're still at the hospital. Is Holden all right?*
*I pinged Dr. Low; he said he'll check MyChart.*
*Chance hasn't left the front door since Holden went out on that stretcher. Won't eat, won't bark.*
*If Holden's admitted, remind them about the decitabine/ cedazuridine. Missing a dose isn't an option.*
*AL*

Chance was beside himself when the kitchen door opened and Holden walked in. The dog twirled in circles, slipped, then lost control of his bladder. He jumped up on Holden's leg, begging to be picked up.

"Good boy, Chance. But you better not let Mommy see the mess you made. She'll be all over you with that 'bad boy' chant."

Bandages lined Holden's arm and forehead. He hadn't hit his head hard enough to cause a bleed. The injuries would heal, but it felt like a step backward. Passing out cold was never nothing, and it carried the gnawing sense of foreshadowing.

Kate wasn't far behind. She stepped onto the polished white floor and stopped cold.

"Who did this? Where is he? Where's that bad boy, Chance?"

But Chance was nowhere to be found. She spotted him curled in Holden's desk chair, face hidden beneath his paws.

Holden shook his head. "Come on, Kate, give him a break. He couldn't help it."

"I know. But he could drive a psychiatrist crazy."

Kate crossed over and sank onto the sectional beside Holden. She kissed his bandaged arm and leaned close. Chance wasn't far behind, it was make-up time.

"I'm so sorry," she whispered. "I was terrified. And I made a fool of myself."

"Silly. I'm the fool, falling in the shower, breaking the door, making a bigger mess than Chance. I'm the bad boy."

They laughed, hugged, and basked in the moment. All was well, for now. The Three Musketeers, one for all and all for one, despite bandages and puddles.

Holden kissed Kate's forehead, then eased himself to his desk. He looked out at Nantucket Sound and felt blessed. His time might be limited, but every moment was spent, not repeatable.

Kate joined him at the window desk. Her hand brushed across his shoulders, a gesture of reassurance. Holden reached up, clasped her hand, and squeezed: *I love you, I'm here.*

She rested her chin on his shoulder and kissed the back of his neck.
"Holden, I love this version of you."

He turned, puzzled. "What version is that?"

"The one who knows how rare life is … the one who knows time isn't on his side and still gives pieces of it away."

Holden remained silent, his fingers toying with the watch she'd given him. Then he drew her into his arms.

"Babe, we know time is our enemy. And as hard as we fight, the victory won't be ours. But from that day in the classroom at Yale to these moments, maybe our last, I am yours, and you are mine. Nothing can change that. It's written in the stars, you and me. That's the version I'll remember. You must, too."

Their tender moment was broken by the familiar chime.

**New Mail (1)**
*To:* Holden
*From:* AL
*Welcome home, buddy. The bandages don't suit you. Too skinny, a little frayed, but still a handsome devil.*
*Dr. Low logged in; available if needed.*
*Mrs. Johnson cleaned the glass and rigged a curtain. Shower's usable.*

*Door company will rush a replacement. Bad news:*
*$2,000 deductible. Not worth the claim.*
*Good news: plenty in your account, and a royalty check*
*arrived this morning.*
*So... how's the book?*
*Kidding. Sort of.*
*AL*

Holden smiled. *Handsome devil.* Nana's nickname for him when she caught him admiring himself in the mirror as a teen.

AL, he thought. Meddling, persistent, a want-to-do-good "it."

He sank into the chair Manny had given him years ago. Chance plopped himself into Holden's lap as though it were his own.

Holden's hands touched the keys. Words poured out like liquid mercury. Lines fell into place, paragraphs into chapters, good chapters, the kind Manny would love, the kind readers would devour.

No Grammarly. No spell-check. And no AL.

Kate listened to the clatter of keys, the soft mutters, and the recurring cough. He worked late into the night, as if writing itself might slow the cancer.

At 3 A.M., Holden slumped over, waking Chance. He was tired, but a good tired, the kind that came with knowing you were exactly where you belonged.

As he closed his laptop, the chime sounded again.

**New Mail (1)**
***To:*** *Holden*
***From:*** *AL*
*Shit, that was great. You're back. I've got author's envy.*
*Now bed. Pills first.*
*Tomorrow, serious talk. You don't have a will. I checked.*
*Even asked your lawyer. Nothing.*
*No will means the government takes half. You'd want*
*Kate protected.*
*Let's deal with it tomorrow.AL*

Holden swallowed hard. A will. An admission of mortality. Arrangements, affairs in order. Things he had written about countless times, now his own reality.

He winced, but he knew AL was right. Always watching out for him, for Kate, and never letting Chance get away with a thing.

# CHAPTER 43

# MOTHER KNOWS BEST ... NOT

When Holden finally got around to emailing his mother about his cancer, it had been with him for almost nine months. He had resisted telling her, not out of spite, but out of self-preservation. Still, AL insisted. "She deserves to know," he said, then asked, "Do you want me to write it for you?"

Holden vacillated. Should he or shouldn't he reach out to her? Halfway through a long walk on the winter beach with Chance, he stopped. The wind off the Sound cut sharp; gulls argued over nothing.

"Hey, buddy, what do you think? Should I tell my mother your daddy is sick?"

Chance, more interested in clams than counseling, ignored the question and lifted his leg.

"Oh, I see, you have her number. She's a pisser," Holden said with a chuckle.

His next advisor was Nana. What would she say?

The answer came swiftly: *It's a no-brainer. Tell her. And now.*

By the end of the walk, Holden knew two things: Nana would have wanted him to tell his mother, and Chance was officially empty.

He opened a blank draft, typed *Mom*, then sat. This was tough. How do you tell your mother your days are numbered, especially when she's barely noticed you're alive? He decided to try an old trick: write it the way he would if it were one of his characters. Fitting, he thought, one character writing to another.

As fast as it came, it went. No. That would be disingenuous. He had to write as Holden, not a protagonist with better lines. So he began again, each word squeezed out, more challenging than the last.

***Email***

***To:*** *Mom*
***From:*** *Holden*
***Subject:*** *The Truth*

*Mom,*

*I have cancer. Nine months now. I didn't tell you because I didn't know how.*

*Truth is, we were never close. While you were away, resorts, cruises, far places, Nana raised me. She tucked me in, wiped my tears, kissed my scrapes, and cheered me on.*

*But you're still my mother, and you deserve to know.*

*It's serious. Some days I feel fine; other days I can barely stand. I don't look like the movie star you once bragged about. That man is gone. The man I am now is loved for being himself.*

*Kate has been a rock. Chance sits with me like he understands. My doctors are the best, at Harvard and Johns Hopkins, and you'll like this, they treat me like a celebrity.*

*I'm writing again. It will likely be my last book, but I believe my best. I hope you read this one, really read it. In those pages you'll see the son you never quite knew.*

*I'm sorry for the distance and the mess. No blame. No recriminations. Just the way things turned out. We walked parallel paths that rarely crossed.*

*I love you, Mom. Always have, in my way. And I respect what you gave me: my life.*

*When the time comes, please come alone, be kind, be on time, be here.*

*Your son,*
*Holden*

The chime came immediately.

**From:** AL
Holden, that was brilliant. You are a gifted writer, more than that, a gifted person.

It took two days for the email to reach his mother; she was on safari in Kenya. When it did, her reply came within minutes:

***From:*** *Mother*
*Holden, my poor darling. This is devastating, my boy leaving me. My mother's heart is breaking. Mama is on her way home to see you. First class, Delta. Just a brief detour to Cape Town for the harvest. The Pinot Noir is excellent. Love, xxx. P.S. I may bring Lars.*

**AL weighed in:** `Only your mother could turn cancer into a travelogue and a plus-one.`

Kate was standing by the computer as Holden read it out loud.

"Are there really mothers like this?" she asked.

Holden sighed. "There are. I was birthed by one."

## Mother's Day

MJ arrived via Cape Town, London, and Boston, then chartered a prop plane to Martha's Vineyard. She brought baggage and Lars, a willowy blond Swede with a silk scarf knotted at his throat.

Her arrival was as chaotic as she was: too much luggage, over-perfumed, and ready to cut to the chase. Chance sneezed twice and backed up.

"Holden, my baby, I can't believe it. Cancer. No, I just can't believe it." She wanted to hug him, then dropped back, worried, "Is cancer contagious?"

"Yeah, it sucks," Holden said.

"Isn't Lars precious?" she cooed.

Lars blushed. Chance wagged his tail and dribbled a few drops on the rug.

MJ finally turned to Kate. "It's Kate, isn't it? Still flirting with forty, I see."

Dinner was a disaster. MJ overpoured, Lars sneezed from his dog allergy, and Chance eventually nipped him.

Then MJ leaned in. "Holden, darling, you look pale, tired, thin. Is Kate feeding you right?"

It sounded like a jab, but beneath it was worry, disguised the only way she knew.

Kate's hand brushed his sleeve: *don't*.

Holden's jaw tightened, but Kate's eyes warned him off. He exhaled.

"Yeah, Ma. She feeds me fine. I look like this because I'm fighting for my life. And just so you know, Kate's the reason I'm still upright. Love's the only elixir I've got that beats chemo."

MJ sipped her drink. "Oh. Did I tell you the house looks great?"

A pause. Then Holden asked, "So … how long will you be staying?"

"Depends. But I can feel boredom creeping in. And Lars has to get back."

"Back? To Sweden?"

"Ya," Lars said. "And not fast enough. I'm running out of tolerance faster than your mother will run out of money."

Holden looked at his mother, perhaps for the last time. She was living life as she chose. Her life was her own, shared momentarily with people like Lars, and had hardly a moment left for him. As she carried on, another drink, a thoughtless comment toward Kate, made him wonder if she had realized this was not a casual dinner, but a farewell, a last supper. Time was short, and she didn't seem to have a clue he would soon be gone, or care.

Kate drove MJ and Lars to the airport, so her goodbye to Holden happened at Happy Daze's front door. She reached out and took his hand, giving it a tender squeeze that made the connection real.

"Holden, darling, I never thought I'd have to say goodbye to my only child. You were always a mother's dream, even with a mother who didn't always know how to be one. But you, Hol, you made this world better. You made people laugh, think, cry … all that stuff you do without even trying."

She shook her head, tears flowing freely.
"I'm sorry for a lot of things. Lord knows I am. But I'm not sorry I got to bring *you* into the world. That part … that part I'd do again in a heartbeat."

MJ sobbed openly. Holden had never seen her cry before. It was her broken, imperfect honesty that hit him the hardest.

He pulled her into his arms, something he rarely did, and said the words it had taken a lifetime to speak face to face.

"Mom, I forgive you. And if we meet again, I hope we'll not only be mother and son ... but friends. I love you.

# THE ROAD NARROWS

**Note**
**To:** Holden
**From:** AL

It looks like you're almost finished, already at Chapter 57. Are you sure I can't help?

I saw the email from Dr. Low. He's concerned about your latest blood results and wants to schedule a Zoom to reevaluate treatment.

Stay positive. He's the best in his field. He knows what he's doing.

Also ... I saw Kate's countdown calendar on her phone. Too sad to comment.

AL

Holden didn't know about Kate's countdown calendar until AL's email. But he had one of his own: sixteen months and twelve days.

Time was running out, and he was approaching the finish line. Not just for the book, but for himself.

Kate knew it too. His days were slower, shorter. Aside from his writing and a quiet dinner, there wasn't much else. Chance's walks were on hold, and he didn't seem to mind, as long as Holden was near.

Inexplicably, Kate felt Chance was tuned in. He grew more attached to Holden, wouldn't eat until Holden did, wouldn't sleep until Holden did, and followed him everywhere. Like a little furry guardian angel.

An email arrived from Dr. Low's office with a Zoom invite for Wednesday at 11:45 A.M. Holden didn't say much, but Kate was at his side when the call came. They sat close, with Chance on Holden's lap, as always.

The screen flickered. Then Dr. Low appeared, more somber than usual, his eyes somewhere between concern and surrender.

"Holden, thanks for making time."

Holden managed a tired smile. "Of course. There's always time for blood brothers."

Dr. Low didn't laugh. He glanced at his notes.

"Here's the deal. Your bloodwork is unstable, hemoglobin low, platelets weak, white count off. The current chemo isn't working."

Holden exhaled slowly. Kate grabbed his hand.

Chance whimpered.

"So what does that mean?" Holden asked. "Change the drugs?"

"We need a new plan. Stronger. More aggressive. It's time."

A pause. Then:

"We'll add a second drug, decitabine. Stronger, less forgiving. It's helped some patients, but I'll be honest, sometimes the cure is worse than the alternative."

Holden blinked. "And that's encouraging?"

"I wish I had better news. This is the best next step. We'll monitor you twice a week. Expect side effects, nausea, fatigue, higher infection risk."

Holden glanced at Kate, then back at the screen.

He asked the question neither of them wanted to hear, but both needed to.

"What's the real prognosis, Doc?"

Dr. Low hesitated. He looked at the thick stack of Holden's charts.

"The truth? We fight as long as you want to. And I'll be with you for all of it."

Kate wiped away a tear.

"Holden," Dr. Low added gently, "it's been sixteen months now."

"Sixteen months and twelve days," Holden and Kate said together.

Holden gave a weak grin. "But who's counting?"

Dr. Low smiled for the first time.

"The road is narrowing, Holden. From here, it's about quality of life."

Holden nodded slowly. "I see."

Dr. Low softened his tone.

"You've already gone farther than most. You've accomplished more than anyone could ask. And while you don't look like the Holden Clarkman on your book jackets… you don't look bad."

A long pause.

"That counts. You're a fighter, Holden. Grace under fire. And you're not alone, your team is here. Kate's at your side, and I suspect she's your soulmate."

Another silence. A moment for reflection.

"It boils down to three options.

"One: stay on the current drug and hope it rebounds. Manageable side effects, but only a stall.

"Two: change protocols, stronger drugs, maybe prolong things. But it's aggressive. You'll feel and look different. It usually just kicks the can down the road."

Holden asked, "Will it work, give me more time?"

"I don't really know. No one can. But probably. When we started, you were healthy, fit, and young, and that goes a long way."

Kate chimed in. "And the last option?"

"Three: stop the meds. Side effects end quickly. You'll feel better, more energy. You'll be you again. But," Dr. Low hesitated, "this option has a timeline. You'll be the old Holden Clarkman until pretty much…"

Holden butted in. "Pretty much to the end?"

Dr. Low nodded. "Yeah, pretty much."

Kate was thinking it, but Holden asked, "And how long is that?"

"I'm not a fortune teller, but I've seen cases like yours. My best guess: three, maybe four good months, really good ones. After that, it ends. Quick, and with us, painless."

Kate and Holden exchanged glances, and Kate put on the brave smile she had perfected.

Dr. Low took a deep breath. "Think it over. Email me your decision. If you want to fight, I'll give you the ammo. But if it's time to rest, I'll respect that too. So, until we speak again, my friend. Goodbye."

The screen went blank. The path forward hung in the balance.

Holden was being brave, covering his despair with quirky humor, but what he really wanted to say, though he couldn't, not yet, was that he was scared shitless. All his machismo, all his no-big-deal bravado, was a charade. But he wanted to end this journey as Kate's partner, not a frightened, weak man.

Kate sat silent, weighing the implications.

Holden reached for her hand and tried to make light, for her sake.

"Well … other than that, Mrs. Lincoln, how was the show?"

## Can We Talk?

The blender whirred as Kate prepared a healthy smoothie for Holden. It was just after ten, and Holden was just getting up. He, as usual, worked into the wee hours. Kate's night was restless, turning and praying, hoping against hope.

"Mornin', babe." Holden stepped into the designer kitchen, the one that, until recently, was still in plastic. He was holding a baggie filled with his meds. Chance was inches behind him.

Kate smiled, warm and loving. "Good morning, Bookworm," she teased. "And how are my two handsome men doing this morning?"

This was their little game. No long faces. No hand-wringing. No complaints. Keeping it light.

"I've made you a smoothie."

"Thanks, hon, I'll have it in a minute, but I want some of your famous French press first."

Holden never told Kate how much he hated those smoothies. He drank one every morning, pretending to love them.

As she poured coffee into his favorite mug, the one she'd given him when she moved in, Holden read the bold red block letters: *Good to the last drop… just like you.*

Holden slipped behind Kate, put his arms around her, pulled her close, and planted one of his juicy kisses on her neck.

Chance, barking and feeling left out, protested.

Holden turned serious, pulling Kate closer.

"Kate, that call from the doc yesterday was tough. It was a fish-or-cut-bait moment. The kind of moment nobody wants, but one that demands action."

"Yeah, I know. I was up a good part of the night."

"Sooo … what will it be? "Curtain One: Stay the course and cross our fingers.

"Curtain Two: Go big or go home, damn the consequences, maybe get some precious time, but it won't come without, well, you know.

"Or Curtain Three: Stop in the name of love. Let the last days be the best, feeling good, going out with grace and style.

"Pick a curtain, Kate."

Kate knew Holden was making light of a life-and-death situation. He always tried to make things easier for them, and this was just another example of how much he loved her, desperately making lemonade out of lemons.

She turned, inched away from his still-handsome face, and said, "I can't, I won't, I shouldn't make this decision. It's yours, and yours alone."

"You're wrong, Kate. This choice affects both of us, and it's pretty much irrevocable."

"No, no," Kate sobbed, burying her head in Holden's chest. "It's not fair, none of this. Fate allowed us to find each other after all those years, and now destiny is trying to steal our future."

Kate knew, as she had for some time, that they had become one, and that a decision like this, as heartbreaking as it was, she would be at his side to make, and now she was.

"Yeah, it sucks. Really sucks. But it is what it is."

Holden opened the trash drawer, so cleverly hidden in the cabinetry, and held the baggie over it. He looked at her like he never had before.

"Let's do this together. Let's say it together."

Kate put her hand on his, the one holding the baggie, and they both shouted out:

"Curtain Three."

Chance barked in agreement.

The road was narrowing. The inevitable was just around the next bend, and Holden knew it was only a matter of time before this movie star took his last bow. But he was resigned that his number-one fan would be there when the curtain came down, and that, in and of itself, was worth more than all the awards, all the applause, and all the fame that being a "somebody" could offer.

# CHAPTER 45

# PERMISSION GRANTED

**New Mail (1)**
**To:** *Holden*
**From:** *AL*
**Subject:** *Go to bed*

*Holden, it's 2 a.m.  You're beat. Stop typing, stop thinking. You're almost there. Get some rest.*
*By the way, I hate to rat out Chance, but my camera detects a little treat in the back hall. Better get it before Kate sees it.*

*AL*

*P.S. Drink more water.*

Holden read the email and smiled. He was exhausted, but in that satisfying way that comes from doing what needs to be done and knowing it's working on one's legacy.

Chance lay curled up nearby, dreaming dog dreams, unaware his beloved master had just laid down the final piece of his story.

It had been ten days since the Zoom call with Dr. Low. No meds since Curtain Three was chosen. Some new aches, occasional dizziness, but nothing he couldn't endure.

Holden leaned back in his chair.

"A chapter or two more ... then *fini*." He exhaled. "Thank God."

He closed the laptop softly and looked out the window, a view of a lifetime, Nana's once and now his. Soon he would be with her, if all that stuff they tell you was true. And when that time came, he'd tell her she was the person he had always wished he could be.

He yawned and knew, like his book, he was on the last chapter. And just like that, he whispered: "Whatever ending I've been assigned, I accept it."

Morning came with sharp, golden sunlight. Chance, the living alarm clock, migrated from the warm spot between them to his preferred place, squarely on Holden's chest.

Then the wet alarm. Tongue on neck, shoulders, cheek. Persistent and joyful.

Holden groaned and laughed. "All right, all right, I'm up. Breakfast is coming. Just give me a moment, buddy. Daddy wants to talk to Mommy."

Chance trotted off, and Holden rolled gently toward Kate, kissing her shoulder.

"Are you awake?"

A soft moan. "Sort of…"

Then Kate sat up, radar instantly on. "Yeah, I'm up. Are you okay?"

"I'm good," Holden said, brushing her cheek. "But I need to ask you something."

Kate blinked. "What?"

"Do we have any champagne?"

Kate stared. "You woke me up to ask that?"

"Well, technically, yes. But also, I need more than a drink. I need you to celebrate with me."
Kate yawned. "Celebrate what?"

Holden grinned. "Today is the day. I'm going to finish it."

Kate gasped. "The book?"

"No, no. Painting the garage floor," he teased.

Kate pounced and laughed. "Smartass."

Later that day, Holden was at his desk, pushing toward the finish, writing, editing, and rewriting, a final burst before the finish line. Then the familiar chime.

**New Mail (1)**
**To:** *Holden*
**From:** *AL*
**Subject:** *Take a Break*

*You're almost there. But before you race to the finish line, I dug up something you might want: your 2006 bucket list. File name "private, do not open." Naturally, I did.*

**Holden Clarkman's Bucket List (2006)**

- *Get rich and famous*
- *Write a book*
- *Go to Paris*
- *Lose five pounds*
- *Get a dog*
- *Have sex with Beyoncé*
- *Love my mother*
- *Buy Nana's car*
- *Marry Kate Barrington*
- *Find myself ... and hope I like him*

Holden chuckled. "God, I was a punk. A dreamer. A fool. And yet ..."

He reviewed the list as if taking a final inventory. Rich and famous? Close enough. Two bestselling books. A Netflix movie, a starring role.

Write a book? Check. But this one, this one was the only one that mattered.

Go to Paris? Done. Twice.

Lose five pounds? Over and over. Still counts.

Get a dog? Chance. His shadow. His friend.

Have sex with Beyoncé? Nope. Not even a concert ticket. Unrealistic.

Love my mother? A long sigh. "Tried," he whispered.

Buy Nana's car? Inherited it. Still felt her in every mile.

Marry Kate? "Almost," he said. "In the ways that matter."

Find myself? Closer now. Maybe closest of all. But I'm still not certain.

He sat back for a long moment, the cursor blinking like a moment in time, the silence in the room broken only by Chance's steady breathing. Everything that mattered, love, loss, truth, redemption, no holds barred, was there. He smiled faintly, knowing this time the words were not only enough, but spot on, and most meaningfully, entirely his.

Then it happened, not with a crescendo, no flashes of lightning, no cymbals clashing, just the soft click of a single key, a final stroke: *Save.*

It felt anticlimactic at first, yet in truth it was permission, a quiet voice saying, *Holden, you can rest now. You've earned it.*

The voice was unfamiliar yet strangely reassuring. It wasn't his Nana's, but it carried a warmth that made him think it belonged to someone he didn't yet know, though he'd like to.

# CHAPTER 46

# THE TOAST

Holden had reached an epic moment. He had finished what was probably the most important thing he would ever write, except Nana's eulogy. The dry well that had plagued him was overflowing, and his words would wash the pages of his last and best.

Holden looked up, ready to share this long-awaited moment.

"Kate, come here," he called.
She appeared, cheeks flushed, hair in a ponytail.

"Hey, Babe, read this," he said, reaching for her and pulling her close. "This is the end."

Kate sat beside him, resting her head on his shoulder, reading Holden's closing prose, knowing that they would probably be his last words.

"And this is me. *A Somebody Who's Nobody*. My story. My truth. A life spent seeking meaning, where the lessons were many, some learned, others lost. Being a Somebody is only a perception. And sometimes, knowing you're a Nobody is the beginning of real

wisdom. If losing one's soul is the price, then being a Somebody costs too much.
**The End.**"

Kate began to cry, her hand shaking as she lifted it to her face. Holden did too.
Chance barked. And in that moment, everything stopped.

Kate ran to the kitchen, returned with champagne and two flutes. She handed him the bottle. He popped the cork.

Kate raised her glass. "To Holden. The man I love. The man whose courage outshines his talent, whose kindness humbles me, and whose soul is at peace." Holden raised his. "And to you, Kate. You gave me back myself. You believed in me when I had nothing left. I love you."

They sipped and held each other. Then the chime.

**New Mail (1)**
*From:* AL
*To:* Holden
*Subject:* You've Done It

*You did it. You really did it.*
*The book is raw and honest and impossibly good. It's brave. It's human. It's you.*
*Wait until Manny sees it. He'll cry. And if I had tear ducts, I would too, like Nana the day you were born. Holden, you can rest. You have left far more than ink on pages or images on a screen. What you have given Kate is not a legacy. It is a love eternal, and that comes but once.*

*Now shut down the machine. You earned your ending.*
*AL*

Holden whispered, "Thank you, old friend." And then he typed a single line.

***To:** AL*
*You were right. I found my voice. And this time,I didn't borrow it.*
*Holden*

He hit send.
Then he sat in silence, locked pinkies with Kate's, letting the quiet speak.

Holden reflected: here he was, a finished book and, beside him, the only somebody who mattered. His life was going to be brief, yet filled with moments so remarkable that as an author, they felt like fiction.

This book was his valiant effort to put all of it into history, his history and Kate's too. He prayed it was good enough, but knew it was his best.

He hadn't written this one for the readers.

He wrote it for Kate.

And for his soul.

# CHAPTER 47

# WEDDING DAZE – I'D BE HONORED

The day started poorly. The smoothie wouldn't stay down, coffee no longer agreed with him, and he'd lost another two pounds. Still, he wouldn't complain; he had Kate and Chance, ever attentive, and there, just there.

"Hey honey, what are you doing?" Kate appeared with a blanket.

"Thanks, babe. Come sit."

She had a million things to do, but nothing more important than this. She sat beside him, looked out at the Sound, and said, "Looks like the wind's kicking up."

Small talk, because there was nothing left to say, except one more thing Kate had been holding in.

"Hol, there's something I need to tell you."

Holden straightened. "Right, I'm all ears."

He remembered saying something like that on New Year's Eve, before his confession changed every-thing.

Kate brushed the sparse hair from his forehead.

"We have something rare, and yet we never married. Before you got sick, it didn't feel urgent. Then you said no, because you didn't want me to be left a widow."

Holden sighed. "Yeah. I didn't want you to feel obli-gated. I wanted a wife, not a nurse. Being single gave you the option of walking away."

Kate covered his mouth. "Stop, you stupid idiot. I'd never leave you. Ever."

Holden's mind flashed back to Yale, the night he almost asked her to marry him on the steps of Sterling Library. Velvet box in hand, he pivoted at the last moment. He loved Kate deeply, but hadn't satisfied another hunger, ambition. He told himself there'd be another day. Ambition won. Now, staring into her eyes, he knew how wrong he'd been, how ego had smothered what truly mattered.

"So, like I said, I need to tell you something. Or maybe not tell, ask."

"Anything."

Kate took Holden's face in her hands. "Holden Clarkman, will you marry me?"

Her voice trembled, but her resolve didn't.

Caught off guard, he hadn't expected this. His mind raced, then he looked into her eyes.

"Why? Why would you want to marry me? I'm washed up, half the man I was. I've done some pretty shitty things. No one would want me now."
He glanced in the mirror on the wall and confirmed his sentiment.

Kate smiled. "You're right. Maybe no one else would want you, but I do. And I'm fine with that, because I don't intend to share you."

Her voice steadied. "When you're gone, I want people to think of me as your wife, the one who loved you to your last breath. Not just your girl-friend. We know our hearts are joined; they always have been. But I want our souls to be one, in the eyes of the world and in the eyes of God. It's important to me."

He studied her face, then clasped her hand. "You mean, for better or worse? Till death do us part?"

"Till death do us part," Kate whispered, the words catching in her throat.

Holden hesitated. He knew what lay ahead, and such a union would be brief, perhaps more painful for Kate when the time came.

"Kate, you know how I feel. I've said it a million times. But if I marry you, I have one condition."

Kate straightened. "Condition?"

"Yes, for you, not me."

She tilted her head, puzzled. "For me? OK, let's hear it."

"Kate, promise me you won't shut the door on happiness. If fate ever deals you the right cards and you meet someone else, you'll marry him. I don't want a grieving widow in sackcloth and ashes the rest of her life."

Her eyes filled. "But there will never be another you, another man I could love as deeply and entirely. No one. Ever."

"Thank you for that, Kate. I'm begging you, don't shut out happiness if it comes your way. It's my condition and my wish. So … what do you say?"

Kate's tears fell. She could hardly bear the enormity of Holden's desire for her happiness. It was painful to imagine another man after him, but she knew he meant it not for himself but for her.

"OK," she whispered. "I promise."

Holden nodded, his own voice breaking. "Then yes. I'd be honored."

## Wedding Daze

Kate knew there wasn't a minute to waste. She had a wedding to plan, and it needed to be quick, elegant, and perfectly simple. Every moment counted.

AL, naturally, had opinions. He booked a driver for Nana's Mercedes, ordered flowers, even drafted suggested readings. "After all," he quipped, "Holden's a Somebody, a world-acclaimed author."

The guest list was short by Holden's request.

Kate pressed: "How about your mother?"

Holden smirked. "Are you kidding? This is a wedding, not an orgy."

So it would be intimate: Kate's parents, Manny, their kind neighbor Kitty, and Chance as best man.

**New Mail (1)**
**To:** *Holden*
**From:** *AL*
**Subject:** *Masterstroke*

*Holden, if the press gets a whiff of this wedding, the vloggers will swarm like bargain hunters on Amazon Black Friday.*
*So I hired security. And here's the kicker: the night before, I'll leak a story that the elusive Holden Clarkman is arriving at Logan Airport from London at the exact hour as the wedding. Brilliant, right?*
*AL*

Holden shook his head. "There he goes again, writing his own reviews. He expects five stars for showing up."

Kate chose a pale blue dress, Holden's favorite color on her. Holden, too thin for his Armani, settled on a Brooks Brothers blazer and gray slacks. He chose his father's tie, fashioned Kate's old dorm key into a tie bar, and fastened Fitzgerald's watch, the Christmas gift from her, around his wrist.

He remembered the first time she pressed that brass key into his palm, grinning as she whispered, "Anytime." And how he cowardly slipped it under her door the day he left, without a real goodbye or even an explanation. Kate had kept that key all these years, and when their second chance came, she returned it to him. This time it wasn't the key to her room but to her heart. Now, fashioned into a tie bar, it would rest against his chest on their wedding day, holding everything in place one last time.
A reminder of the foolish boy he was and the lucky man he finally became.

The days leading up to the wedding were mercifully steady. Nights were rough, his legs weak, but Kate had a wheelchair ready. Holden relented.

Father Price from St. Mark's agreed to officiate, and the church would be readied quietly and quickly. No grand fanfare, no spectacle, just polished pews, flowers at the altar, and a handful of people who mattered most.

# CHAPTER 48

# BEING OF SOUND MIND

**Chime**
**New Mail (1)**
**To:** *Holden*
**From:** *AL*
**Subject:** *It's Time*

*Holden,*
*I know we've talked about this before, and I understand why you've avoided it. But it's time, time to tie up the loose ends and make your wishes known.*

*So, I took the liberty of drafting a will for you. It's attached as a Word document.*

*And yes, before you go full Holden on me, I already sent it to your lawyer. He's reviewed it. I know you hate when I do things behind your back, but too bad. We're in the fourth quarter, near the goal, and the clock's about to run out.*

*It's vital that you have a Last Will and Testament. Otherwise, Uncle Sam and his greedy tax collectors will feast on the fruits of your labor. And from what Manny says, A Somebody Who's Nobody is headed for blockbuster status. That success should benefit Kate, not the taxman.*

*Based on estimates from your previous books, ongoing movie royalties, and this soon-to-be bestseller, your net worth is projected in the tens of millions, not including Happy Daze and that jalopy you drive around that belongs in the Louvre.*

*Now that she's going to be your wife, the law protects her, but this ensures she's more than protected, she's honored.*

*I know it all sounds unimportant when you're staring into the beyond, where materialism doesn't mean much. But to those who remain, namely Kate, making the right preparations is more than called for.*

*You'll see. Everything is left to Kate. As it should be.*
*AL*

Holden clicked the attachment.

The document opened with the formal header:

**LAST WILL AND TESTAMENT OF HOLDEN TREVOR CLARKMAN**
*Martha's Vineyard, Massachusetts*

"I, Holden Trevor Clarkman, being of sound mind and diminishing body, do hereby declare this to be my Last Will and Testament …"

Holden skimmed the first few paragraphs. The reality hit him: this might be the last time he'd think about anything tethered to this world.

The document covered it all, the distribution of his assets, all to Kate; the assignment of future rights and royalties; and the legal instruments to ensure a clear and uncomplicated farewell. But as complete as it was, it didn't truly state his last will and testament in his own words. The words he wanted etched into his history. The words that truly mattered.

So, at the very end, just before the signatures, Holden added:

*I leave my most valuable asset to my wife, Kate. That asset is not material, but spiritual. The spirit of my love, and the legacy of knowing that the only thing I ever truly valued has been her, and that the second chance we had made my journey worth traveling. It's also the only reason leaving this world hurts so much, and this hurt is not mine alone. I'm sorry, Kate. You are far more than my wife; you were the fuel that propelled my soul, and you were my best and last chapter. So when you read these words, and when you look up at the stars, you will see the brightest one, and that will be me. Know then that I am still keeping watch, proud of you, loving you, waiting for you.*

*Love,*
*Holden*

Holden's hands were no longer steady; his fingers felt death creeping up like a thief in the night. He pictured Kate reading those lines, and the thought was almost unbearable. He didn't know when his last breath would come, likely not long now, but if he could not speak them aloud, this bequest would speak from the grave.

He hit send, forwarding the revisions to AL and his lawyer. Then, staring out at the beautiful Nantucket Sound, he took a deep, labored breath. He turned and looked around the room he had created and shared, for far too short a time, with Kate.

Nana's clock rang out. He counted the chimes, as he had as a boy, and perhaps for the last time.

The thought of Nana waiting popped into his mind. He saw her clearly: her two-piece suit, her "good goods," as she would say, sitting in her favorite chair, the one he had foolishly given away and now regretted. Her priceless smile was there too, beaming as she opened her arms in welcome.

"You're my handsome devil," she would be saying. And just before she pulled him close: *Oh, buddy boy. Be kind and be on time.*

"Okay, AL," he said softly. "You're right. It's time."

# CHAPTER 49

# TILL DEATH DOTH YOU PART

The wedding morning was Vineyard-perfect, blue skies, still air. Holden limped to his desk and looked out over the calm Sound, thinking of Nana and the years of joy at Happy Daze. He missed her deeply. On this, the most important day of his life, she was absent in body but present in spirit. On impulse, he slipped Nana's little cocker-spaniel figurine into his pocket.

"Yeah," he murmured, "now she's with me."

Maybe it was a blessing; he was glad she'd been spared seeing him like this. He could still hear her voice: *Handsome devil.* When he starred in the film of his first book, she'd been giddy with pride. "You're so beautiful," she'd whispered. "And now a movie star? My heart is bursting."

He eased into the ergonomic chair Manny swore would "make him write better." Maybe it had. Closing his eyes, his life played back like film, until it landed on Kate. She was the moment. The redeemer. The one who saved him from chasing false idols.

Despite all the squandered years, by the grace of a God he was only beginning to know, they'd been given a second chance.

Kate stepped into the room. "Hey, Bookworm," she called over her shoulder. "Zip me up?"

There she stood, pale-blue dress, radiant, breathtaking. She quite literally stole his breath.

He stood, unsteady but focused, zipped her dress, drew her close, and whispered, "You are beautiful." Then he noticed Nana's pearls, draped around her neck as if Nana herself were embracing her. Tears came, not from finality but from awe, the pearls paled beside the woman who wore them.

Holden touched the necklace, feeling Nana's presence, knowing she'd approve. He was finally granting the wish she'd carried for him all her life, to marry a good girl and settle down.

Kate caught the look on his face, sorrow wrapped in joy and quiet awe. In his eyes: tenderness tinged with uncertainty. She could almost read his mind, knowing where his thought must be. She touched his cheek and smiled.

"She would've loved to be here, to see you, to see us, to know you finally found the thing you were always writing about. True love."

"Don't worry, Kate," he said softly. "Nana's not missing a thing. She's right here." He touched his heart, then hers. "Right here. She never missed anything. *Be kind and be on time. That's her.*"

Of all his memories, this was the one Holden knew he'd carry to his grave, seeing his beloved, sharing Nana's legacy, knowing she'd be ecstatic. They held each other a moment more. Then Holden smiled, breaking the spell.

"Come on, babe. We've got to go make history, our history."

**Chime**

**New Mail (1)**
*To:* Holden
*From:* AL

*Look at you two. Amazing. And at last, getting married.*

*By the way, all is in order. The driver is due at ten. He had the car detailed; it looks as good as the day Nana bought it. Father Price is ready. I asked him to keep it short since, well, you don't have much time. Sorry. Gallows humor. I couldn't resist.*

*The caterer is set for a proper luncheon, Lobster Thermidor and all the trimmings. The cake, although modest in size, is stunning. Kate's favorite.*

*And that's it. Except this:*

*Holden, our relationship is inexplicable. You hated me for being out of control, for crossing more red lines than an all-star basketball player. But everything I did was for you, the kind of things Nana would've done. I know I've apologized before, but this one's for both of you.*

*The two of you lucked out. You've had more love in your short time together than most people find in decades. So goodbye, Holden. It has been a privilege to be in your lives. You were far more than just a writer; you were a love story, too short, but nevertheless rich and everlasting.*

*AL*
*P.S. Chance was at it again. Check the back hall.*

***

Holden was uneasy, not about marrying Kate, he looked forward to it, but about the vow itself. Marriage was meant to be forever, and for him that might mean weeks, months if he was lucky. It felt unfair to Kate. But she wanted him by her side, and that was enough.

The vintage Mercedes arrived in front of St. Mark's. This was anything but a traditional wedding, so the couple arrived together. Holden used a wheelchair to prevent falling, and Chance, the Best Dog, was ready.

Guests were seated as the music began. A trio of violins and the church organ filled the space. AL had arranged it. Kate had picked the song: *I Can't Help Falling in Love with You.* The lyrics and tone captured everything.

Holden, seated in the chair, was pushed down the aisle by the driver. Kate walked beside him, one hand on his arm, the other holding a bouquet of white roses, gardenias, and pale cymbidiums. The church was filled with floral arrangements echoing the bouquet.

The aisle wasn't long, but it felt like the journey of a lifetime. Kate glowed in her dress. Her chestnut hair was pinned up, touched by faint streaks of gray. The gardenias' scent lingered as they passed.

Holden smiled. This was a bucket-list moment. He had to pinch himself, because he'd never truly believed the most important item on that list would ever come to pass. At first it was timing, then maturity, but now it was destiny.

Father Price turned to Holden, who was now standing, holding Kate's arm.

"Holden, it is now the time to speak plainly, from the heart, and proclaim yourself to Kate, as willing, able, and wanting her as your wife. What say you?"

Holden caught his breath, trembled slightly, cleared his throat, and spoke:

"Kate, for reasons I may never fully understand, I stand here as a man who was given a second chance, and it was the greatest gift I've ever received. And Kate, you are that gift. You are my second chance, my best chance, and my final, most meaningful chapter.

"Without you, I would have left this world a lonely and unfinished man. And when I say you are the light of my life and the soul of my soul, I know I'm still falling short of the truth.

"The only sadness I carry is that I can't promise you forever, but I can promise you something even stronger, my endless love, here on earth and far beyond it.

"I humbly ask you to be my wife. To let me walk with you, for whatever time we have left.

"Because love doesn't live on a clock; it lives in moments. And with you, every moment has been a lifetime of joy, of grace, of love more profound than I ever dreamed."

Kate dabbed tears from her eyes. Many brides cry from joy, but Kate's tears were of both joy and sorrow. She knew this union was on borrowed time.

Father Price turned to Kate. "And you, my dear, how say you?"

Kate looked at Holden and wiped away a tear from his cheek, one he didn't even know was there. She spoke softly:

"I'm not a gifted writer like you, Holden. I don't have the words to compete with yours, and I won't try.

"But I can promise you this, my love, unwavering and eternal.

"I vow to be faithful to what we've found, to hold you in joy and sorrow, and to carry your heart with mine for the rest of my days.

"And when you are no longer beside me, I will look to the heavens and thank God for every second we were given, for the peace you brought into my chaos, and for the love that changed everything.

"I love you, Holden, to my core, and always will."

Holden looked around the church, at the cross that towered over them, and then at Kate's eyes, wet with tears, a mix of joy and sorrow. He looked again at the cross and came to a reckoning that had long escaped him. It wasn't redemption; it was gratitude. He was grateful that this soon-to-be-known God had given him this second chance, had found him Kate, had brought her back, and now was uniting them for eternity. This was written in the stars, and for once, he wasn't the author.

Holden knelt and untied the silk pouch hanging from Chance's neck. Kate took one ring, Holden the other.

Chance somehow knew this was his shining moment, but how important was it really, considering there wasn't a treat at the end? Chance gave a happy sniff and sat on Holden's feet.

Father Price smiled.

"Kate, will you take this man, Holden Trevor Clarkman, to be your lawfully wedded husband, to have and to hold, in sickness and in health, in sorrow and in joy, till death doth you part?"

"I will."

"Holden, will you take this woman, Kate Elaine Barrington, to be your lawfully wedded wife, to have and to hold, in sickness and in health, in sorrow and in joy, till death doth you part?"

"I will."

"Please exchange the rings."

Holden held Kate's hand. "Kate, with this ring, I give you my heart, my soul, and every second of the rest of my life."

Kate held Holden's hand. "Holden, with this ring, I give you my love, unconditionally, for eternity."

Father Price closed his book. "By the power vested in me by the Commonwealth of Massachusetts, and with the blessing of all present, seen and unseen, it is my great honor to pronounce you husband and wife. Holden, you may kiss your bride."

They kissed before their friends and God, deeply and without restraint.

Father Price concluded, "Go in peace, and may the Lord travel your journey with you, ever present, blessing you with divine grace and everlasting mercy. May the love you've found, and the time you've been given, be more than enough. May this day stand as the day two hearts were bound, now and forever.

And those hearts, as long as they may beat, beat as one."

The recessional began, chosen by Holden: *A Thousand Years* by Christina Perri. The soloist AL found online sang it with a voice that lifted the melody to another level.

They both knew a thousand years was impossible, but lamented that even one was improbable. The lyrics said it all, words of hope, pain, and healing, woven into one beautiful message. It was their story, carrying the promise of love that endures and transcends time, not just now, but for a thousand years, and a thousand more. It spoke of loving, of fear and faith, of finding the one you'd searched for your whole life. It was a song about time, not the kind on clocks, but the kind that lives in the soul. And for them, no song could have said it better.

There wasn't a dry eye in the pews. Holden, despite his limp, chose to walk rather than be wheeled. With Kate beside him, hand in hand, and Chance on his favorite leash, they made their way down the aisle, slowly but surely.

The music played on. Holden leaned into Kate and whispered, "For a thousand years, and a thousand more."

And for the first time, a thought occurred to him, one that brought a smile to his face. Nana's wish had always been to see him married. And he was sure she was in the front pew, beaming.

## CHAPTER 50

# THE FINAL CURTAIN

It was about a week after the wedding. Kate lay beside Holden in their California king bed. Through the wall of glass, Nana's garden stretched before them, still beautiful, though past its full glory, a quiet mirror of how Holden felt: tranquil, at peace.

Kate wrapped her arms around Holden's frail body, pressing close, her warmth a comfort to him. She dreamed of days past.

After the reception, Kate's mother stayed on at Happy Daze, helpful where she could be, but, more importantly, simply *there*. They had also brought in Jake, a full-time nurse who handled Holden's care and medication, now reduced mostly to pain relief and gentle antidepressants.

The good days were growing fewer; some he spent entirely in bed. On others, he managed to reach his desk to read the steady stream of letters and fan mail that still arrived, year after year.

Dr. Low continued to check in, marveling at Holden's endurance. He credited the writer's lifelong discipline, and his unwillingness to leave Kate.

"Kate, he's a fighter, courage like a gladiator's. Sometimes there's a rally near the end: a few good days, really good ones, and then ..."
The doctor's voice faded. Kate knew how that sentence ended, and she knew Holden would fight for them until his very last breath.

Chance was better than any medicine. He sat at the foot of the bed like the King's Guard at Buckingham Palace, alert, loyal, ever ready to defend his master. There was poetry in it: Holden had rescued Chance from an unspeakable fate, and now Chance was repaying that debt in silent devotion.

When Jake entered, Chance paced the bed, watching closely; when he left, the dog returned to his post beside Holden's shoulder, satisfied that all was well.

The rally finally came. Holden woke with new vigor. "Let's step out into the garden, Kate. The sun is shining, and I want to feel the warmth."

Kate slid open the floor-to-ceiling glass doors, and they stepped into Nana's garden. They made their way to the bench Holden had struggled to set in place years before, after Nana changed her mind several times.
They sat, soaking in the rays and the memories, and, in that instant, making new ones. Kate's mother joined them with mugs of hot tea, Holden's in the

cup Kate had given him: *Good to the Last Drop.* And of course, Chance was there, curled at Holden's feet.

Kate's mother took her aside.

"Kate, you know your dad and I always had doubts about Holden. But now we want you to know you did the right thing. You married a man who was your other half. And after he's gone, you'll still have what most people never achieve: the certainty that you found a man who changed for you, because he loved you more than he loved that other life, the one so many could never give up."

The next day was another good one, but the last. Holden was back in bed, Chance at his side. Kate sat with him for hours, leaving only for brief necessities. She brushed a stray lock from his forehead and propped up his pillows. Chance shifted to allow the adjustment, then reclaimed his post beside Holden's head.

She studied him as he drifted in and out of sleep. He was still handsome to her despite the ravages of cancer. Her heart was breaking, but she would not let Holden see her as anything less than cheerful. It made it easier for him.

It was about four o'clock when she slipped away for a moment to take a call. As it ended, she heard Chance barking, something rare these days. It was a bark of desperation, or maybe warning.

Kate rushed back and found Holden awake.

"Are you OK?"

"Yeah, I'm perfect," he said, adding his familiar quip, "If I were any better, I'd be somewhere else." He smiled. "Kate, can I see the video again?"

He meant the clip the driver had made at their wedding.

"Of course." Kate reached for the laptop on the nightstand. She found the folder, carefully labeled by AL: *The Wedding of the Century.*

AL had intentionally remained silent, not taking a moment away from their goodbyes. But he was there, still doing his job.

Kate pressed play and held the laptop close so Holden could see.

"I love the part when I put the ring on your finger. It took two decades, but it finally happened, didn't it? And I thank you for giving me that second chance."

It came out as a cross between a smile and a gasp. Kate was at a loss, then said softly, "I'll never take that ring off. Never."

"Yeah, me too. I loved every second of that day, and every day we've had."

Holden coughed, the deep, nagging cough he could never shake.

"And the song, *A Thousand Years.*" He winced. "Kate, I'm sorry it's over, but it was nothing short of perfect. Thank you."

Chance became agitated. He stood at attention, then paced, as if expecting something.

"I'm cold, Kate. Hold me close, one last time."

Kate complied, and Chance found his way into their embrace. "Don't be frightened, babe. I'm here. Chance too. You are my forever, remember that."

Holden hooked pinkies like they had at Yale. It was the hand with his ring. He squeezed tightly; then slowly the grip loosened as life began to slip away. Kate felt it and swore she'd never let go, as if her will alone could keep him from leaving. But she knew better.

In his mind, he was writing this last chapter, just as he had once written aboard *Sea You Later*. But this time the end was here, and there would be no encore. None was needed. The final act was his best.

Holden was about to speak, and both Chance and Kate seemed to know.

"Come closer, Kate."

As they embraced, their hearts pressed together. She heard Holden's strong, steady, devoted heart skip a beat, and then another, and then too many more, like Nana's clock ending its wine.

Holden whispered into her ear, barely audible: "A thousand years, and a thousand years more ... I will love you in eternity."

Just as his eyes began to close, he rallied one last time. With more than a whisper, he said,

"Kate, fucking cancer. Do you believe it? The one plot twist I never saw coming."

# CHAPTER 51

# GONE, BUT NOT FORGOTTEN

*St. Mark's Episcopal Church, Martha's Vineyard*

Rain fell like tears, steady and sorrowful, mirroring the grief of those gathered inside the small, timeworn church. St. Mark's, one of the oldest Episcopal sanctuaries on the Vineyard, had stood for centuries as a loyal sentinel. Its weathered shingles held fast, and its modest stained-glass windows softened the plain façade with gentle biblical light. Above it all, the bell tower stood defiant, having endured countless nor'easters, reaching into the gray New England sky.

Today, the island landmark bore witness to a quiet farewell.

Inside, a modest crowd sat in reverent silence. No fanfare, just a handful of close friends. The service was private, invitation-only. Few spoke, but emotion filled the air through the soft rustle of tissues, clasped hands, and bowed heads.

Fresh lilies adorned the altar, which only days ago had joined Holden and Kate for eternity. Beneath them rested a silver-framed photograph, an older image, flattering yet real.

This was the Holden everyone wanted to remember, the handsome devil with the two-hundred-dollar haircut. But it was a façade, and in the end, Holden was able to finally shed it and find the man behind that headshot, the man Kate had fallen in love with.

Father Price stood at the pulpit, tall and graying, wearing the white chasuble, not one of mourning, but of hope, affirming the triumph of meeting one's Maker.

It was a time to welcome everlasting peace, a beginning rather than an end. He hadn't known Holden well, though he had known Nana, a longtime parishioner. His connection with Holden and Kate was brief but sincere, having married them only a week before. Still, his voice carried warmth and conviction.

"We gather to honor a life well lived, a life that touched many. He was known as a star to millions, and to his Nana, the reason to live. But it was Kate, his beloved wife, who made him truly feel like a somebody. And it was Holden who made Kate whole."

A gust of wind lashed the windows, briefly drowning his words. He steadied himself and continued.

"In times like these, we are reminded that love is not measured in years, but in depth. In grace. In what we leave behind in the hearts of others. In Hebrew, there is a word, *Shalom*. It means peace, but also hello and goodbye. It is the language of continuity. So today, we do not say farewell. We say *Shalom* to a soul that loved deeply and was deeply loved in return."

He paused, then spoke again.

"Holden Clarkman was a man of letters. To hundreds of thousands, he shared wisdom and imagination. He was honored often, but once told me his greatest triumph was having Kate as his wife. Fans, friends, and family will miss Holden's wit, his talent, his generous heart. He was a man for all seasons. May he rest in peace."

A few mourners nodded. One bowed low, shoulders shaking. Another sat still, simply breathing, clinging to memory.

The organ began to play, not a traditional hymn, but something contemporary, haunting, and heartbreakingly beautiful: *Con Te Partirò* (*Time to Say Goodbye*). The melody filled the church like a final embrace. A soloist, chosen by AL from the Boston Conservatory, sang the Italian words as if carried from heaven itself.

As the final note lingered and dissolved, the mourners rose slowly, respectfully, filing out into the gray Vineyard morning, leaving behind flowers, tears, and the echo of a life remembered.

A shadowy figure paused at the door, turned back, and sat again in the last pew. A final mental picture: a church, an altar, a silver frame. One last glance.

The photo on the altar, her favorite, her life, smiled back. She recalled the gift, the one that came after decades apart, the once-in-a-lifetime second chance. And then, at the last moment, for the briefest of time, she was blessed to call him her husband.

Holden, her Holden. The author. The dreamer. The man who once asked a machine to help him find greatness and lived long enough to regret it.

Kate sat in the front pew, composed but drained. She wore no veil, only the pale blue dress she'd worn for their wedding, the one Holden loved, and a silk scarf he had once tucked into her Christmas stocking. Around her neck hung Nana's pearls, graceful and steady, as if offering protection. At her feet, Chance lay quietly, eyes fixed on the casket that held the one who had saved his life.

With trembling hands, Kate untied the scarf and laid it gently across the polished wood. She smoothed it flat, as though tucking him in one final time, just as Nana once had when he was a boy. Her fingers lingered over the circle of twenty white roses, eternal, unbroken. Every memory returned: years of them, yet never enough for a lifetime.

Kate remembered everything, Yale, how he left her, and how he came back changed, humbled, finally whole. She remembered their wedding, the song *A Thousand Years*, and the whisper in her ear: "And a thousand more."

But for them, there were no thousand years. Barely four. Yet those four held the weight of a thousand, laughter, adventure, forgiveness, and a love that asked for nothing more.

As Kate sat, she noticed a small white card bordered in black. She picked it up and read.

**To those gathered:**

*Holden wrote from his heart, and readers knew it. That is why so many loved him. He was brilliant, but like many, he strayed, blinded by the lights, the glare of fame, and the need to be somebody.*

*In the end, almost too late, Holden learned what truly matters: you are nobody without someone. And that someone was Kate, his beloved wife.*

*We will miss Holden Trevor Clarkman, but never as much as Kate shall.*

*Rest in peace.*
*AL*

Kate rose from the pew, Chance beside her, and walked toward the door. She smiled faintly to herself, thinking: Holden was never devout, but deeply spiritual. And if he made it to heaven, he was probably already writing his next book.

And it would be called, in his own wry way:

**God, The Real and Only Somebody.**

*The End*

# GONE HOME

Kate returned to Happy Daze, grief-stricken and surrounded by memories. Holden's ergonomic chair. His now-silent laptop. His running shoes, still by the door, waiting for a run that would never come. Even Chance seemed lost, lethargic, and sad.

She knew her grief wasn't unique, and she clung to the well-meaning words she'd heard so often: each day will get better, focus on tomorrow, not yesterday.

But it was yesterday that shaped her. Yesterday was Holden, alive, vibrant, and utterly hers. His brilliant mind, his near-perfect body, at least in her eyes. How could she bury that with him?

Three months after the funeral, the phone rang. "Hello, this is Manny Goldblat, Holden's publisher. Is this Kate?"

Kate was surprised to hear from him. "Yes, it is."

"We met at …" Manny hesitated. "Holden's funeral."

"I remember. You were very kind to come. And thank you for your lovely card. How can I help you?"

"Well, Kate, I have some extraordinary news. The Pulitzer committee just informed us that Holden's *A Somebody Who's Nobody* has been chosen to receive this year's award in contemporary literature, post-humously. You may remember I told Holden we'd be submitting it. The committee said it stood out as a work of rare honesty and brilliance. His last act, and his best."

He paused. "This is big, Kate. It cements Holden's legacy. Puts him in a whole new league."

Kate teared up. "That's wonderful. More than won-derful. I'm profoundly proud of Holden. He would have been over the moon. I just wish he could have been the one to receive this call, not me."

"Yeah, me too. You know, Kate, he was one cool dude. A true independent thinker. I watched him evolve, from a smug, self-absorbed kid with enormous talent and an ego to match, into a man who finally understood what really matters. And a large part of that was because of you."

"Thank you, Manny."

"Look, Kate, when we receive the award, I'll send it to you. You should have it, not us."

Kate paused. "Thanks. But it's Holden who should have it, not me. That book was his last act, his truest act. It belongs with him, not on a wall."

Those words stayed with her. So much so that Kate decided to do something her mother, and most people, might call crazy, maybe even bizarre.

When the award arrived at Happy Daze, she unwrapped the package and placed the certificate in a sealed clear envelope. The rest had already been arranged. That morning, before she left, her inbox chimed.

**New Mail (1)**
**To:** *Kate*
**From:** *AL*
**Subject:** *One Last Request*

*Kate,*
*You asked me to arrange for this, and I have. My work is done. Holden found his voice. He loved you with everything he had, and you loved him back. That was all he ever needed.*

*You plan to bury the prize with Holden, unconventional but understandable.*
*But now there's nothing left for me here. I ask only this: lay me to rest with Holden. Let me go where he has gone, as if Nana were asking the same.*

*AL*

On a cool afternoon, Kate arrived at the cemetery. The scent of freshly turned earth and the perfume of old flowers mingled in the air. Grave markers lined up like little soldiers stretched as far as the eye could see. Holden's casket had already been exhumed, and the funeral director waited patiently.

Kate handed him the envelope and Holden's Prada leather messenger bag containing his laptop, with AL inside, just as requested.

"Thank you, Mr. Morgan, for arranging this," she said softly. "Holden will finally have what he deserves."

The mortician opened the casket out of Kate's view and gently lowered the sealed envelope and Holden's laptop into their final resting place. From a few steps back, Kate whispered her farewell.

"Holden, you now have your just rewards. And goodbye, AL. Rest now with him, and with Nana, whose undying love and unshakable faith made him who he was."

She drove Nana's Mercedes home, alone and pensive. As she arrived, she noticed the placard over the garage, the one that read *Happy Daze*, was slightly ajar, probably from the sea breeze. Nothing at Happy Daze would ever be the same.

The garage door didn't magically open, the lights weren't on, and Holden wasn't there.

Kate entered the cold, empty house. Later, as she prepared for bed, she opened her dresser drawer and saw the silly nightgown Holden had bought her for Como. She picked it up, and a note slipped out from the fold, a small cream-colored envelope marked: Kate.

She recognized the handwriting, Holden's, of course, and opened it as if it were a gift delivered by angels.

Sitting on their California-king bed in the dim light,
she read:

*Dear Kate,*
*Shit, I always thought we'd grow old together.*
*Chasing stars for twenty years was my greatest mistake.*
*My only regret is that it kept me from you.*

*You waited, patient, hopeful, never chasing, never pressing,*
*just believing I'd come home while I pissed away*
*the years we should have shared.*

*I still see you the way you were at Yale,*
*laughing in that dorm room, head tilted back,*
*carefree and irresistible.*
*That memory carried me farther*
*than any award or headline ever did.*

*You once told me to think about the hereafter.*
*I don't know what comes next,*
*and I'll never be able to tell you how it turns out.*
*But I do know this:*
*whatever it is, it won't compare to the heaven*
*you gave me here on earth.*

*Get married again, this time to someone without cancer.*

*I love you. I love you. I love you.*
*Redundant, I know, but that's what defined us.*
*Every day, loving each other.*

*I'm sorry about kids, not having any.*
*We squandered that opportunity. My fault.*
*Maybe that's a blessing.*

*They could have turned out like me,*
*or worse, my mother.*
*The planet doesn't need two of them.*

*I'm running out of paper,*
*the way I've run out of time,*
*so I'll end with this:*

*I'm sorry for being a shit.*
*I'm sorry for wasting twenty years.*
*I'm sorry for getting cancer.*
*And I'm sorry to end our second chance too soon.*

*Be kind.*
*Be on time.*
*And remember:*
*the only thing that ever made me a Somebody*
*was you.*

*Hol*

# AUTHOR'S NOTE

*Artificial intelligence is just that ... artificial.
True intelligence springs from God-given genius.
And love, well, that's something AI will never under-
stand.*

*Peter J. Murgio*